THE FOREVER FEET

A NICK DRAKE NOVEL

DWIGHT HOLING

The Forever Feet
A Nick Drake Novel

Print Edition
Copyright 2022 by Dwight Holing

Published by Jackdaw Press
All Rights Reserved

ISBN: 978-1-7347404-9-3

For More Information, please visit dwightholing.com.

See how you can **Get a Free Book** at the end of this novel.

For those who walked ahead

1

The blacktop ended ten miles east of Cedarville at the California-Nevada line. If I'd been riding Wovoka instead of the front seat of my government-issued pickup, the buckskin stallion would've whinnied his approval at the switch to hoof-friendly dirt. I gave the horn a couple of taps to signal my own satisfaction at being back in the high lonesome even though I still had 250 miles of rough road ahead before reaching my home in Harney County, Oregon.

I was on the last leg of an early summer circuit that began with a patrol of the three Klamath Basin national wildlife refuges in northeastern California. The plan was to wrap up the ten-day-long workweek by cutting across the Sheldon refuge in the northwest corner of Nevada. I needed to check on a radio collar fastened around the neck of the strongest ewe in a band of bighorn sheep. It was part of a population and herd-movement study following the reintroduction of the species after its eradication during the frontier era.

Barring washed-out roads, engine trouble, or the wary matriarch playing hide-and-seek in the rugged 900-square-mile preserve, I planned to be hugging my wife Gemma and four-year-old daughter Hattie before midnight. That warranted two more beeps from the horn, partly to celebrate, but mostly to drown out the little voice in my head reminding me Scottish poet Robert Burns had been right about the best-laid plans of mice and men. It was a lesson I'd learned the hard way during three years of combat duty in Vietnam and again over the past six years as a US Fish and Wildlife ranger where the only thing to be expected was the unexpected.

The dirt road swung north through Long Valley, an endorheic basin of evaporating soda lakes and frying pan playas. It was formed when sheets of ice once scoured the continent and liquid basalt shooting from the planet's mantle formed a series of mountain ranges that rose and fell across the breadth of the Silver State in the fashion of swells on the open ocean. I passed by the last pair of still-standing buildings in the ghost town of Vya and a handful of few-and-far-between cattle ranches where graze was sparse and drinking water even more so.

To the east ran a dark-crowned plateau bisected by the hauntingly named Massacre Lake Valley while the unfathomable enormity of the Black Rock Desert retreated in the rearview mirror. I downshifted as the road climbed sagebrush-covered tablelands dotted with clusters of mountain mahogany and isolated stands of aspen peeking from the folds of mountaintops that bent the horizon 7,000 feet above sea level. No other vehicle was in sight, but if past was prologue, I didn't expect to see any.

My last patrol of the refuge was in spring and a sun-bleached wooden sign welcomed me back. Established in 1931 by Herbert Hoover, the Sheldon was an enduring legacy of an otherwise forgettable one-term presidency that had been poleaxed by the Great Depression. Thinking of Hoover reminded me of the current occupant of the White House. News reports on the pickup's radio about the recently begun impeachment hearings made it seem a foregone conclusion that President Nixon's tenure would be cut short. That would have an impact on me, since he'd handpicked my boss. Another lesson I'd learned in the military was a change in commanding officer always triggered repercussions felt all the way down the chain, especially on grunts in the field like me.

I put current events out of my mind as I navigated toward the heart of the refuge. The Sheldon was a sanctuary for pronghorn, the fleet-footed mammals whose speed was second only to cheetahs. I spotted a large herd as I passed Fish Creek Table. Unused to the sight and sound of a vehicle, they bolted with a lightning-quick flash of their white rumps and disappeared over a rise.

Fortune was with me when I cut east on a single track that ran through Mud Spring Canyon. No rockfalls blocked it and the even more rugged turnoff to Hell Creek was also passable as long as I kept the four-by in low. The area was a favorite for bighorn sheep because of its access to fresh water and steep high ground that allowed them to stay out of the clutches of hungry cougars. I parked at the end of the road and took a boxy VHF receiver, earmuff-sized headphones, and hand-held directional antenna from a padded case and fiddled with the knobs to try catching a signal.

The clicks and pings coming through the headphones didn't translate to a radio call from the bighorn's collar announcing her whereabouts. I glanced at the top of the gorge and considered leaving the bulky equipment behind before making the trek. The electronic gear had recently joined a Smith and Wesson .357 magnum sidearm and pair of long guns as part of a wildlife ranger's standard arsenal.

While I favored tracking animals by following signs on the ground and searching for movement by eye, I kept the headphones clamped to my ears in case they could speed my task and get me on my way all the sooner. Ten days was a long time to be away from home when my little girl was sprouting up faster than a tumbleweed rolling in a windstorm. Every time I left on a road trip, I clipped a new snapshot of Hattie to the pickup's visor to keep pace with her ever-changing appearance.

With the receiver hanging from a leather strap around my neck, and holding the antenna aloft, I scrambled up a faint trail that led from creek to peak. Disappointment awaited me at the top when no positive signal sounded. I turned off the receiver to save battery juice. The only sign of bighorns was scat. Wild-sheep droppings ranged in size from apple seeds to deer pellets, but a sharp point on one end made them distinguishable from those of their more common ungulate cousins. The ones I toed were old and crumbled easily. The next most likely place to find my wandering ewe was atop the tableland in the next drainage.

I raised my binoculars, but the distance was too great to tell boulders from bighorns and so I hoofed back down the trail, fired up the Ford, and rolled out. Mud Spring Canyon widened the farther east I drove. Greater sage-grouse scuttled between clumps of bitterbrush while vesper sparrows and loggerhead shrikes zoomed past. I kept an eye out for pygmy rabbits, but had little chance of seeing one with the powerful V8 rumbling under the hood and the knobby tires churning up dust. The burrowing bunnies were half the size of a guinea pig and the smallest rabbit on earth. Despite a doe capable of producing three litters a year, the pygmy's population was declining. It was only a matter of time before I'd be trying to buckle a radio collar around a tiny neck.

The road delivered me into Virgin Valley where a network of springs and a postcard-pretty lake attracted birds and mammals alike. Thick bands of pink sandstone cliffs streaked the valley's walls while entrances to dark gorges offered mystery. It was my favorite camping spot in Nevada and I'd never spent a night there without witnessing a sunset and sunrise as colorful as the opals that speckled the area's historic pick-and-shovel diggings at Rainbow Ridge and Royal Peacock.

I stopped in front of a pool ringed by rocks and stands of rushes. Despite the summer heat, steam rose from it. I'd soaked in the hot spring plenty of times, and the thought of easing my road-weary backside into the soothing waters was tempting. The middle of the pool suddenly erupted and a man's head broke water. He looked in my direction, slicked back his long, black hair, and got out. There was a bundle by the water's edge. He picked it up without getting dressed and walked toward me. It was Searcher, a Paiute who traveled the Great Basin on foot and lived by the old ways. We'd crossed paths a few times, both in the Sheldon and on other wildlife refuges I patrolled.

"Greetings, Searcher," I said as I hopped out of the pickup. "I'm surprised to see you back here. When we spoke in the spring, you were journeying to Duck Valley." It was a Shoshone-Paiute reservation on Nevada's border with Idaho, a walk of two hundred miles each way across open desert.

"I went and now I return."

I pegged Searcher to be around thirty-five years of age, but I could've been off by ten years in either direction. Despite a life-time spent outdoors, his skin was bronzed and unwrinkled from exposure to sun and wind. Searcher was rightly named, for he was always on the move, always looking for something, be it other Paiute people, known as *Numu* in their tongue, or cacti, mushrooms, and other plants that he made into medicines. He never rode a horse or in a vehicle. The one time I offered to give him a lift, he declined, explaining his feet must always touch the ground except when he was in the dream world.

"Where are you going now?" I asked.

"Summit Lake." It was another reservation about thirty-five miles by foot from where we stood. "I bring medicine from the

Tule Eaters for the Fish Eaters. The old ones of both bands have sickness."

"I'm sorry to hear that, but I'm sure the medicine you carry is powerful."

I nodded at the bundle he held. It was wrapped in a pair of buckskin leggings, but Searcher didn't pull them on or even a breechcloth. He never seemed self-conscious about his nakedness. He once told me he considered clothes the same as shoes, barriers between him and Mother Earth and Father Sky.

"And you?" he said.

"Back home to No Mountain. I'm passing through the refuge to look for a bighorn sheep I radio-collared last time I was here. Have you seen any?"

His wet hair sent a spray of water that caught the sunlight as he shook his head. The drops glistened. "I arrived last night and slept beside the spring, but they did not come down to drink. They are staying high in the mountains."

"To keep out of the reach of cougars."

"That is not all they fear. There is too much noise and light."

"From what?"

"I do not know because I was there one sleep ago." He pointed northeast toward the Pueblo Mountains. "Perhaps I will find out on my journey to Summit Lake."

Both walks were a considerable distance to complete in a day, but not for Searcher. His treks were legendary as he kept alive the Paiute tradition of being a long walker. His ancestors were nomadic and roamed the Great Basin at will for thousands of years.

"I'm headed in that direction and would offer you a ride, but I know it's not your way," I said.

"If you hear the noises and see the lights, be careful they do not deafen and blind you to what they really are. Coyote takes many shapes and many forms."

And with no further farewell, Searcher walked away.

I got back in my pickup and followed the main road east and then turned south on another jarring single track that wound through a steep-walled gorge cut by Sagebrush Creek. The rough road was one of the few that led out of the refuge. I parked in a wide spot in the shadow of Big Mountain where I bet my split-hooved quarry was nibbling on tufts of summer grass somewhere above.

While the trail promised to be steeper than the last, I added more weight to my backpack by stowing a powerful spotting scope and tripod along with the tracking gear and extra canteen. The sun arced past noon as I set off and sweat soon yoked my khaki uniform shirt and dripped from my brow. The pitch gained elevation quickly and demanded both hands and feet to keep from backsliding. A scraped knuckle and banged knee later, I reached a wide bench that provided a sweeping view of the tableland and an endless sea of sand and sagebrush that spread beyond the refuge's southern border.

When the antenna didn't pick up any telltale sounds, I exchanged the electronic gear for the spotting scope and began sweeping from left to right. A twister soon filled the field of view. Dust devils that towered three thousand feet were common in the high desert, but this was no bucking, twirling column of grit kicked up by the wind and carried aloft by thermals. The dust storm had been unleashed by a brontosaurus-sized dragline excavator scooping gigantic buckets of earth from an open-pit mine that hadn't been there on my last visit.

It had all the hallmarks of a cyanide-leaching operation. Crushers were pulverizing the rocks unearthed by the dragline. Conveyors and earthmovers piled the ore in heaps that were sprayed with a mixture of cyanide and sodium. The poisonous brew percolated through the ore and leached out gold. Toxic runoff was channeled into wastewater ponds the color of old pennies. The surrounding desert was barren of plants as if scorched by the napalm I'd witnessed turn jungles to ash.

Though the new gold mine was operating right outside the refuge's boundary, distance was no guarantee the runoff would stay out. The high desert was prone to flash floods unleashed by summer monsoons that rushed down washes and through underground channels. Contaminated water escaping from cyanide-bathed ore heaps and unlined waste ponds could easily bubble up miles away where pronghorn, bighorn sheep, and other animals might drink it.

Rivulets that pointed like guilty fingers ran from the dikes impounding the nearest pond. I scoped the one aimed at my position. The carcass of an animal was beside a channel of runoff. It was a buck mule deer. While the course of poison that had killed it finally disappeared into the sandy soil, the toxic brew was certainly still spreading.

I angled the scope to search a gully inside the refuge that was closest to it. Sure enough, another carcass was there. I sharpened the focus, hoping it wouldn't be my collared bighorn. It was a burro. The once-domesticated beasts inhabited Sheldon along with herds of mustangs. But this was no wild burro. It bore a packsaddle. I continued panning before halting abruptly. A man was sprawled facedown. I zeroed in on him and made out two holes darkening the back of his shirt. Holding my breath to keep the scope steady, I willed him to move, praying it was a mirage, not only for his sake, but my own.

Until that moment, I'd come to believe that in the four years since I'd gotten married and become a father, I was finally free from a destiny charted by war, crime, violence, and death. My life now revolved around family and work. Serenity rose each day with the sun. I no longer felt the need to seek danger to remind myself I was alive, that I'd survived a brutal war and its traumatic aftermath.

A minute ticked by, another did too, and finally a third. I lowered the scope as the reality of what I saw bore down. The weight was not the horror of murder or sadness for the victim, but the understanding that I'd become an unwilling part of it. I could either turn my back and leave the killing for someone else to find or go down and investigate it. One would result in forfeiting my soul and the other becoming involved in a homicide to make sure justice was served.

As I mulled the choice over, the elemental spirit of the mountains, gullies, and desert washed over me. The Sheldon was the least visited and most remote refuge I patrolled. That didn't mean I had any less of a duty to protect it from mines that killed with toxics and murderers who killed with guns. My wife was the daughter of a lawman; she'd understand why I couldn't walk away. I hoped in time my daughter would come to understand too.

With my decision made, the prospect of seeing Gemma and Hattie anytime soon evaporated as quickly as blood spilled beneath the hot desert sun.

2

The winding track along Sagebrush Creek roller-coastered between steep rock walls. I glanced at the climbing speedometer, but adrenaline had hijacked caution. I didn't let up on the gas despite fishtailing around one curve and nearly plunging into the boulder-strewn waters below. The absence of turkey vultures circling the bodies told me the killings were recent. The carrion eaters relied on their keen sense of smell to detect gasses escaping from corpses, but that typically took twenty-four hours after death. The killer could still be there.

The road straightened when the gorge opened onto an hourglass-shaped playa. I swung onto the open desert. The four-by handled the jarring cross-country trek without blowing a tire or busting an axle. Even the muffler managed to survive a right jab from a rock whose height I'd misjudged.

I skidded to a stop at the edge of the gully and jumped out. The wind was blowing from the direction of the gold mine and I could taste ore dust. The location markers I'd committed to memory—a boulder with a cleft face, a burn scar from a lightning strike on a hillside behind—proved accurate. The body was no more than fifty yards away. I scanned the gully, but saw no one but the dead man.

Still, I strapped on my service revolver and took the Winchester .30-30 from the rack behind the front seat and levered a round into the chamber before clambering down the slope. Nobody jumped out from behind a rock. Nobody sprang an ambush. When I approached the two bodies, I took everything in the same way I did when making a pen-and-ink drawing of an animal in the wild: the setting, the position of the subject, light and shadows, and the essence of the moment. Not what was visible, but what could be felt.

The man wore patched jeans cinched by a wide leather belt and tucked into the tops of scuffed calf-high leather boots with worn-down heels. A sweat-stained brown hat had been knocked off when he fell. The wide brim was turned up in the front and the inch-wide band was made of jackrabbit fur. His hair was gray and tumbled to the top of his shoulders. Though he was face down, I made out the sides of a bushy gray beard that seemed to cushion his chin from the ground that served as his eternal bed.

The two black marks on the back of his long-sleeved cotton shirt with frayed cuffs were definitely bullet holes. The absence of muzzle burns indicated the rounds had been fired from a distance. One slug had struck him in the top of his right shoulder. The other was lower and surely the kill shot, since the entry was in line with the back of his heart.

The Sheldon refuge was part of the Paiute's ancestral homeland. Thinking of Searcher, I plucked a handful of sage from a nearby bush, crouched next to the old prospector as I now thought of him, and waved the sweet-smelling stalks in a circle over him. "You're not alone. You've been found. And you have my word, your killer will be too."

I went to the burro. It was a jenny. Her packsaddle was

covered by a dirty canvas tarp that had torn loose when she went down. Some of the contents had spilled out, including a short-handle shovel, a deep-sided prospecting pan, and a ripped five-pound cloth sack. Pink pinto beans littered the ground.

At least two rounds had struck the jenny's hindquarters and another the side of her shaggy neck. Blood splatters marred the rocks behind her. I could see the imprints her knees had made in loose dirt when she stumbled. I closed my eyes and heard the jenny's pitiful brays as she was hit over and over, and then her last gasp for breath as her lungs from the neck wound filled with blood and she collapsed on her side and died.

Paiute considered animals the first people—*Nuwuddu* in their language—and themselves as the second people. I waved the stalks of sage over the burro too. "You're not forgotten and your killer won't be either."

The scene of what likely happened played out. The prospector was being chased. He ran into the gully to escape while leading his loyal burro by her halter. When the jenny was fatally struck and went down, the old man lost his cover and was felled by the slugs to his back.

I retraced the pair's steps in the direction they'd run from, alternating between looking for brass casings gleaming among the rocks and footprints in the sand. I stopped when I reached a dirt road named Quartz Creek that intersected with the mouth of the gully. The gold mine loomed close by. I turned around, shouldered my Winchester, and aimed at the burro with no intention of pulling the trigger. It would be a long shot for the .30-30, but there were no jutting boulders or overhanging bushes to obstruct the bullet's flight.

Sensing I was standing where the killer had been when he fired, I looked down at my boots. The road was hardpacked and there were no discernible footprints to determine what kind of shoes the shooter wore or tire tracks to help identify a vehicle. It was time to call for help.

I hiked back to my pickup and radioed the Humboldt County Sheriff's Department in Winnemucca. "Your name again?" the dispatcher said in a gravelly voice.

"Nick Drake. I'm a ranger with US Fish and Wildlife. I was working in the Sheldon refuge when I spotted a murdered man's body. His burro's too."

"How can you be certain the cause of death wasn't the result of an accident or natural causes?"

"Two bullets to the back rules out both, wouldn't you say?"

"No reason to be a smart aleck."

"Would you put the sheriff on, please?"

"No can do."

"But I'm a law enforcement agent reporting a capital crime in his county. Isn't Winnemucca the county seat?"

"It is, but how can you be sure you're in Humboldt County? Part of Sheldon is in Washoe County. That is unless the body is in the little itty bitty panhandle part that crosses the state line into Oregon."

"Because I'm southeast of Virgin Valley and looking at a new gold mine that's on Quartz Creek Road."

"Yep, you're in Humboldt County, all right. That'd be Oro Holdings Limited. Quite the setup they got there. Foreign money behind it, so the gossip goes. Had it up and running quicker than you can say jackpot. Lot of fellas from town got hired. Good paying jobs too. Our chief deputy took early retirement to head mine security. Bull Hammond says it's the easiest money he's ever made. Doesn't have to worry about getting a beer bottle smashed across his face busting up bar brawls any longer."

"About the sheriff. Can you connect me?"

"Like I said, no can do."

"Why not?"

"Because he's not here is why not. He's in the hospital in Reno recuperating from bypass. He'll be on sick leave for about a month. That's how long it took me when I had mine. 'Course mine was a double and his a triple, so maybe that'll take him a couple extra weeks. Two per pass." He chuckled.

"Who's in charge?"

"That'd be our new chief deputy."

"Put him on, would you?"

"I can try, but there's no guarantee. He's young and pretty new and has had to be in three places at once ever since the sheriff's ticker stopped ticking. What did you say your name was again?" I told him. "Hang onto your hat, Ranger Drake, and I'll give it a go."

I looked at my field watch. Winnemucca was more than a two-hour drive away, much of it on unpaved roads.

The radio squawked. "Chief Deputy Manning Dobbs here. What's this about a gunshot victim?"

I told him about discovering the old prospector. "He was killed no more than twenty-four hours ago."

"What makes you such an expert?"

"I'm a wildlife ranger. I know about the scavenging behavior of turkey vultures. They haven't smelled the body yet."

"And buzzards give you experience with dead men?"

"Three tours in Vietnam do."

I could hear him suck in his breath. "When was that?"

"Sixty-five to sixty-eight. Were you in country too?"

"I served stateside. Military Police. Which Fish and Wildlife office are you out of, Fallon or Reno?"

"Neither. I'm based in Oregon. Harney County."

"Is Pudge Warbler still the sheriff there?"

His tone had turned wary and something told me it wouldn't help if I mentioned Pudge was my father-in-law. "He is."

The radio was silent except for the bumblebee buzz of static. Dobbs finally said, "I need you to stay put and preserve the crime scene until I can get there to investigate. That means don't say a word about it, not over the radio or to somebody who might be driving by and stop to see what's going on. I don't want anybody disturbing anything. I'll be there in the morning."

"The morning! But a man's been murdered."

"That's why I need you to stay put and stand guard. I'm shorthanded here. The sheriff is out on medical, my original position hasn't been filled yet, and another deputy is transporting a prisoner to the state penitentiary in Carson City. The rest of us are working back-to-back shifts. The casinos and bars will be crowded with long-haul truckers, cowboys, and miners who show up every Saturday night. Our hands will be full by sundown and the drunk tank by sunup."

"What time will you get here?"

"Right after church." And with that, he clicked off.

I stared at the radio and debated calling Gemma, not that I'd given her a firm return time when I left a week and a half ago. After Hattie was born, we agreed not to set exact schedules for work trips in the belief it would keep our daughter from worrying if one of us ran late. Gemma's large-animal veterinarian practice covered all of Harney County's ten thousand square miles and was no nine-to-five job. Anything from delivering multiple breech births, fighting an epidemic sweeping through a herd, or having her single-engine airplane grounded by a surprise storm could delay her by days. The unpredictability of nature and wildlife ruled out my ability to stick to a timetable too.

While our parenting strategy seemed sound in theory, it was having an unexpected side effect. Hattie was not only growing up to be worry-free, she'd become downright fearless. When she was three, she set out to walk to town on her own. There was the time she brought home a baby snake. Luckily, it was a Pacific gopher snake, but could've easily been a similarly marked northern Pacific rattler. She once held a tea party with her dolls in the middle of a field that was home to the orneriest bull in the county. Her language was a combination of *Numu* and English, the result of being around November, the Paiute healer who lived with us.

I glanced at my watch again. It was a long time until morning and there were still hours of summer daylight. I returned to the gully with tarps, covered the dead prospector and burro, and anchored the corners with rocks. Then I climbed back in my rig and headed for the gold mine.

3

The windshield wipers were losing the battle against dust as I pulled up to a hand-operated boom pole that was striped like a candy cane and blocking the entrance to Oro Holdings. The man sitting inside the plywood-sided guard shack appeared reluctant to brave the gritty air because he opened the sliding window only a crack.

I told him I needed to speak to the person in charge of the mine's wastewater system.

His chin drooped. "What?"

The rumble of heavy machinery was loud. "The mine's wastewater ponds are leaking and the escaped cyanide is poisoning wildlife," I shouted. "That's a violation of federal law."

"I dunno nothing about that. You need to talk to somebody at the home office."

"Where's that?"

"It's not here."

"Do you have a radio channel or phone number I can get patched through to?"

"Look pal, all I do is lift the pole for employees and delivery trucks during my twelve-hour shift. Another fella does the same for the other twelve. If they're not on this, they don't get in." He waved a clipboard.

I slapped the duck-and-fish emblem on the pickup's door and then patted my badge. "This automatically puts me at the top of your list. Call the mine foreman and tell him US Fish and Wildlife is on its way and then raise the boom."

Before he could respond, the shack shook and my rig rocked. An explosion's roar filled the air and a new column of dust black with smoke rose from the open pit.

The guard's grin showed missing teeth. "Why we keep people out. They go through TNT like my three brats do a bag of Chips Ahoy."

"Make the call," I said.

"It's your funeral."

He slid the window shut and picked up a walkie-talkie. While he was on it, another explosion thundered and my rig's springs squeaked. A surging wall of dust chased a pickup heading toward me. It had an emergency light bar on the roof and post-mounted spotlights on the doors. The driver stopped on the other side of the barrier pole and slid out from behind the wheel. He wore a light blue uniform with a black holstered sidearm buckled around his waist. A silver hardhat was perched on his block-shaped head.

"Bull Hammond, Chief of Security," he said when he reached my vehicle. "What's this all about?"

I told him who I was and that I'd spotted a dead mule deer next to runoff from a leaking waste pond. "Other wildlife may have come into contact with the spill too."

He looked over the roof of my pickup and scanned the desert. After a moment, he bent down so we were eye to eye. "This is private property, not state or federal game refuge land. You have no authority here."

"Tell that to the poachers I've arrested. They shoot an animal that's inside a national wildlife refuge, the law is the same no matter which side of the boundary the gunman was standing on when he pulled the trigger or if the animal fell over the line after it was hit. Same goes with a toxic spill. It leaks into a refuge, that makes it my business."

The flint-gray pupils in Bull Hammond's eyes hardened. "Show me the dead critter. I'll follow you."

As he walked back to his pickup, he gave the guard a thumbs up. The man rushed out of the plywood shack, jotted down my license plate on his clipboard, and then raised the boom by pushing down on the cement block counterweight. I turned off the gravel drive and cut across the desert. Hammond stayed right on my tail despite the dust. We got out and he gave the deer a quick once-over.

"Okay, it's a dead buck. So what? I worked sheriff's out of Winnemucca for twenty years, the last five as chief deputy. You know how many deer we pulled off the interstate that got flattened by a big rig or clipped by a family sedan on the way to visit grandma in Salt Lake City? The two-lane to McDermitt during rutting season is like a shooting gallery at a carnival. Bam. Bam. Bam. The bucks keep trying to cross no matter how many in front get knocked flat."

His silver hardhat shimmered as it shook back and forth. "You don't know this one wasn't struck by someone driving on Quartz Creek Road or maybe one of your poachers gut shot it and this is where it finally bled out."

"Take a sniff. Smells like almonds, but the nearest grove is in Sacramento Valley three hundred miles west. That's cyanide in the water trickling past our boots and it's coming from one of your ponds."

Hammond had fifty, sixty pounds on me, easy. He stepped in close and jutted a rock-hard jaw. "I don't much like your attitude."

"I'm not asking you to. What I am asking is, what's your employer going to do about this? The ponds are leaking and spilling into federally protected land. I could see the stains all the way from the top of Big Mountain." I hooked my thumb toward the tablelands behind me.

He didn't take his eyes off me. "What were you doing up there, spying on our operations?"

"Looking for a bighorn sheep I'd radio-collared for a population study. Your mine with all the noise and dust being kicked up is pretty hard to miss. So are the leaks from your toxic ponds."

Hammond continued the stare down. "All right, if there's a leak, operations will take a look and patch it. That still doesn't prove we killed this buck."

"A toxicology test will."

"I said, operations will check it out and do what needs doing. Go back and look for your damn sheep. We're done here." He made to turn away.

"It may have been a deer today, but who's to say it won't be a person tomorrow? Anybody passing by could come in contact with the runoff. Paiute kids from the reservation over at Summit Lake. Rockhounds looking for opals like they do in Virgin Valley." I gave it a couple of beats. "I'm sure prospectors are likely picking and shoveling around here too since your mine must've found gold or it wouldn't be operating around the clock."

Hammond rolled his broad shoulders as if working out a kink. "The company takes security serious, why they hired me away from the sheriff's department. We put up fence, posted keep out signs, and my team runs regular perimeter patrols. If Fish and Wildlife or any other big government agency has a problem with the way we're doing business, they can take it up with the company's pinstriped lawyers who eat caviar for breakfast and bureaucrats for lunch."

He picked up the dead buck and swung it into the bed of his pickup. It was an impressive feat of strength that also showed he had the stomach for getting up-close and personal with a corpse.

"Does that mean you're going to perform the tox test yourself and send me the results?"

Hammond's jaw jutted again. "I'm going to spell this out since you seem particularly thick about what you poked your nose into. Nevada is a mining state. Gold is king and Oro Holdings holds the keys to the kingdom. Anybody comes to our mine without permission is considered a thief out to make off with our treasure and treated as such. And I mean anybody. Is that clear enough for you?"

"As cyanide."

I returned to the bluff above the dead prospector and his burro. As day turned to dusk, the sky showed pinks and reds everywhere except behind the open-pit mine. The clouds of dust refracted the setting sun's rays like big city smog and turned them into a sickly pall of orangish brown. I made camp and built a small fire in a circle of rocks and set a pot of water onto boil. My stores were thin after being in the field for so long and supper would have to be peanut butter slathered on a heel of store-bought bread, the last slice in the bag. At least I still had the fixings for tea tonight and coffee in the morning.

I pulled a camp chair from the back of my pickup, balanced a sketch pad on my knees, and made a series of quick pen-and-ink drawings of the gray-bearded prospector and his jenny, not as they were now, but as I imagined them to have been. In one, he was leading her through a landscape ablaze with desert paintbrush and buckwheat blooms. In another, he was busting a chunk of quartz apart with a rock hammer while she grazed nearby. In still another, he was panning for gold as the jenny looked on with resignation in her eyes.

When the sun disappeared beyond the horizon and whorls of brown bats took to the sky, I put away the sketch pad and threw a few pinches of dried white sage and wild spearmint leaves into the pot to brew. I poured myself a mug and leaned back in the chair and ate the sandwich as colors gave way to shooting stars and spinning planets. I didn't even notice the bread was stale.

As night wore on, more lights joined the stars, not up in the sky, but low on the horizon. They were coming from the gold mine. Large booms and pounding drowned the crackle of wood and hiss of embers from my campfire. The sounds and lights from the mining operations must've scared off the coyotes because none howled. That was fine by me because I didn't want to shoot at any that might try to scavenge the bodies; coyotes were omnivorous—live prey, dead animals, even plants, they ate them all. I wanted the prospector and jenny to lie in peace. I knew firsthand how precious peace was, how difficult it was to come by, and how slippery to hold onto. War had taught me that. So did rangering.

So did living in the high lonesome where nature could soothe in one moment and lash out in the next. Four years prior, Gemma and I had been flying over the mountains in her little plane when a sudden lightning storm blasted us out of the sky and plunged us into a snowy wilderness. Our precious daughter was born during our fight for survival and I came to understand how fragile life was and how strong love could be.

I finished the tea, rolled out my sleeping bag next to the campfire, and fell sleep.

The moon had climbed halfway across the sky and midnight was two hours gone when the sounds of murmuring and footsteps woke me. I held my breath and listened. The sounds grew closer. The footsteps were soft, not loud like boot soles slapping on rocks. The murmurs were low, guttural. Maybe it was a herd of deer, maybe a cougar and a pair of cubs she'd birthed in the spring.

I turned my head in the direction of the sounds and made out moon shadows of human figures walking in a single file between me and the edge of the gully. Bull Hammond said he had a team that made regular patrols around the gold mine. Had they found me up here? Were they trying to surround me?

Reaching under the folded jacket I'd been using as a pillow, I drew the Smith and Wesson from its holster. The figures kept walking, kept murmuring. Gripping a flashlight in my left and the .357 in my right, I slipped out of the sleeping bag, thumbed the flashlight on, and hurled it as I bolted toward my pickup.

The metal flashlight clanged when it struck rocks and the beam rolled toward the edge of the gully. I reached into the cab and pulled the headlight knob, backing away quickly so as not to become a target. Twin beams stabbed the darkness. The murmuring stopped. So did the sound of footsteps. Nothing was there, no single file of humans, no herd of deer, only clumps of sagebrush that stood stock-still in the windless night.

I retrieved the flashlight and searched for footprints, but didn't find any. Whoever, whatever, had been walking by was gone. So was the possibility of falling back asleep, and so I gathered more sticks, rekindled the fire, and put the water on for coffee.

4

Deputy Manning Dobbs must've attended the sunrise service because he pulled up to my campsite at half past eight in a white Jimmy with "SHERIFF" painted across the doors in big green letters.

"You got an early start," I said by way of greeting.

"Last night never ended," he said without smiling.

The chief deputy was even younger than I expected. Thin and boyish, he still had traces of acne. His khaki uniform shirt was offset by dark green pants. Instead of a peaked cap or Smokey Bear hat, he wore a ballcap that had an embroidered patch of the Humboldt County sheriff's emblem above the bill. The design featured a silhouette of a mountain behind a bighorn sheep.

I pointed at his cap. "One of those is why we're standing here."

"Come again?"

"I was trying to locate a bighorn sheep I'd radio-collared when a dust devil at the gold mine caught my attention. I saw runoff from a wastewater pond and a dead deer next to it. That drew me to look at this gully. I never found my sheep, only a dead man and his burro."

"Another deputy is escorting the coroner. They'll be along shortly. Show me the victim."

I led him down the trail and waited at the bottom. He was favoring his right leg. I didn't comment on it, but he saw me staring. "A typical Saturday night. Someone threw a barstool."

"I hope you threw it back."

"I believe in turning the other cheek."

"As a lawman, that'll likely get you a broken jaw more often than not."

Dobbs frowned. It made the acne on his cheeks darken. "You put a tarp over the deceased. That disturbed evidence."

"I was careful how I placed it. Mind if I ask you how long you've been on the job?"

"A little over two years. Why?"

"I was wondering if this is your first homicide."

"As a matter of fact it is, but I took a course at the Police Academy in Las Vegas before joining Humboldt Sheriff's. I've studied up on investigation techniques. I know the protocols. I know what I'm doing."

Dobbs lifted one of the flat rocks anchoring a corner of my tarp and slowly peeled it back to the center. The other three corners got the same treatment until the tarp was folded into a neat square. He handed it to me and then stood over the body.

"The victim is male. The position of his arms and legs are consistent with involuntary collapse. Two wounds that are consistent with those made by gunfire are visible in the back." The young deputy spoke as if he were reading a manual. "No other signs of bullet entries or wounds inflicted by other forms of weaponry are readily visible."

Dobbs crouched and carefully examined the ground around

the body. There was something about him that was familiar. His
boyishness, his acne, his earnestness. He reminded me of a
cherry in my squad, a kid from Minnesota who'd enlisted right
out of high school. His name was Danbury, but the men called
him Danbaby. They didn't do it to be mean; they did it to buck
him up. They knew there was precious little time in war for a
cherry to get his act together. Those who didn't rarely got a
chance to grow old.

Private Danbaby was pious and innocent and followed me
around like a kid brother, always asking questions, always trying
to measure up. He never called me Sarge like the rest of the
men; it was always Sergeant Drake. I didn't consciously go easy
on him, knowing that could put him in even greater danger, but
when I was lying to him, telling him he'd live as a medic tried to
plug a sucking wound in his chest while I had my palm jammed
hard against his femoral artery that had been severed when he
stepped on an NVA mosquito mine, I wondered if maybe I had.

Deputy Dobbs said, "Help me turn him over."

"You're not going to wait for the coroner?"

"I believe I can ID him."

I put the tarp down and crouched beside him. He placed his
palms under the old prospector's left shoulder while I did the
same under his left hip. We rolled the body over. The front of his
shirt didn't have bullet holes. The rounds that killed him were
still in him. The man's gray-bearded jaw had dropped in death,
leaving his mouth agape and swollen tongue sticking out. The
tip was speckled with dirt. His eyes were also open, but long past
caring that particles of sand were stuck to the lashes.

"Jump Diggins," Dobbs said.

"That's his name?"

"It's what he went by. Most people who live around here
knew him or at least have heard of him. He'd show up in

Winnemucca from time to time and pose for snapshots for tourists. Jump would charge them fifty cents. A dollar if Ruby was in the picture."

"Ruby being?"

"His donkey."

"Was he a real prospector?"

"If by real, you mean a dream chaser, yes. He was like all the rest, throwing their lives away thinking they're only a day away from striking it rich. Swinging a pick or pulling a slot machine arm or sticking up a bank, it's all the same."

"Have you seen a lot of that in your two years on the job?"

He bristled. "I've seen what it does to their families. Honesty and hard work are the only virtues I put any stock in. That and obeying the law and being penitent, of course."

I looked at the dead man's face and couldn't decide if the frozen expression was one of fear, surprise, or resignation. Maybe Jump Diggins would finally find what he was looking for in what the Paiute called the spirit world.

"Any idea who would've wanted to kill him?" I said.

"A robber, more than likely. They chased him in here and shot him."

"Does he look like he owned anything valuable?"

"A stranger wouldn't know that, would they?" Dobbs said quickly. "They see a prospector and believe he's carrying gold."

"The burro, Ruby did you say her name was? Her packsaddle spilled when she fell, but nobody pawed through it looking for hidden treasure."

"You searched it?"

"No, but I looked for tracks around it. The killer never came up here. I backtracked Diggins' and his burro's trail to Quartz Creek Road. I believe the shooter was standing there when he fired. He hit his targets and left, confident in his kills."

"Then it was probably somebody Jump crossed. Maybe a dispute over a map or a claim he'd jumped or a game of cards. The person held a grudge and finally caught up to him."

"Anybody out for revenge or looking to settle a personal score wouldn't have shot him from a distance. They'd do it face-to-face so they could see his reaction. That'd be the payback they were after."

Dobbs shifted his weight off his bum leg. "For a wildlife ranger, you sure have a lot of opinions about murder."

"Saigon was thick with corrupt officials and criminals. Paying off the cops to look the other way was cheap and taking a life even more so."

"I never got over there. Being an MP, well, most of the job was hauling drunk soldiers back to the base and manning the front gate."

"It takes a team, no matter what the duty," I said.

His shoulders straightened. "Who do you think shot him?"

"I'm not sure about the who, but my guess is it had something to do with that." I pointed at the gold mine looming in the distance.

"What makes you say that?"

"Proximity, for starters. The mine's fence line is a rifle shot away from here. There's no shortage of firepower over there either. The security guards conduct armed patrols to keep people out."

"But that doesn't make any sense. Why would a mining operation the size of Oro Holdings give two shakes about a desert tramp like Jump Diggins? More to the point, why would the people running it risk everything they have on killing him? Do you know how rich they are, how powerful? This is Nevada."

"So Bull Hammond told me."

The deputy's head jerked. "You spoke to Bull? When?"

"Yesterday afternoon."

"I distinctly told you not to tell anybody about this in order to preserve the crime scene."

"And I didn't. I know about protocol too. I only talked to him about a dead mule deer that took a drink from water leaking from one of their waste ponds that holds runoff from their cyanide-leaching operation."

"Why did you do that?"

"It's my job. I'm sworn to protect wildlife."

"What did Bull say?"

"Beat it and don't come back."

Dobbs chewed on that for a moment. "Do you think he knows about this?" He glanced at the dead prospector and burro.

"Jump and Ruby were killed when the sun was up because only a lucky shot would've hit them in the dark. I doubt somebody firing off multiple rounds from a rifle in broad daylight would've escaped his attention."

When Dobbs didn't say anything, I asked him what he thought. "You must know him pretty well. He told me he served with the sheriff's for twenty years before hiring on at the mine."

"We only worked together a couple of years," the deputy mumbled.

"The sheriff sure must've seen something in you to hopscotch you over the other deputies and make you his second-in-command."

"None of the others wanted it. The pay bump isn't much and they're comfortable doing what they've always been doing. I had the MP experience and that training course I took at the academy, plus I'm dedicated to the profession. I've always wanted to be in law enforcement." He bowed as if standing in front of an altar receiving Holy Communion. "It's my calling."

"Following someone like Bull Hammond, I imagine it's tough being the squad leader."

"I think the men appreciate a change." He hesitated. "At least, I hope they do."

5

The sound of a vehicle approaching the top of the gully reached us. An engine turned off and doors slammed. A man's voice called out. "Anybody home?"

Dobbs cupped his hands around his mouth. "Down here."

A uniformed deputy peered over the side. He was middle-aged and overweight. "I got the croaker with me. He's putting on boots. Worried about snakes." He snickered.

"Give him a hand to get down, okay? I'll wait here."

I told Dobbs I'd help them take the body up.

"Thanks, we could use it. The deputy's rig has a power winch. We can skid the litter up the side."

"What about Ruby?"

"We'll collect any gear she was carrying."

"That it?"

"The coroner's not going to want to do a postmortem on a dead donkey."

"You can order him to. It's your investigation."

Dobbs hesitated. "I suppose I could ask him, but I think the slugs in Jump's body should be all the evidence we'll need."

"To match to the murder weapon." I looked toward the gold mine. "If you can find it."

The overweight deputy worked up a sweat helping the coroner get down. "Well, if it isn't ol' Jump Diggins. They say he struck it rich twenty, thirty years ago and forgot where he buried his treasure. Dumb cluck. He's been looking for it ever since."

"That's nothing but an old wives' tale," the coroner said. He had white hair and a drinker's nose. "Pull up his shirt so I can get a reading."

"You do it," the overweight deputy told Dobbs. "I don't want to touch him."

I wasn't surprised when the chief deputy didn't chastise his subordinate. I pulled up the dead man's shirt before Dobbs did it himself.

The coroner opened a black satchel and took out what looked like a meat thermometer and plunged it into the upper right hand side of Diggins' stomach. "Liver temperature will give me time of death after I do some calculating to take into account the thirty-degree swing in air temperature from day to night and back again this time of year."

After moving the prospector's head from side to side and lifting his arms and letting them fall, he scribbled some notes. "Rigor's come and now it's going." He turned to me. "You're the one who found him? When was that exactly?"

"Yesterday early afternoon."

"By my rough calculation, if you'd been a day earlier, he would've still been alive. I'll know precisely when I get him on my table. Okay, boys, he's all yours. Take me back up."

"What about the burro?" I said.

"What about it?" the coroner said.

"Aren't you going to take a look at her?"

"What for? I can see she's dead. I don't need to take her

temperature to know time of death even if I could find her liver. She died the same time ol' Jump here kicked the bucket."

The overweight deputy snickered again and then led the coroner up the embankment.

I asked Deputy Dobbs if he needed me to come to his office to give a formal statement.

"I don't think that'll be necessary. I can remember what you told me when it comes time to file my report."

"Look out below," the overweight deputy shouted.

A litter clipped to a wire cable tobogganed down the side. I grabbed it and maneuvered it next to the prospector's body. Dobbs unzipped a body bag and we wrestled Diggins into it. After strapping him to the litter, the chief deputy said, "Okay, bring him up. Nice and easy."

The sound of a winch motor whirred and we held onto either side of the litter and walked alongside to keep it from overturning. Once we were up top, we lifted it into the back of the overweight deputy's rig.

"Come on," I said to Dobbs. "I'll help you retrieve Ruby's packsaddle."

We scrambled back down the embankment. I took my tarp off her and we unfastened the packsaddle.

"His entire life's possessions fit on her back," Dobbs said with a shake of his head. "What kind of life is that?"

"The one he chose."

I gave a last look at Ruby, and then grabbed a load and carried it up. Dobbs did the same. When we reached the vehicles, another rig had joined them. Bull Hammond was talking to the coroner and deputy. When he looked over, his chin jutted at me.

"What's he doing here?" he growled.

Dobbs flinched. "Helping out."

The overweight deputy grinned at Hammond. "The ranger

found Jump Diggins and called it in, Chief. Manning let him stay."

Hammond jabbed a finger at me. "Did you find Jump before or after you talked to me yesterday?"

Dobbs stepped between us. "The ranger was under my orders not to discuss this with anybody until I got here. I had to wait until this morning because the department is understaffed since you left and the sheriff got sick."

Hammond aimed his finger at Dobbs. "I'm not just anybody, got that, boy?"

When the young chief deputy cringed, I said, "I'm surprised that a man with twenty years of law enforcement experience wasn't curious to find out why someone was shooting off a rifle in broad daylight outside his front door, but came running the minute he saw dust being kicked up by a passing vehicle."

Hammond bulled past Dobbs to get at me. "Who the hell do you think you are telling me what I should or shouldn't be doing? Huh?"

"A man who answers a simple question with a question is a man who's got something to hide. A lawman in Harney County with a lot more experience than you do told me that."

He balled his fist. "I didn't like you the first time we met and now I like you even less."

I was ready for him to throw a punch, but Dobbs said. "Now, hold on. Everybody calm down. No one is accusing anybody of anything. I'm sure there's a reasonable explanation for everything."

"You don't know what the hell you're doing," Hammond spit.

Dobbs' acne reddened. "I'm the chief deputy now, Bull. This is my investigation. Did you hear any gunshots or not?"

The other deputy stepped closer to Hammond, signaling whose side he was on. "Manning's never investigated a murder like all the ones you have, Chief. Never put any killers behind bars like you done either."

Hammond spit again. "I don't have to answer you, boy, but I will, seeing you clearly don't know your ass from the gully you pulled Jump Diggins out of. No, I did not hear any gunshots. Yesterday was my first day back at the mine after taking two days off. But if you pulled your head out of your own gully, you'd know that even if I had been at work, I wouldn't have heard anything because there's so much noise there between the TNT going off and all the heavy machinery running, everyone wears earplugs to keep from going deaf."

Dobbs blinked. "I hope you understand why I had to ask." He nodded to the other deputy. "Take the coroner and body back to town. I'll be along shortly."

The overweight deputy didn't move. He looked at Hammond for instructions. When the former chief deputy nodded at him to move out, he got in his rig. The coroner did too.

After they left, Hammond said, "Waste of time trying to find whoever shot Jump. Most likely it was some Indian driving to Summit Lake and mistook the donkey for a deer and hungered for some easy backstrap. He either shot Jump by mistake or decided he didn't want any witnesses. Now he's holed up on the reservation and no one there will give him up unless you ride in there and force them to at gunpoint."

Hammond turned to me. "You call yourself a wildlife ranger? You of anyone should know what a poacher is willing to do to cover his tracks."

He didn't wait for me to answer, but got in his rig and drove away.

I asked Dobbs what he was going to do next.

The deputy exhaled. "My job."

"Do you need any help?"

"No, you've done enough already. The coroner will conduct

an autopsy and we'll know what kind of weapon was used. I'll take the packsaddle and Jump's belongings back to the office and go through them. Maybe there's some evidence in them. I'll give Bull some time to settle down, and then I'll give him a call and ask him to ask around the mine to see if anybody there might've seen or heard something the day of the murder."

"Since he didn't, because he says he wasn't at work that day."

Dobbs rubbed his bad leg. "Why would Bull lie about that? It'd be easy enough to prove. That is, if I thought I needed to, which I don't."

"What did you think about his theory of someone mistaking the burro for a deer?"

"Anything's possible, but Bull's right. It'll be pretty hard to track down. Quartz Creek Road is no highway, but it gets its share of traffic. Workers going back and forth to the mine. Hunters and fishermen use it. So do the Indians who live at Summit Lake."

I didn't like it that Dobbs was already making excuses not to look. Being short on staff and short on experience wasn't a great combination for building a successful murder investigation. The fact that the old prospector had no standing in the community or a grief-stricken family clamoring for justice would make it even easier for him to justify giving the homicide a low priority.

Easy for Dobbs, maybe, but not for me. In combat, every man counted, no matter if he was in my squad or my squad's unit or my unit's division. No death was any less important than another. It was a belief we all shared and it held us together when the fighting was the toughest.

"I know from experience that trying to solve a homicide is hard," I said. "My first year on the job, a man turned a wildlife refuge into his personal graveyard for girls. I helped the sheriff's department find the killer. This is your first case and that makes it an important one even if the victim doesn't seem important. Important for your calling, as you put it."

"I know that," he said.

"If you decide you need some help, give me a call. I have an office in No Mountain. The number's in the book. The same goes when you find the killer. Call me. I'll want to know."

"How come? You don't know Jump Diggins."

"True, but since I found him, I feel obligated to him."

He seemed puzzled by that. "All right, I will."

I started to walk to my rig, but then stopped midstride and looked back at the young deputy. "Pudge Warbler. When you mentioned the sheriff's name on the radio yesterday, I got the impression you didn't care for him. Do you two have some kind of history?"

"Why do you want to know that?"

"I married his daughter. We have a little girl."

"Lucky for you. My father never got to meet me. Pudge Warbler shot and killed him two months before I was born."

6

I crossed into Oregon at the border town of Denio. As Nevada retreated with every spin of the pickup's tires, I tried to erase the image of Jump Diggins' death mask. Ruby's too. I didn't want them haunting me when I got home and kissed my wife and daughter. As much as I wanted to believe Chief Deputy Dobbs was up to the task, instinct told me it was only a matter of time before I'd be turning my rig around and driving back south.

Familiarity grew as I pressed north through Harney County. The great white salt flat of the Alvord Desert shimmered like a beacon. I gassed up at the lonely outpost of Fields Station before climbing up and over Long Hollow Summit. The two-lane dropped into Catlow Valley and there was no stopping now. The road was straight, the sky blue, and the speedometer had numbers to the right that begged burying. My 8-track tape of *American Beauty* was three years old, but still unstretched and unscratched despite heavy playing because it was among the best road music ever recorded. I shoved it into the player bolted below the dash and cranked up the volume. Jerry Garcia and the rest of the Grateful Dead kept me company as I sang along:

"Truckin', I'm a goin' home. Whoa, whoa, baby, back where I belong."

Passing between Hart Mountain National Antelope Refuge and Steens Mountain, I rolled down the window and breathed in the hot, dry air. It carried the scent of sagebrush and juniper that tasted as good as it smelled. Seeing the Donner und Blitzen River winding through the grasslands of the Malheur National Wildlife Refuge and the blue water of the big lake that gave the sanctuary its name felt good too. These were more than landmarks, they were my neighbors, as familiar to me as houses on any block on any street in any town were to a husband and father arriving home after a hard day's work.

The last stretch was always the longest coming back from a patrol and I found myself pressing both hands against the steering wheel as if I could push myself across the finish line that much sooner. I grinned back at the impish smile in the snapshot fastened to the visor, knowing how fast Hattie would scamper when she heard my pickup rattle over the cattle guard that marked the entrance to the ranch, knowing how good it would feel to pick up my daughter, swing her around, and then tuck her under my arm as I bounded up the steps to the front porch and pulled her mother into an embrace that didn't need any whispered words to go along with it to say how much I'd missed her.

Flashing red lights ahead snapped me back to the moment. A Harney County sheriff's vehicle was stopped broadside on the two-lane into No Mountain. I turned off the music and came to a chary halt. Deputy Orville Nelson sat in the driver's seat with his police band radio's mike to his lips. Questions ricocheted in my head. Had a big rig T-boned a rancher's pickup up ahead? Maybe some cows had busted loose and were moseying down the middle of the blacktop. Or was this a roadblock aimed at intercepting a fleeing criminal?

Orville glanced over and his eyebrows rose in recognition. The grin that accompanied their sudden elevation was reassuring. By the time I put it in park and got out, the young deputy had finished his radio call.

"Ranger Drake, it is good to see you," he said cheerfully when I reached his specially equipped rig that allowed him to control the gas and brake pedals with his hands; he'd lost the use of his legs when a cattle rustler shot him in the back. "You have been gone some time."

"What's with the roadblock?"

"The movie. They are filming a scene at Blackpowder Smith's today and the action inside is supposed to spill out into the street. I have been tasked with traffic control. Another deputy is doing the same north of town."

"What are you talking about?"

"You have not heard about the movie?"

"My radio's more no-way than two-way when I'm on the refuges."

Orville's grin widened. "You will never believe it. No Mountain has gone Hollywood! They are shooting a Western starring Garth Scott and Amber Russell." When I didn't react, he said, "The biggest movie stars in the world?"

"I don't watch much TV."

"Their films are blockbusters. You cannot pick up a magazine without seeing Amber Russell on the cover. Garth Scott was nominated for an Academy Award for his last role."

I shrugged. "I'm sure Gemma's heard of them."

"She has more than heard of them. Your wife is working on the movie set. The producer hired her as the on-location veterinarian to look after the horses, cows, and dogs. Actually, there is only one dog in the movie, but they use three different ones to play him. It is like the stunt men they use for Garth Scott. One for riding, one for shooting, and one for fighting. He does the love scenes with Amber Russell himself."

"Smart man."

"A lot of folks are working as extras. Blackpowder Smith landed a speaking part. He says 'What'll it be?' when the bad guy enters. The set designers have turned his tavern and dry-goods store into an old fashioned, Wild West saloon complete with card tables, a piano player, and dancehall girls."

"Knowing Blackpowder, he probably stands in front of a mirror all day practicing that one line."

Orville grinned again. "He certainly appears to have been bitten by the acting bug."

"I hope you're not going to tell me they shanghaied Pudge into putting on a costume and fake moustache. I need to talk to him about a murder that happened in Nevada."

"A murder? Whose?"

"An old prospector. I found his body when I was at the Sheldon refuge and called the local sheriff's office."

"That would be Humboldt County sheriff's."

I nodded. "It's their case, but I wanted to talk to Pudge about it."

"Of course. To answer your question, Sheriff Warbler is the least star-struck of all. He is focused on making sure none of the movie people get hurt or into trouble while they are in Harney County. We deputies have to clear any calls for help and citizen complaints through him first. The sheriff does not want to see something wind up on the front page of the *Burns Herald* that could get picked up by big city newspapers and television news."

"Although Bonnie LaRue wouldn't mind that one bit." She was the paper's formidable editor and publisher whose on-again, off-again courtship with Pudge was always making head-lines of their own among the town gossips.

I asked Orville where the movie crew was staying since No Mountain didn't have a motel.

"They have taken up residence at the Crossed Bars Ranch. There are plenty of bedrooms built by the religious cult that owned it. I understand it is still in top-notch condition after they abandoned it. An encampment of equipment trucks and trailers along with a mobile kitchen and dining tents has been set up on the outskirts of town."

"How much longer are they going to be filming?"

"At least another week, possibly two according to the schedule they gave us."

"I meant, right now."

"I will radio the location manager and ask. She has been very helpful. There are always breaks in filming, either for repositioning the cameras or reshooting a scene because someone flubbed their lines."

While Orville made the call, I looked in the direction of town and wondered what else had changed since I'd been gone. I hoped not much, because No Mountain was perfect just the way it was. Peaceful, beautiful, and as far off the beaten track as a person could get.

Orville re-cradled the mike. "You are in luck. They are on break for another five or ten minutes, which, in the movie business means at least thirty. You will want to drive down the center of the road and keep it under five miles per hour."

"How come?"

"Because No Mountain has returned to being the wild, Wild West town it once was."

Orville backed up his rig to let me through. I passed the old lineman's shack with its cockeyed stovepipe that had been my home when I first moved to No Mountain. Since marrying Gemma and moving to her family's ranch, it had become an official field office for the US Fish and Wildlife's Western Region, part of a deal I'd struck when I turned down my boss's offer to move to Portland to become the district supervisor. The patch of open desert on the town side of the shack was now occupied by the movie company's trailers and equipment.

No Mountain itself had been transformed. The block of false-fronted wood-sided buildings that dated back a century had received artfully applied makeup in the way of paint, a change of signs, and pre-automobile fixtures. A foot of soft dirt covered the two-lane blacktop that served as Main Street. Saddle horses were tied up at a newly placed hitching post in front of Blackpowder Smith's. There was a wooden horse trough too. Klieg lights were positioned across the street to illuminate the exterior while a camera dolly on tracks was set up on the sidewalk.

Extras were milling about. The men were dressed in cowboy getups and the women in bonnets and prairie dresses. I drove slowly so as not to spook the hitched horses. Two women with lots of makeup were sitting on director's chairs, drinking Coca-Cola from bottles. They wore frilly red dancehall dresses that showed off garters and black fishnet stockings.

Catching me staring, one batted her false eyelashes and said in a Mae West drawl, "Come on over here, big boy, and I'll give you a," she gave it a couple of beats, "autograph."

"Don't scare him off, Dani," the other one said in a Betty Boop voice. "We might need a big, strong man to come rescue us from a bear one night."

She gave an exaggerated shudder and it nearly caused her breasts to spill out of the lowcut bodice. The actresses laughed and clinked their Coke bottles.

The dirt covering the blacktop ended past the post office and I sped up. A few minutes later I turned left, rattled over the cattle guard, and parked in front of the Warbler ranch house. I waited for the screen door to swing open and slam shut followed by the echo of little cowgirl boots thumping down the front steps and crunching across the gravel drive.

I gave it thirty seconds. Sixty seconds. A full two minutes. Dismayed that no one realized I was home, I got out to see what other changes had occurred in my absence.

Neither my wife nor daughter was inside, but November was in the kitchen tending to two soup pots simmering on the stove. The healer whose birth name in *Numu* translated to Girl Born in Snow harrumphed at the sight of me.

"Your own eyes cannot see I am busy with soup? Take the cornbread out of the oven before it burns. It is no good to anyone when it becomes like wood in a campfire put out by rain."

"I missed you too, *Mu'a*," I said, using the *Numu* word for grandmother that Hattie called her.

I pulled a hot mitt from the drawer and opened the oven door to find four, square cake pans of cornbread with crusts the color of honey. "This is a lot of food. Are you having a home-coming party for me or cooking for the movie crew in town?"

November's tsk was sharp. "Who has time for make-believe when real life and death is happening."

"What's that supposed to mean?"

"Many of the elders are sick. Some have already made the journey to the spirit world. I am making healing soup for those who cannot feed themselves."

"I ran into Searcher yesterday. He said there was sickness at Duck Valley and Summit Lake too. What is it, a summer flu?"

"This sickness knows no season. Cut the cornbread into squares and wrap them in paper and place them in a sack. Hurry. We are late."

"We?"

"While my own two feet can carry my pots, it is better for the elders if you drive us so the medicine will be hot when I ladle it into bowls."

Steam rose from the crosshatches I sliced into the cornbread like the vapors that hissed from volcanic vents scattered throughout the high lava plains. In the rising mists, I could see the faces of Paiute elders. I asked if my old friend Tuhudda Will was sick.

November's ladle stopped clanking against the side of a pot. The gray hairs that wove through her hair like spider's silk seemed whiter than before I'd left on my trip. She was in her late seventies, the same age as Tuhudda.

"Our first stop will be his camp. I will sing a healing song while he drinks the soup."

My stomach churned. "And Nagah Will?"

"He has the strength of youth."

I'd seen Tuhudda's grandson grow from a shy boy into a confident eighteen-year-old. Nagah now worked as Gemma's assistant. She'd taught him everything, from how to fly her plane to injecting vaccines and treating hoof-and-mouth. Hattie worshipped him. He was the brother she never had.

"Is Nagah taking care of Tuhudda?"

"Not today. He is with Gemma. They flew to Warm Springs to treat many cows with blackleg. Girl Fell from Sky is with them." That was the *Numu* name she'd given Hattie.

"I wondered where they were."

"Hm. Your eyes say missing, not wonder. If you would spend less time talking and more time cutting cornbread, we can be home by the time they return."

We finished preparing the meals and loaded them into my pickup, whose engine hadn't had time to cool. November kept her striped Pendleton blanket wrapped around her shoulders as she sat next to me. I took the road east across Harney Basin. It led over both forks of the Silvies River that emptied into Malheur Lake.

A pickup headed toward us as we neared the junction to the rutted track that led to the Will camp. I pulled over to give it room to pass. Four adults crowded the front seat. Three, maybe four, children sat on their laps. I didn't recognize them, nor the half-dozen people riding in the back. November murmured as the rig eased by us. The tailgate was down and a shrouded body was in the pickup's bed.

"Who's that?" I said.

"Donna Has Many. The fever took her."

Donna was a spry woman who tended a garden a couple miles past the Will camp. She would shake her hoe at crows and ask them to leave a little corn for her or she'd become too poor to feed them.

"The people in the pickup must be family, but I don't recognize them. Where do they live?"

"They are *Agaipaninadökadö*, Summit Lake Fish Eaters, from her husband's side. He moved here when they married to live with her family as is the *Numu* way. He journeyed to the spirit world several years ago."

"Are they taking Donna to Summit Lake?"

"No, her journey ceremony is at Lyle Rides Alone's ranch. He and Donna are cousins."

"Searcher was walking from Duck Valley to Summit Lake, but he is neither a Tule Eater nor a Fish Eater. I've asked him who his people are, but he never answers. Do you know?"

She shook her head.

When the cortège had passed, we completed the turnoff. The Will camp comprised a few single-wide trailers, cabins, and outbuildings. Rusty junkers littered the yard. Horses grazed in an adjoining field. In winter, the same field would be crowded with the family's herd of sheep that was now pasturing down in the Catlow Valley.

Tuhudda's middle daughter was sitting on a sagging couch in the front room of his trailer mending clothes.

"I have brought soup," November said.

"Ah," the woman said, inhaling deeply. The thimble on her index finger flashed as she tapped the side of her broad nose. "I smell wada root." The women were both *Wadadökadö*, the Wada Root and Grass-seed Eaters.

November asked if her father had slept last night.

"His dreams broke often. The coughing has left him weak. If not for the poultice you made, I don't know if . . ." Her voice drifted off like a dying echo.

November set the pot on the counter, took a bowl from one of the open shelves, and filled it with soup. Plucking a spoon from a drawer, she said to me, "Put some cornbread on a napkin and bring it."

Tuhudda was propped up in a narrow bunk in a room at the far end of the single-wide. The red bandana he usually wore as a headband to keep his long, white hair away from his face was clenched in his fist. Rheum clouded his eyes and his craggy cheeks were pale as sheets.

"Hello, my old friend," I said, making an effort to swallow my shock at his appearance.

"Nick Drake. I knew you were coming before you left," he said. His manner of speaking was even slower and more deliberate than usual. Tuhudda was soon wracked by coughing. He held the red bandana to his lips until the fit subsided.

"Do not spend your breath on words," November chided. "You will need it to help me sing when it is time to sing. Now, it is time for soup."

His hands shook and the spoon clacked against his few

remaining teeth. November took it from him and held the bowl
to his lips. He lapped at it like a kitten at a saucer of milk.

Tuhudda pushed the bowl away. "My eyes have not seen you
for many days."

"Work," I said. "I drove up from the Sheldon refuge today. I
was looking for a bighorn ewe that I put a radio collar on last
spring."

"Does the sheep like to listen to music?"

I could see the twinkle behind the rheum in his eyes and it
was good he still had his sense of humor. "It sends a signal that
makes the animal easier to find. She's the leader of a band of
ewes and their offspring. I find her, I'll find them and can make a
head count. A collared ram wouldn't lead me to the rest of the
herd as easily since most only come around during the rut."

"To find a ram, you must listen for butting heads. This is so."

Tuhudda's words seemed to leave him exhausted. He
slumped back onto the pillow. November tsked. "Eat some cornbread. I used extra honey for you."

A thin smile appeared on the old man's lips. "Everything is
better sweeter."

I broke off a piece and was preparing to hold it to his mouth,
but his hand reached out and took it from me. "I will feed
myself."

When Tuhudda swallowed the last crumb, November held
the bowl to his lips. "To help the cornbread on its journey."

After a few more sips of soup, he laid back on the pillow and
was soon asleep. November started murmuring. It was the same
sound she'd made when the pickup carrying Donna Has Many
passed us. It also sounded like the murmuring I'd heard last
night when camped above the gully.

Tuhudda's daughter collected the bowl, spoon, and napkin.
She placed them in the sink and then returned to stand between

November and me. "My father told me stories of how fever took our ancestors. Perhaps he will survive this one."

"When Tuhudda and I were the age Nagah is now, the fever white men called Spanish flu took many of our people," November said. "There have been many fevers since. Small pox. Tuberculosis. Measles. No matter the name, all spelled death for *Numu*."

The old healer murmured some more and started chanting. "We sing to our ancestors to give Tuhudda strength. We sing to them to welcome Donna Has Many. And we sing for the Forever Walkers who fled their camp to escape a fever long ago and left behind only the echo of their footsteps on a path that has no end."

7

Dusk was already settling over the eastern horizon when the sun dipped behind the Cascades to the west. November and I clattered across the cattle guard and pulled up to the ranch. This time the screen door swung open. Hattie squealed as she flew down the steps and across the gravel drive. I barely had time to jump out of the cab and stretch out my arms to catch her as she leapt. Her pert nose had sunburned since I'd been away and was peeling. Her freckles seemed browner.

"Daddy, guess what? I gave a cow a shot and didn't close my eyes. Guess what? I sat in the front seat while Nagah flew us home. Did you bring me anything?"

"I can't remember. I'll have to unpack and see."

"You're teasing." She tightened her arms around my neck and looked over my shoulder. "Why is *Mu'a* with you? She didn't go on your trip."

"I got home early and we took soup to Tuhudda Will. Is Nagah still here?"

"He went home."

"We must've passed him on the way. Here, let me put you down so I can bring in the pots."

By the time I followed Hattie up the front steps, Gemma was on the porch. Her ponytail swished and her eyes sparkled.

"Well, if it isn't a door-to-door salesman. I hope you brought something besides old pots and pans."

"Tall tales and this." The pots clanged like cymbals when they hit the floor and I threw my arms around her waist and pulled her close and gave her a kiss that shouted the three most important words ever spoken.

"My, you have been gone a long time," she said with a laugh when we came up for air.

I carried the pots to the kitchen where November was putting a kettle on to boil. Hattie was running back and forth to her room dragging out drawings and talking a mile a minute about all the things that had happened while I'd been away.

"I rode Sarah every morning while Mama led her around the corral. Grandpa took me fishing." She took a breath. "How come you can hear pots when they fall, but not falling stars?"

"I've been asking that my whole life. Did you go see the movie being made?"

Her head bobbed. "There are three dogs that look the same and do tricks. Everybody sits around in dress-up clothes and then some mean man yells and they all run around."

I glanced at Gemma. "I ran into Orville on the way in. He gave me the what's what."

"I couldn't say no when they asked," she said. "They were bringing a vet from California, but he got derailed at the last minute."

"Orville said Blackpowder has gone Hollywood. How about you?"

"Not a chance. There are more egos on the set than red

anguses grazing at the Rocking H. I'll take being out on a ranch hip deep in cow flop any day."

Hattie sat at the dining table to color while I went to take a shower. When I first moved to the Warbler ranch, Gemma and I slept in her room with our baby in a crib next to us while Pudge and I built a bedroom wing that had a view of open desert and the Stinkingwater Mountains beyond. It went up fast thanks to a couple of old-fashioned barn-raising parties.

After a late supper, and with Hattie put to bed, Gemma and I sat on the porch drinking tea. We took our time filling each other in on what we'd done over the past ten days. I told her about the bighorn ewe. She spoke about working with the horses on the movie set and the fever that was plaguing Harney County.

"It seems like it's targeting the old ones," she said. "I've worried myself sick about November and Tuhudda. Pudge got mad as a hornet when I told him I was worried about him too. He said he wasn't old, only well-seasoned."

We sipped our tea and gazed into the still of the night broken only by the snorts and nickers from the two cutting horses in their corral and the steady whine of crickets sawing their wings.

Gemma leaned her head on my shoulder and said, "Something happened on your trip that you're not telling me."

"Nothing gets past you. I didn't want to mention it because I didn't want to put a dampener on being home."

"But now you have, so you'd better spill it."

I breathed in the steam rising from my mug and then told her about finding the old prospector and his jenny, meeting Chief Deputy Manning Dobbs, and my suspicion that somehow the gold mine was involved.

"Jump Diggins and Ruby. For some reason when I sketched them, I pictured an old married couple. I must be getting soft."

"That'll be the day," Gemma said. "It'll also be quite a day if you ever tell me you see me as an old jenny. You'll find out I can kick even harder."

That earned a smile and a squeeze.

"But I agree with the chief deputy," she said. "Why would a big gold-mining company have anything to do with the prospector's murder, and if it had, why leave the body to be found? Why not bury it there or hide it under a pile of crushed ore or in the bottom of a cyanide pond?"

I gave her a look. "Maybe being around moviemaking is wearing off on you. Chuck a body in a vat of poison?"

"Go on, admit it. You wondered the same thing yourself." My silence answered for me. "You are going to leave this to the Winnemucca deputy, aren't you?"

I wondered if she knew her father had killed his, but I wasn't about to mention it. "I have plenty of my own work to do. There's the visitor's center under construction at Malheur, a trail sign project at Hart, not to mention the honey-do list I put together when I was at the Lower Klamath refuges."

"But . . ."

"But what?"

"The bighorn at Sheldon. You told me you weren't able to find her."

"That's true. I'll have to go back and check on her if I'm to keep up with the study."

Gemma nudged me. "Don't prospectors call iron pyrite 'fool's gold'? So, who's fooling who now about going back to look for a lost sheep?"

That earned another squeeze from me. "Speaking of, want to go fool around?"

"I thought you'd never ask."

Gemma picked up our mugs and took them to the kitchen on her way to the bedroom. As I got up to follow, a pair of headlights turned off the main road. I recognized the sheriff's rig. I could either wait for my father-in-law to park and say hello or hurry after Gemma.

The screen door didn't even come close to hitting my backside when it slammed shut.

8

Hattie and Pudge were already eating breakfast by the time Gemma and I joined them. The four-year-old's lips and fingertips were covered with powdered sugar. "I helped *Mu'a* make frybread."

I filled a mug from the blue enamel coffee pot that took center stage on the dining table and plucked a piece of the sugar-coated treat from a basket with a black triangle pattern that November had woven.

"How were things on the California refuges?" Pudge said. The sheriff was dressed for work. The seven-point star on his chest was polished as usual and his short-brim Stetson and holstered .45 were hanging by the front door.

"With lots of miles and no soft beds between them," I said.

"Did you hear about all this Hollywood hoopla?"

"Orville said you're trying to keep the movie people from turning No Mountain into the Sodom and Gomorrah of the high lonesome."

The lawman's bulldog jowls jiggled when he clicked his cheeks. "They act up more than they act in front of a camera. A lawman I know was working in Navajo County when they were shooting all the Westerns in Monument Valley. He told me a liquor distributor out of Phoenix wore through a set of tires each movie."

November was pushing through the kitchen's swinging doors carrying a skillet of fried eggs. "That valley is the home of Di'neh but they called them Apache in the movie."

"How on Earth would you know that?" Pudge said.

The old healer tsked. "One night I heard people shooting. I grabbed my skillet, but it was the television set. You were asleep. A man in it said Fort Apache."

"The name of the movie. One of my favorites," Pudge said. "John Wayne starred, but in my book, the scenery was the biggest star. Almost as pretty as Harney County."

"Are they making a cowboy and Indian movie here?" I said.

"It's a range-war story," Gemma said. "Homesteaders versus an evil land baron who controls all the water and graze. Garth Scott is a mysterious gunslinger with a past who shows up and helps the homesteaders."

"Let me guess. He falls in love with a homesteader's beautiful daughter. Then he has a showdown with the bad guy and they let their six-guns settle things."

"Close, but with a twist. Amber Russell plays the bad guy's wife. She meets Garth and while they're rolling around the hayloft the sparks between them all but light the barn on fire. She winds up shooting her husband and rides off into the sunset with the handsome gunslinger."

Pudge pushed away from the table. "Speaking of riding off, I got to scoot. The director wants to drive a herd of cattle right through No Mountain and I'm the one who's gonna have to educate him about cows not being very good in the listening department. He stands in front of them and shouts 'Cut,' he's likely to wind up on the wrong side of a hundred hooves."

He kissed Hattie on the head, buckled his holster, and

slapped on his Stetson. I bolted the rest of my coffee. "I left something in my pickup. I'll be right back."

I caught up to Pudge as he was climbing into his rig. "Got a minute?"

"Depends on what it is you're so hellbent on telling me without my granddaughter hearing it."

"I stumbled onto a killing while I was working at the Sheldon refuge."

"Oh Lord. I knew it was too good to be true that these past few years going by without you getting yourself into the middle of a homicide meant you never would again."

"I didn't go looking for it," I said.

"You never do. Trouble always finds you even if it takes some time off. Better go on and tell me about it while I still have the patience that comes with a new morning."

I described the prospector and his burro lying in the gully. "His name is Jump Diggins."

"I've come across plenty of desert ramblers over the years, but I don't recollect that moniker. Blackpowder might. He did a little prospecting in Nevada back in the day. That is if you can tear him away from preening for the cameras. He's convinced he's gonna be the next Dub Taylor."

"Thanks, I'll make a point of it."

"If you were at the Sheldon, you were probably in Humboldt County since it has the lion's share of the refuge. You must've met Sheriff Jim Coons. He's worn a star even longer than me."

"I didn't. He's recuperating from bypass surgery."

"Probably has eaten a whole lot more frybread and chicken-fried steak than me too. Who's in charge, his chief deputy, Bull Hammond?"

"You know him?"

"I met him a couple of times chasing bad guys over the state line. A real blunt-instrument sort."

"That's an underestimate. He retired to take a job as head of security of a new gold mine that's right next to where I found Jump Diggins. I talked to him twice. The first occasion was about a buck mule deer that was poisoned by wastewater leaking from one of the mine's cyanide wastewater ponds. The second time was when I asked him if he'd heard all the rifle fire in broad daylight that killed Diggins and his burro."

Pudge arched an eyebrow. "What was his excuse after he got done telling you off?"

"Hammond said he wasn't at the mine that day."

"You think there's something not jake about a fellow lawman?"

"You're the one who's always told me to trust my gut."

"That's a fact. Your gut also telling you there something not jake about the gold mine too?" When I nodded, he said, "Tell you what. I'll ask Orville if he can find something out about the owner. So, if Jim Coons and Bull Hammond aren't trying to track down the killer, who's leading the investigation?"

"The new chief deputy. Manning Dobbs."

"Well, how about that? The kid gone and went into law. I expect he told you about me and his daddy."

"Only that you shot him."

"Reggie Dobbs didn't leave me a choice. It if was to happen all over again, I'd still shoot him. That doesn't mean I don't think about it from time to time, same as I do with any of the men I put down. Except for the ones on Iwo Jima. There was no time to count bodies and no time to feel sorry for nobody, not even my foxhole buddies. I had plenty of time afterward to get a lump in my throat and shed a tear for my fellow leathernecks who died on that godforsaken rock. Still do, and not only on Veterans Day and Memorial Day."

"How do you know about Manning Dobbs? He said he was born after his father died."

"I found out later. Reggie's widow sent me a letter with a photograph of her holding a baby. She wasn't more than a child herself. Teenage bride, I reckon. She asked me to put in a word for her so she'd get a twenty-five hundred dollar reward a bank had put on her husband. She was of the mind that I was gonna get it and I had to set her straight it doesn't work that way for people who wear a star. Later, I got to thinking about her hard-luck story, and, well, I mailed her some money. It wasn't anywhere close to the reward, but it was all I could afford. Hundred fifty bucks, half-month's pay back then. I had a child of my own to feed."

"I'm glad you did. Feed Gemma, I mean."

"Years later I got a call from a teacher in Winnemucca. He'd given his students an assignment to write about what they wanted to be when they grew up. Manning Dobbs wrote he wanted to be an honest sheriff because his daddy was a bank robber and he mentioned my name when he described what happened to him. The teacher said the essay was so well-written he thought the kid had either made it up or copied it from a book. He called me to see if it was true." Pudge paused. "What sort of man did he grow up to be?"

"To borrow one of your expressions, he's still mighty wet behind the ears. The sheriff named him Bull Hammond's replacement even though he only has two years on the job. It sounds like it was by default because no one else wanted to take it. Dobbs never worked a murder case before. He doesn't even know where to start."

"Then he'll have to learn on the job like most deputies who work in big territories do."

"What about his father? You say he robbed a bank in Harney County?"

"In Burns. Killed some people doing it too. Reggie Dobbs was as cold-blooded as they come."

"What happened?"

"The Devil came to town. I was no doe-eyed deputy, mind you. I had four years on the job after getting my discharge following VJ Day. I came home from the Pacific, signed on with the sheriff's, and got married, all in the span of three weeks. Nine months later we were blessed with Gemma. That's the way we did things back then. War taught us time was precious and don't waste any of it because life was short and death certain. But, I got to tell you, what Reggie Dobbs and his cutthroats did put some gravel in my gizzard."

Pudge told me the story as we stood beneath a daisy-yellow sun in front of the ranch house. The then-young lawman was driving back to the sheriff's office from Crane where he'd been investigating a missing-horse case when his radio crackled. It was a quarter past two on a wintry afternoon. There was more electricity in the dispatcher's voice than in the overhead power lines running alongside the road. A hold-up at the First National Bank. Shots fired. Two dead. Two injured. One taken hostage. Three suspects. All armed and dangerous. Weapons included a Guide Lamp M3 submachine gun. Pudge had fired one in the war. It was a light version of the Thompson machine gun. GIs nicknamed it a grease gun because it resembled a tool used by auto mechanics.

The robbers got away in a Lincoln Continental, a red cabriolet with a rag top the color of sand and whitewalls so big it made the car look like it had spinning clouds for tires. Pudge thought it was a mighty conspicuous car for outlaws to use in a part of the country where pickups and tractors outnumbered sedans twenty to one. They were either cocksure or plumb loco. Turned out he was right on both accounts.

Pudge hit the siren on his pickup and gave chase even though he was miles behind the Lincoln and the posse of sheriff's vehicles chasing it. The dispatcher was reading off last knowns like a caller at a thoroughbred racetrack. The Lincoln tore up Broadway, screeched around the corner at Adams, sped back down on Alder, and careened onto Highway 20 heading west. It blew through Hines where it just missed striking a pedestrian, but forced an oncoming car to swerve and crash into a sign post. The red Lincoln was last seen traveling at a high rate of speed on the straightaway past Riley, heading for the county line.

The sheriff bet that the bank robbers were bound for Bend. He called his counterpart in Deschutes County and asked him to send his deputies east on Highway 20 for an intercept. He also alerted Oregon State Police troopers and requested a roadblock be set up on Highway 395 in case they tried to make an end run south.

Pudge pushed his rig to the limit to catch up as the dispatcher provided updates on the robber's victims. One of the two dead was the bank guard, a moonlighting pensioner who'd served with the 6th Marines at the Battle of Belleau Wood in the Great War. Pudge always traded salutes with him when he went to the bank to deposit his paycheck. The second fatality was a teller, the mother of two children whose husband had been left an invalid after a horse kicked him in the head. Pudge knew the two injured customers too—one by a gunshot in the leg, the other by a pistol cracked across the skull. There weren't many people in Burns he didn't know, or in all of Harney County, for that matter.

The name of the hostage forced air from his lungs and a curse from his lips. Connie Barstow was a childhood friend of his wife, Henrietta. She was also engaged to Blackpowder Smith, who was as close to being a best friend as the young deputy would allow himself to have.

Pudge crested a rise and saw emergency flashers and brake lights a mile ahead reddening the otherwise leaden sky. The only thing illuminated between the faceoff between Harney County and Deschutes County sheriff's vehicles was a snow flurry blowing across the two-lane. He slammed on the brakes.

"The Lincoln's a bullfighter's cape," he shouted into his mike. "They've ditched it for another vehicle and are doubling back."

He didn't wait for the sheriff to agree or argue. Pudge hung a U-turn and sped back toward Burns, figuring the bank robbers had turned off on one of the dirt roads that led to ranches along the highway where they'd stashed a second getaway car or stolen a new one. There were only a handful of houses between the county line and Burns. He replayed the chase, trying to picture any oncoming cars he'd passed. Pudge recalled a couple of big rigs—the wakes from their trailers nearly blew him off the two-lane—and also a pickup. All had solitary drivers behind the wheel.

Then he remembered a fleeting image of a dark blue, late model Buick. He could see the shiny vertical bars in the Roadmaster's oversized chrome grille flashing like teeth as it barreled toward him, but couldn't recall the driver or any passengers. The car stuck in his mind because Doc Wooster had one just like it. He drove it in the annual Fourth of July parade with red, white, and blue ribbons streaming from the antenna and his signature chalkboard propped in the rear window with the ever-changing number of babies he'd delivered written in big, white numbers. Doc had a hearty laugh, a penchant for fly fishing using flies he tied himself, and lived in a tidy ranch house between Chickahominy Creek and Silver Creek with his wife Belinda.

Pudge got back on the radio. "I got a hunch the suspects stole Doc Wooster's Buick and are heading east. Put an APB on it. I'm coming up on the turnoff to his place now."

"Wait for backup," the sheriff barked. "You don't know the robbers ain't holed up there waiting til dark to get away. Need I remind you they're armed with a machine gun?"

And so were plenty of Tojo's boys on every Pacific Island he'd stormed, Pudge thought to himself. He pulled his gun out of the holster and held onto it as he steered. It was a standard US Marine Corps Colt .45 automatic that he'd been issued and brought back from overseas. When he was offered a new weapon upon becoming a deputy, he said he'd just as soon keep this one. It was as familiar as his thumb and four fingers.

Pudge ruled out trying to sneak up on the Wooster house. This wasn't the time nor place for a sneak attack. Only a full frontal assault would do. He left the lights and siren on as he turned into the drive and gave the accelerator another punch to raise dust. When the house neared, he slammed on the brakes and cranked the wheel, shooting up a wave of dirt and gravel that peppered the front porch. When he came to a stop broadside to the front door, Pudge jumped out of his rig and crouched with his .45 aimed and ready. No doors slammed. No machine gun bullets stitched across the pickup's body. No one cried for help.

He counted to three and then charged the front door. It was ajar, but he kicked it open anyway while sweeping the room with his sidearm. Doc Wooster was slumped against the entryway wall. His wire rim glasses were askew. The bullet hole in his forehead was not. It had been placed dead center one inch above the bridge of his bulbous nose.

Pudge made a quick search of the house and garage. Neither Belinda nor the Buick were to be found, but the red Lincoln was. He didn't wait for the rest of the posse to arrive. He jumped back in his rig and tore up the road and fishtailed onto the highway.

"Doc's dead in the house. The Lincoln's in the garage," he radioed. "Belinda's not there. If she's not dead or hiding in a field, then they grabbed themselves a second hostage. Suspects are in Doc's Buick. I'm in pursuit."

Impatient to learn the ending, I said, "They had a fifteen-minute head start on you, at least. The entire Harney County sheriff's department was still miles behind you. How did you catch up to Reggie Dobbs and his gang?"

Pudge pushed the short brim of his Stetson back and rubbed his jaw. "Well, son, with a little horse sense and a lotta luck. Not to mention some help from the Good Lord and a good friend. You see, I knew they were determined to get out of Oregon. There were only three ways they could go, what with the state troopers blocking three-ninety-five south. One was to head straight east to Idaho, but that would mean crossing over the Snake River. The last thing a man on the run wants is a bridge between him and freedom. Going north to Washington meant having to figure out all the backroads over the Blue Mountains, but remember, this was in wintertime. No, their only choice was to go south to Nevada."

The old lawman shrugged. "Plus, I had a hint that's where they'd come from. The red Lincoln? It didn't have any plates on it, but I found a Winnemucca car dealer's business card in the glovebox."

"You couldn't have caught up to them sticking to the main road through Burns, but you knew about the dirt road shortcut near Hines."

"That's right. If I recollect, you were driving that same one a few years back and hit one of those three convicts on the run."

"Taking it would've put you in No Mountain around the same time as the bank robbers. Is that where you had it out with them?"

Before Pudge could answer, his radio squawked. He reached over and clicked the mike. "Sheriff Warbler here. Go ahead."

It was Orville Nelson. He said the sheriff was needed right away at the Crossed Bars Ranch. A fight had broken out there and one of the movie stars had gotten hold of a pistol. Shots were fired.

"The director's assistant Mr. Briscoe called for you personally," the young deputy said. "He sounded overwrought."

"That the one who wears a polka dot neckerchief and talks with an English accent? He always sounds like his pants are on fire. Did you happen to remind him all their guns are loaded with blanks?"

"He said this one is a star's personal weapon."

"Garth Scott or the one playing the bad guy? I forget his name."

"Neither. The gun belongs to Miss Russell. She fired it and now she has locked herself in her room and says she will not come out until you come assure her that you will personally take charge of her safety."

"Great day in the morning! Now that woman wants me to be her babysitter too?"

"Mr. Briscoe said the director will be ever so grateful and give you a special title in the credits."

"You can tell your Mr. Briscoe where the director can put that special title of his." Pudge exhaled noisily. "All right, I'm on my way. But Orville? Keep this on the QT. Nobody, and I mean nobody being Bonnie LaRue gets wind of this."

The sheriff slammed the mike down and turned to me. "These Hollywood folks. The one who fired the gun, Miss Russell? She gets fresh cucumbers delivered to her room every day. Slices them with a fancy silver knife and puts them over her eyes when she sleeps. Says it keeps the wrinkles away, especially here in Harney where it's so dry."

"How do you know that?"

"She told me when I saw them in her room."

"You were in her bedroom?"

"I was walking by and heard her screaming. It was only a little hobo spider that scared her."

"Did you throw a cucumber at it or her silver knife?"

"My bootheel."

"I don't know what I want to hear about first, how you stopped Reggie Dobbs or how you became a Hollywood sex symbol's leading man."

"Son, I'll take facing down a bank robber armed with a grease gun over a mad as a hen actress any goldang day of the week."

9

No Mountain was quiet. The mouthy dancehall girls who'd been sitting in director's chairs in front of Blackpowder Smith's tavern and dry-goods store were nowhere to be seen. The Klieg lights aimed at his establishment had been turned off and fitted with protective black hoods. No saddle horses were tied to the recently installed hitching post. While Blackpowder's was open for business, the store aisles were empty.

I found the proprietor leaning on his elbows at the bar with his eyes glued to a book. "Going over your lines?"

"Well, howdy there, young fella. Didn't hear you come in." He tapped the side of his head. "Got 'em all memorized."

Blackpowder sported a white billy-goat beard and a black cowboy hat with a snakeskin band. He wasn't wearing a costume for the movie; it was the way he always dressed. I asked him what he was reading.

"It's a book about method acting. I'm studying on using my own experiences and throw 'em into the role I'm playing. See, the more I make the character my own, the more authentic it'll be. Russian fella name of Stanislavski invented it. Marlon Brando? He was all method all the time in *A Streetcar Named Desire*. Earned him an Oscar nomination. Three years later he won the prize straight out for *On the Waterfront*. I liked that one better. More action." The old codger closed the book. "Haven't seen you 'round for a spell. Where you been?"

"California and Nevada."

"Did you get down to Hollywood? I'm hankering to see all those handprints in cement in front of that fancy Chinese theater."

"The Lower Klamath refuges were as far south as I ventured."

"Well, you sure have missed a lot." He swept his hand to encompass the interior of the tavern. Old-fashioned oil lamps with glass chimneys hung over rustic wood tables and chairs. A roulette wheel and an upright piano were positioned near a stage set against the rear wall.

Blackpowder winked. "After they're done filming, they're goin' leave all these fixings as payment for using my place. I'm goin' advertise it in the *Herald*. Get people to come down to take a gander. Might even charge admission. I'm getting a stack of photos of yours truly and will autograph 'em, the fans want." He struck a pose.

"Could be a boost for your new acting career."

"My thoughts precisely."

"Do you still have time to make coffee?"

"You betcha. Folks from the film crew come in special for a cup of my joe even when they can get it for free over at the canteen they set up next to your old lineman's shack." He chuckled. "Pardon me, I mean the US Fish and Wildlife office."

Blackpowder poured two mugs from a tarnished percolator, but didn't add a healthy dollop of whisky to his own like he usually did.

"Got to stay on my toes in case they need me for another scene," he said. "They got a script, but they go off trail more often than they stick to it. Makes the writer mad, but he always simmers down and reworks it lickety-split. Smart fella, that writer. Starlets are always buttering him up in hopes he'll write 'em a bigger part. One thing I've learned about the movie business, it's more competitive than bull riding on the rodeo circuit. Everybody's jostling to stay on camera the longest."

Blackpowder's brew was bitter from having been reheated without the dregs ever being discarded even when he added more water and fresh grounds.

"That cutie-pie daughter of yours sure is a ball of fire," he said. "The other day Hattie was here while they was filming. She walks up behind the man billed as the lead stuntman while he was bridling a horse and starts telling him he's doing it all wrong, that using a two-shank broken-mouth bit was making the horse toss his head. Wyatt Clark, that's his name, begins cussing her out for telling him his business before he turns around and sees she's only a kid."

"Did that make him change his tune?"

"You betcha, especially when Gemma mama-beared right over. She showed Wyatt where the shanks were cutting into the corners of the horse's lips 'cause the straps were fastened too tight. Gemma re-rigged it for him on the spot and from then on that stallion's head was quieter than a knight's on a chessboard."

"I'm guessing he didn't like being shown up."

"And you'd be right, but Wyatt was smart enough to keep his opinion to hisself seeing Gemma has the power to shut the filming down if she sees anyone being cruel to the stock, dogs included. I imagine later that night it wasn't only coyotes yipping and yowling their displeasure."

He chuckled and I did too at the thought of a rough, tough stuntman being no match for my two girls. I took another

swallow of coffee and thought about how I could ask him about
Jump Diggins without mentioning Manning Dobbs. As far as I
knew, Blackpowder had never been married, and maybe the
reason why was because it had turned out for the worst for his
fiancée, Connie Barstow.

"I need your help with something," I said. "Pudge thought
you might know, and if you don't, maybe you could put the word
out on your grapevine."

He waved his mug. "Fire away."

I told him about driving through Sheldon and climbing up
the tablelands looking for my bighorn and spotting the old
prospector and his burro in the gully. Blackpowder's head
snapped back at the mention of Jump Diggins' name.

"Now, ain't that a kick in the shins! Been a long time since I
thought of ol' Jump and now I wished I hadn't, given the circumstances. Shot in the back, you say? And they shot his neddy too?
Only a no-'count dirty SOB do such a thing."

I asked him if he knew where Diggins was from and if he
had a family. Maybe they knew who might've wanted him dead?
It would be information I could pass on to Manning Dobbs.

"Can't say I know 'cause it never come up. See, ol' Jump was
like most men who take up prospecting as a way of life. Instead
of wanting to find something, more often than not they're trying
to lose something, and it's usually heartbreak. I know that as a
plumb true fact 'cause it's what drove me to be like Jump for a
spell. How I met him."

Blackpowder tossed the rest of his coffee into the sink,
reached under the bar for a bottle of whisky, and poured a
couple of fingers into his mug. When he closed his eyes and took
a drink, I knew my hope of not dredging up Connie Barstow's
memory had been in vain.

"I had this Willys I'd bought surplus after the war," he said.

"I'd never driven a jeep in the war 'cause I was never on land. I enlisted in the Navy. Growing up in the high lonesome I wanted to see the ocean. Never had before."

He wetted his whistle again. "I saw it, all right. Looking down at it from a pitching deck and looking up from it while I was floundering around in it. Hitler's U-boats torpedoed two ships out from under me while we was escorting convoys across the Atlantic. My first sinking, we barely had enough life boats to go 'round. Second sinking, we didn't have enough men to fill 'em 'cause they was blown to bits when two torpedoes hit us midships.

"Anyway, I had this Willys and drove off into the desert four years after the war ended with nothing more than a bedroll, case of whisky, a couple five-gallon jerry cans full of gas strapped to the back, and the heaviest heart a man could carry. I'd just lost the most precious thing a man could ever hope for and I didn't care what happened to me. Where I was goin', I had no idea. All I knew was I never wanted asphalt beneath my wheels and no bright lights on the horizon neither 'cause people was the last thing I ever wanted to see."

Blackpowder told me days, weeks, and months passed by in a blur of dusty backroads and sleeping under the night sky. He zigzagged from No Mountain to Idaho and crossed the arid vastness of the Snake River Plain south into Utah. He camped on the northern shore of the Great Salt Lake until he could no longer tell sunrises from sunsets. He shot rabbits and quail for food and only bought gas from country stores with a single pump out front.

Most of the people he saw were Indians who were traveling through the Great Basin on backroads like him, although they had purpose and he didn't. He came across a band of Goshute on horseback riding home to their reservation in Skull Valley from a wedding one hundred miles away. A party of Shoshone on a deer-hunting trip gave him a cut of venison, but were not offended when he declined to eat with them, saying to each other that the white man was on his own version of a vision quest.

One morning in Nevada he woke to find a Paiute elder sitting cross-legged next to him. The man hailed from the nearby Pyramid Lake reservation and asked if he wanted to trade for coffee. Blackpowder gave him his last bag of beans, but when he said he wanted nothing in exchange, the old Paiute pressed an animal figure carved from soapstone into his hands and said it would replace what he'd lost.

"I still have it and wouldn't trade it for a starring role, but to this day I don't know if it's an antelope or jackrabbit," Blackpowder said. "A couple days after he gave it to me, I was driving through the Carson Sink area. A rainstorm had left standing water in spots. Wouldn't have met Jump if I hadn't heard his neddy braying her fool head off. Tracked the cries down on the other side of a stand of willows and found man and beast chest deep in a mudhole. Closest thing to seeing someone swallowed by quicksand as you're ever likely to see outside of a Tarzan movie."

I asked him how he got them out.

"I tied a rope to the rear of the Willys and threw Jump the other end. Told him to loop it around hisself and I'd pull him free. You know what he did? He said no siree, not until you pull her out first."

"Ruby," I said.

Blackpowder did a double-take. "How the heck could you know that? This was twenty-five years ago."

"I was thinking of the dead burro I found. The deputy who responded to my radio call recognized Jump and said that was her name. It could be the same burro you freed. Wild burros can live thirty years. If they're treated right, a burro used as a pack animal can live upwards of fifty."

"The SOB killed Ruby?" His expression of surprise turned to wistful and then to anger. "Makes me even madder about Jump's murder knowing that. If the deputy who answered your call down there needs help finding the killer, he can count me in."

"What happened after you pulled them out?"

Blackpowder said that Jump and Ruby had been stuck in the sucking mud since daybreak and were plumb tuckered out, not to mention starving. It was already dusk, and as determined as he was to avoid people, he couldn't leave them in that condition. Blackpowder made camp, staked Ruby out in a patch of Mormon tea to graze, and made a pot of jackrabbit stew with wild onions and turnips for Jump and him.

"He wasn't a bad supper companion even though I wasn't looking for one," Blackpowder said. "Jump didn't ask questions nor offer any sad stories about how life had done him wrong. He told knee-slapping jokes and played a pretty good harmonica. 'Streets of Laredo' and 'Red River Valley' and, my personal favorite, 'Ghost Riders in The Sky.' " He hummed a few bars.

"When the campfire got down to coals, I tucked into my bedroll and fell asleep. Don't know who snored louder that night, me, Jump, or Ruby."

"Was that the last you ever saw him?"

"Not by a longshot. As we was packing up in the morning to go our separate ways, Jump tells me he wants to repay me for my act of kindness. Says he's come across his fair share of men who'd've pulled his neddy and packsaddle out of the mud and left him there to die. I tell him to forget it, he don't owe me nothing. Jump says, nope, a man's only as good as his gratitude. He takes out a scrap of paper and draws a little map with a stub of pencil and marks it with an X and then also puts down a smaller R in another place. Ignore the X, he says. Everybody marks a find with an X, but Jump fools whoever might get hold of his maps by putting an R for Ruby on the real spot.

"He tells me he and his neddy are headed there because he has it on good authority there's a vein of quartz as thick as a man's leg streaked with gold. Says it'll take them 'bout a week to walk there and we should meet up. I'm to pick up some grub for the both of us and buy myself a pick and shovel and we'll split whatever we dig up right down the middle, fifty-fifty."

I asked him what he did.

"We shook hands and I drove off figuring him and his neddy was having a right good laugh. I continued on my way which really wasn't no way at all since I had no destination in mind. Four days later I stop at an outpost in the middle of nowhere. The man owns it is selling gas out of fifty-five-gallon drums he pumps by hand. When he's done I follow him inside to pay and reach into my shirt pocket."

He patted his breast. "I kept a ten-dollar bill wrapped around the soapstone carving that old Paiute from Pyramid Lake gave me. Out with the sawbuck and carving comes Jump's map. Forgot that's where I put it."

Blackpowder exhaled through his teeth. "Took it as some kind of sign, I did, and so I looked around at the dry-goods the man's selling. First thing I saw was a pick and shovel. On a shelf right next to them was a gold pan and a rock hammer. That sign started flashing brighter. I loaded up the Willys with grub and supplies and drove hellbent until I reached the R on Jump's map. He wasn't there, so I made camp and set to waiting, thinking that if there was a bigger fool in the world, I never wanted to meet him.

"One day went by. Two days went by. On the third day, I woke up to a bray. Ruby caught wind of me and was letting me know she was happy to see the fella who'd pulled her out of the mud. Jump, he wasn't surprised at all. Said he knew I'd be there. Well, to make a long story short and not have to relive every drop of sweat I poured and blister I got, Ol' Jump's vein of quartz was there all right. It took us a while to find it, but find it we did. We busted loose so many nuggets we couldn't count 'em all. Some as big as my thumb."

Blackpowder drained the last of the whisky. "But quartz veins streaked with gold are like dreams and fade just as fast. After a few months of picking and shoveling, the vein played out. I was playing out too. Found more gold than I'd ever be able to spend, and found something worth even more. The hot days, the cold nights, the fresh air, and the clear skies of the high lonesome did as much to cure what was ailing me as the honest hard labor did. You see, a broken heart is like any wound. It'll heal with time and leave a scar you'll always feel, but the scar also reminds you you're still alive."

He nodded to himself. "It was time for me to get back to the business of living and so I told Jump I was going home to No Mountain with my share of the gold and buy the feed-and-grain store I used to work at from the old cowboy who owned it. My plan was to turn it into a dry-goods store and tavern and name it after myself. I also pledged to help my neighbors out with my findings, which I do from time to time when someone needs a hand, but is too proud to ask. Like making a missed bank payment for them when cattle prices fall or if there's a hospital bill needs settling, I settle it. All quiet like, never boasting. And don't you tell nobody neither.

"Jump, he said good luck and God bless, that the past few months had been a pleasure, but him and Ruby, their lives were already set and he was goin' bury his gold in a secret spot and then look for the next vein. And that was the last I ever seen of 'em."

"The place on Jump Diggins' map where you found the quartz vein streaked with gold, where was it exactly?"

"Why, it was within spitting distance of one of your own bailiwicks. In the gully lands beneath Big Mountain at the Sheldon refuge. They put a road near there and I get a kick out of it 'cause they went and named it Quartz Creek."

10

The movie tents and trailers parked next to the old lineman's shack showed little activity as I pulled into the gravel drive and parked in front of the overhang that protected my sixteen-foot skiff and Triumph 650cc motorcycle.

It had been a long time since I took the bike out for a rip across the salt flats. Knowing how much I liked riding, Gemma asked why I didn't keep it at the ranch. I told her I'd bring the Triumph over one of these days, and she seemed to have forgotten about it, but I knew she hadn't. The same as she hadn't forgotten I left behind the tin cans I used to fill with pebbles like twelve-step sobriety coins. While the roar of the motorcycle and rattle of the cans had been a way to silence the howls of heroin addiction that dogged me after Vietnam, all I needed now was to recite the vow I'd made never to let my wife and daughter down.

The shack's door was unlocked, as was the custom in Harney County. The inside was redolent of smoke from decades of heating by a wood-burning stove. When the shack was my home, I could conjure up the scent at will. These days, I summoned the smell of the Warbler ranch, a mix of Gemma's shampoo when she laid her head on my shoulder, Hattie's breath when I rocked her to sleep, November's frybread wafting from the kitchen, and the Hoppe's oil Pudge used to clean and lubricate his guns.

The biggest change to the shack was the installation of an electronic contraption hooked to the telephone. It took up a sizeable piece of real estate on the creaky wooden kitchen table that served as a desk. The machine was a Code-a-Phone, a gift from my boss. Regional Director F.D. Powers had sent a note with it saying he was as tired of me never answering as he was listening to me explain why being bound to a desk and patrolling refuges spread across a territory larger than most states were mutually exclusive.

Several messages had been left during my absence. One was from a birdwatcher complaining that Malheur Lake was dangerously low and if I didn't do something to keep the water from being siphoned by hay farmers, I'd have the death of a million waterfowl on my conscience. He ended his call with perfect imitations of a ruddy duck, black-crowned night heron, and common loon. Another was from an anonymous tipster who said he could name several active poachers in the area. He instructed me to tape one hundred dollars to the front door, and once he retrieved it in the dark of night, he'd call back with their names.

Four messages were from F.D. Powers. All had been recorded in the past twenty-four hours. He implored me to call back immediately, no matter the time in Washington DC. With each message, the urgency in his voice grew.

I dialed his number and Powers picked up on the second ring. "Ranger Drake, are you alone?" I told him I was. He asked me to double-check.

"Sir, if you'd ever seen the size of this field office, you'd realize I'd know if a dust mite was in here with me."

"I will take you at your word." He cleared his throat. "What I am about to tell you is classified and comes from the highest level. It is for your ears only. I understand a major motion picture is being filmed at your location."

I stifled a groan. Was everyone star struck? "Yes, they started while I was in the field, but, no, I haven't talked to any of the movie people."

"My point is, White House Chief of Staff General Alexander Haig called me into his office yesterday morning to tell me the producer is a friend of President Nixon from his days as a California congressman. The producer is acutely sensitive to the political climate roiling Washington and very sympathetic to the president. He has extended him an invitation to visit the set. General Haig believes it could be a positive distraction as well as an opportunity to generate favorable public approval if President Nixon were to be welcomed by celebrities with the star power of Amber Russell and Garth Scott." As was his habit, Powers clicked his ballpoint pen for emphasis.

"The general also believes there could be an additional opportunity to garner public support if President Nixon toured a local national wildlife refuge. It could serve as a scenic backdrop for a speech whereby he extolled his considerable domestic policy achievements to protect the environment." Accompanying each with a click of his pen, he ticked off legislative acts aimed at protecting clean air, clean water, endangered species, and whales. Nixon's creation of the Environmental Protection Agency earned three clicks of the ballpoint. "General Haig has personally selected me to lead the advance team."

"President Nixon is coming to Harney County?"

"Let us not get ahead of ourselves. There are many steps that you and I will need to take first to assess the viability of a presidential visit. Ensuring the president's security must take precedence over any personal agenda we may have for promoting his presence at a wildlife refuge as a vehicle for securing increased appropriations. Our assessment will be scrutinized by the Secret Service and General Haig himself."

Powers droned on for a bit longer, but the words *you* and *I* rang the loudest. When I was finally able to get a word in, I asked him who else would be on the advance team.

"No one, of course. It is imperative that our site assessment maintain a low profile. National security is at stake. The pretense for my visit will be a belated tour of the field office and refuges in the region. That I am there at the same time as the motion picture company is merely happenstance."

"When are you planning on coming?"

"I leave for Boise tonight and touch down at the Burns airport tomorrow morning courtesy of a seat aboard a Forest Service aircraft. They know nothing of the real purpose of my visit."

We agreed I'd pick him up. I no sooner ended the call when the door swung open and my fellow Vietnam combat veteran turned wildlife ranger came in. Loq had to duck to keep the top of his long mohawk from brushing the upper jam.

"Perfect timing," I said. "I was just on the phone with our boss."

"The man in the suit who told me he worked for the Great White Father when he hired me?" the Klamath said. "What did he want?"

"He's coming out for a visit."

"When?"

"I'm picking him up in Burns tomorrow."

"All these years, he's never stepped foot on any of the refuges you and I patrol. Why's he coming now?"

"For a tour. I'll fill you in later. I thought you and I were meeting tomorrow to go over a plan for the California refuges." Loq lived in the town of Chiloquin in Klamath County.

"Today is yesterday's tomorrow." He was wearing blues jeans and a khaki uniform shirt like mine but with the sleeves ripped off to give his biceps room to roam. His nostrils flared. "I don't smell any coffee."

As he filled a pot with water and put it onto boil, I told him about coming home and learning a fever was taking a toll on the Paiute elders. "I saw Searcher when I was at the Sheldon. He said it was the same at Duck Valley and Summit Lake. I drove November to deliver healing soup to Tuhudda Will. It was hard seeing him so weak."

Loq's expression remained stoic. "If it's his time to make the journey, he does so with honor. Tuhudda has always had the heart of a warrior and the spirit of someone who lives in both worlds. He will have many ancestors to welcome him."

"I know, but I'll miss him. He's been a great friend and taught me a lot."

"His lessons won't end when he makes the journey. They only do if you let them."

I asked if the fever had reached the Klamath tribes too. They included Modoc and Yahooskin peoples. The three tribes shared a language and culture.

"I've heard talk of old ones falling sick, but there's been no official word. Maybe the Bureau of Indian Affairs is turning a blind eye. It wouldn't be the first time our people were left to die."

As I mulled that over, he threw a handful of coffee grounds into the water. "Was the bighorn's radio collar still transmitting?"

"I never heard it nor found her," I said. "Something came up."

"That something, was it down there or up here?"

"Down there. Face down in a gully to be exact. I came across an old prospector and his burro. They'd been shot."

"I like what we call a burro better. *Limi'lam t'shíshap*. Gives it the respect it deserves. How fresh was the kill?"

"About twenty-four hours."

"What's the local sheriff's department doing about it?"

"The sheriff is in the hospital and his chief deputy is young enough to be our kid brother. He's never seen a killing before. He's got a manual, but no experience or instincts."

"It was the same for most of the soldiers filling the boots on the ground in 'Nam. Marines like me went through boot camp. Dog Soldiers like you through basic training. But for all of us, it got down to on-the-job-training. It'll be same for the deputy."

"Roger that, but I told him to give a call if he needs help."

Loq filled two mugs with coffee and handed me one.

"So, what's the real reason you're back in No Mountain a day early?" I said. "Is it because you missed me?"

"All these years, you still can't tell a joke. You're supposed to grin after, not before." He tried the coffee and nodded his approval. "I'm meeting up with an old friend I haven't seen for a long time."

"Here in No Mountain. Do I know him?"

"Not a him."

"Does she live in No Mountain?"

"She's here on a job."

"Where?"

"Different places around Harney."

"Wait a minute. Are you telling me your friend is part of the movie crew?"

"That's right."

"What does she do?"

"Acts."

"How do you know a movie star?"

Loq drank some coffee. "I met her in country on my last tour. She was a go-go dancer back then on a Bob Hope Christmas show. The one with Ann-Margret and Rosey Grier. He was a better football player than an actor."

"I want to know about the actress, not football."

"Dani was flying from one base to another with the other dancers and the band on a Jolly Green Giant when the engine crapped out. It went down hard. My unit was a klick away. We hustled over and set up a perimeter while we waited for an evac. What was left of the chopper provided the best cover for the civilians and flight crew. I was point and went inside to tell them to keep their heads down while the corpsman put on bandages."

"And you got to talking with the cute go-go dancer who grew up to be a movie star. Talk about a romantic feature film."

"It wasn't long before we were taking fire from Charlie snaking through the tall grass. Not much time for small talk after that. But Dani, she made an impression. Kept asking me for a gun, said her dad taught her how to shoot. I gave her my forty-five since I was using my M16."

"Did she fire it?"

"Until it ran out of ammo." He took another drink of coffee. "Girl wasn't lying. Her aim was true."

"Did you ever see her again?"

"I drove down to LA one time, but that place was too gray for me. Concrete, freeways, smog. There was a phone call after that, maybe two." He looked down at his mug.

I asked him if she had grown up there and was that how she got into the movie business.

"She moved there when she was little, but Dani was born in Mexico. A village in Oaxaca. Her mother is Zapotec. 'Cloud People' in their language."

"Why did Dani and her family leave Oaxaca?"

"Work. They moved around. First to Mexico City, but they were forced to live in a shack made of cardboard and packing crates. Dani remembers when it rained, the whole neighborhood flooded and rats the size of Chihuahuas would swim down the roads. The family kept heading north. Picked oranges in Veracruz, worked on a cattle ranch. When Dani was six or seven, they crossed the Rio Grande and picked cotton in Texas. Eventually they wound up in East LA. Her father worked at an auto body shop. Sanding scrapes, pounding out dents. He died young."

"Was that before or after she started go-go dancing?"

"Around the same time. She was running with a fast group of kids and, needing money, lied about her age and got hired at the Whiskey a Go Go. It wasn't a strip joint, but close. One night, a man hands her a card after a dance and said give him a call, that he's a talent agent and can get her a real job. Thinking it was just another come-on, she tucked the card in her purse and forgot about it. A few nights later she's riding in a car and it gets pulled over. The kid driving had boosted it and stashed a bag of weed under the seat. They all get taken downtown. Dani gets her one phone call, but she doesn't dare call home."

"And then she remembers the card in the purse," I said.

Loq's long mohawk rippled when he nodded. "The man remembers her and comes right down to the station. He tells the cops if they don't release her, the next person they hear from is going to be the president because Dani is scheduled to fly to Saigon with Bob Hope for his Christmas show. The cops buy it and let her go. Turns out the man really was a bigshot agent. He tells Dani he knew the first time he saw her she was a natural and the sky was the limit. He talks her into taking the job on the Hope tour and when she gets back, he's got her signed up for a movie role. He's still her agent."

"How did Dani find you up here?"

"She remembered where I was from. When she got to Oregon, she asked the operator to connect her to a Chiloquin phone number, said it didn't matter whose. She asked the person who answered if they knew how to get ahold of me. Everyone knows everyone in the Klamath Nation. Only took Dani one more call to reach my mother who got word to me and here I am."

Something poked at my memory. The name Dani. I'd heard it recently. "What's Dani's last name?"

"Reyna. Why, have you seen any of her films?"

"It seems I'm the only one in Harney County who doesn't know a movie star."

"Easy enough to fix. Come over to the Crossed Bars Ranch tomorrow. Dani told me the director's having a barbecue to introduce the producer. He's the money behind the film. Everyone's welcome. His way of showing No Mountain appreciation."

It suddenly dawned on me the timing of the barbecue and F.D. Powers' arrival was no coincidence; it was part of General Haig's plan for conducting a site assessment in advance of a possible presidential visit. I wondered what other tricks the White House had in store.

Loq looked down his high cheekbones. "Now tell me, brother, why is our boss really coming here?"

11

The Burns airfield didn't have commercial flights. It was mainly used by local pilots who were familiar with the challenge of taking off and landing on a short runway battered by fickle winds, extreme temperatures, and within spitting distance of mountains. I stood next to my pickup and watched a DC-3 appear from the east. The Forest Service operated a fleet of the World War II–vintage workhorses to haul smokejumpers and, for my deskbound boss's sake, I hoped this one had passenger seats.

The pilot appeared to have experience landing in Burns because he circled cautiously to make sure no large flocks of birds were present—always a danger, especially during migration—and then headed into the wind to help slow the plane's speed as he made his approach. He steepened the angle of attack and the wheels hit the tarmac hard. The pilot worked the brakes aggressively and brought the DC-3 to a screeching, shuddering stop before tarmac turned into desert.

The air still stunk of burnt rubber when the tail-dragger turned around and taxied to a halt in front of me. A slight man with thinning brown hair and stooped shoulders wobbled down the stairs that folded from the doorway near the tail. He wore a tan summer-weight suit with a black knit tie and carried a dark brown attaché case.

I welcomed F.D. Powers to Harney County. "How was your flight?"

He dabbed his forehead with a white handkerchief. "Memorable. Very memorable, indeed."

As we drove from the airfield, Powers told me he'd transferred to the DC-3 after flying commercial from Washington National to Boise via a connection at Stapleton in Denver.

"You must be hungry. The Pine Room in Burns serves the best food in town."

"We are operating under an extremely tight timeframe," he said curtly. "Please proceed directly to the Malheur refuge for a site reconnaissance. Given the great distances involved, my preliminary assessment has led me to conclude it is the only one suitable for a presidential visit."

I steered south. "Does your plan take into consideration Air Force One can't land in Burns? A seven-oh-seven would overshoot the runway by a thousand feet."

"That is precisely the reason I flew to Boise. I needed to confirm its airport has a runway of sufficient length. The president can transfer there to Marine One and Idaho Air National Guard jet fighters can escort the helicopter to the motion picture set, Malheur refuge, and back."

Filming hadn't resumed in front of Blackpowder Smith's as we drove past, but I pointed it out anyway. "Those are the film crew's equipment trailers," I said, "and here's our field office. Would you like to see it?"

The gold band of his wrist watch shined as he looked at it. "Maybe on our return if there is sufficient time. I have an afternoon meeting with the motion picture's producer."

"During the barbecue at Crossed Bars Ranch?"

"How do you know about that?"

"It's the talk of the town."

"Excellent. Staging a public event as camouflage for our private talk was my idea." The color had returned to his face and he appeared quite pleased with himself.

Powers balanced the attaché case on his lap and thumbed through a manila file folder, read papers, and jotted in a leather-bound notebook with a ballpoint pen. Though it was his first time in Harney County, he was blind to the black-capped buttes, miles of open desert whiskered with sagebrush, and fields filled with threshed hay drying in windrows we drove by. It was some of the most beautiful scenery in the country and changed with the season and each passing cloud and movement of the sun. They were nature's true artists, painting the landscape with light, shadow, and color in bursts of creative energy that refreshed every second.

I slowed to make the turnoff to the refuge. Squadrons of redwing blackbirds flashing their crimson epaulets flew back and forth, but Powers never looked up. I turned into the entrance and drove to the visitor center. His eyes finally left his sheaf of papers when I purposely pulled to an abrupt stop.

"Sorry," I said. "The rig's due for a brake job."

Powers frowned, but then took an Instamatic camera from his attaché case and slipped it into his jacket pocket along with the notebook and ballpoint pen. I led him to a grassy area that was partially shaded by cottonwoods and willows. A tended garden of native shrubs provided an intoxicating swirl of reds, whites, and purples.

"This is one of the best spots in the refuge's three-hundred square miles to see hummingbirds and hear songbirds during spring migration," I said. "Even in June, the president will have a good chance of spotting rose-breasted grosbeaks, black-chinned hummingbirds, yellow chats, and lazuli buntings."

His blank expression signaled I was speaking Greek. "The path over there leads to a pond that attracts shorebirds and waterfowl year-round. This time last year, I saw white-faced ibises and a pair of double-crested cormorants. The background music we're listening to is courtesy of western grebes."

"What about a bald eagle?" he said. "Footage of the president speaking while the nation's symbol soars overhead would guarantee the top-of-the-hour story on every nightly news show."

I said it was always a possibility. "So is a golden eagle."

He shook his head dismissively. "If the eagle doesn't have a white head and tail, no one will care."

Powers jotted in his notebook and then fished out the Instamatic and snapped pictures. "This location appears adequate for accommodating a podium, flag stands, and press box. We need to assess security and confirm a landing spot for Marine One."

"The clearing behind the visitor center is big enough to land a chopper. There's a fire lookout tower where the Secret Service snipers can set up. They'll want an armed speedboat on the lake, roadblocks on the two-lane and at the main entrance, and patrols walking the perimeter. His main security detail will never leave his side, of course."

"Impressive. I forgot you originally joined Fish and Wildlife through a special program for combat veterans."

"The training sticks with you."

Powers checked his watch again. "We have a few minutes. Is there anything else I should see while I am here?"

"That depends, but can I ask you something first?"

"What is it?"

"You and I both joined the Wildlife Service around the same time. You know how I wound up here and I recall you telling me you were asked by the president, but why Fish and Wildlife? No offense, sir, but you don't strike me as being particularly fond of the outdoors."

When Powers hesitated, I knew it wasn't because a western tanager trilling from the top of a cottonwood had captured his attention. I braced for him telling me I'd overstepped.

"It is correct to surmise that the outdoors is not my natural habitat. I am more comfortable in an urban milieu, more specifically that of Washington DC. It is where I first met then Congressman Nixon. I was an intern on Capitol Hill and he was making quite a name for himself, most notably for the role he played in the Alger Hiss case and House Un-American Activities Committee during his first term.

"His patriotism was admirable and I volunteered for his US Senate campaign and again when he was on the presidential ticket as General Eisenhower's running mate. I was hired as a campaign staffer eight years later for his ill-fated race against Kennedy. When victory was finally his in 1968, he asked me to serve in his administration. I'd hoped it would be in a leadership position in Treasury or Commerce."

Powers gave a wry smile. "I see numbers the same way you see birds. I am also quite adept at managing people and, most importantly, politicians."

Wry gave way to serious again. "Imagine my surprise when the president told me he wanted me at the Interior Department. He said he needed a loyal lieutenant there because he planned to make his mark with an environmental agenda. The Western Region directorship position at Fish and Wildlife was open and I took it at his urging with the promise it would be the first step to an undersecretary position and then secretary of the interior. Alas, he was forced to use those appointments to appease Republican party members as well as for bargaining chips with the Democrats."

Powers glanced around the meadow. "What motivates me is

not the position per se, but the proximity it provides to the most powerful man on Earth. The president of the United States has a global reach that makes the eight-hundred-fifty million acres under Fish and Wildlife's jurisdiction seem miniscule by comparison. If I were to use a metaphor apropos of the service's purview, I would say that providing support and counsel to President Nixon is analogous to running with a pack of wolves as opposed to watching one from afar."

I started to explain how wolf packs were known to drive off one of their own when times turned tough, but he cut me off, realizing I was referring to the Saturday Night Massacre triggered by Nixon's attempt to thwart the special prosecutor. "Watergate is nothing more than a witch hunt orchestrated by the president's political opponents. I am proud to stand by him. He will be vindicated."

Pudge Warbler's words spoken during supper one night echoed in my head. The sheriff had slammed the dining table with his palm. "I was all right with old Tricky Dick and his conniving ways until the night he lied right to my face on television in my own living room. In my book, a man who steals the truth makes him no better than a thief who comes in and makes off with the silverware."

I shook it off and changed the subject. "There's another spot at the refuge that could provide good footage for TV coverage. It's on the way back. Would you like to see it?"

"By all means."

We returned to the pickup and took the Central Patrol Road. Powers looked out the window rather than at his papers. A coyote trailed by four frisky pups trotted across the road ahead of us. Flocks of violet-green swallows swarmed over the canal running parallel. Cumulus clouds gathering atop Steens Mountain gave the skyline a dramatic punch.

I stopped at the Buena Vista Ponds Overlook and led Powers

up the short trail. It was my favorite viewpoint because of the eagle's eye view of a colorful patchwork quilt of fields, marshes, and ponds stitched with the blue threads of the Blitzen River. I handed Powers my binoculars without saying anything. He took his time panning the heart of the refuge.

"It is very peaceful," he said. "I can see why this world attracts someone with your history of violence."

On the drive back, I told him it would be better if we went to the barbecue with Gemma and Hattie. "Folks here put a lot of stake in how a man treats his family. If I were to take my out-of-town boss to a big party without them, it'd put you under the microscope and me in the doghouse."

"And your wife knows nothing about my agenda? Very well. Let us proceed."

We stopped off at the Warbler ranch. When I introduced Powers to November and said she was a revered tribal elder whose birth name translated to Girl Born in Snow, he started speaking very slowly, enunciating each word and using his hands to pantomime flying on a plane. The old healer, who'd learned English when she was forced to attend a boarding school for Indian children, asked me in *Numu* if he'd had a stroke. I replied in her language that Powers was uptight.

"Then I will make him a cup of licorice root tea to move his bowels."

My chuckle prompted Powers to ask me what she said. "Can you translate?"

"It's a traditional Paiute welcome and November is very honored to make your acquaintance."

He bowed to her. "And I you."

We transferred to Gemma's red Jeep Wagoneer with Powers riding shotgun and my wife and daughter sitting in the back seat. The entrance to the Crossed Bars Ranch was off the two-lane a few miles north of No Mountain. We passed under a pair of timbers forming an X that served as the gateway to a quarter-mile-long gravel drive leading to a house, barn, bunkhouse, and stables. The first time I'd visited the ranch, garlands of orange marigolds and strings of Tibetan prayer flags hung from the crossed timbers. They'd been placed there by a mysterious religious leader and his followers. The man called himself Vasudeva and had a taste for luxury cars, including a 1968 Rolls Royce Silver Cloud. Three years after his arrival, the Rolls carried him away in a brown cloud of dust with his followers right behind.

I was explaining this to Powers when Hattie said, "It's so pretty, why would anyone want to leave?"

"Ranch life isn't easy, especially for people who aren't used to it," I said.

Powers asked Hattie if she liked living on a ranch.

Her pigtails whisked as she nodded. "I'm going to get a pony for my birthday when I turn five and name her Shell Flower."

"That is a pretty name," he said.

"Mama's horse is named Sarah after a beautiful Indian princess. Her daddy was a war chief named One Moccasin. Sarah wasn't her Paiute name. It was Shell Flower."

"*Thocmentony* in *Numu*," Gemma said. "Sarah Winnemucca was a great leader and champion for her people's rights. Her father was Chief Winnemucca."

"I have always wondered how the Nevada city got its name," Powers said.

"When I have a pony of my own I'm going to ride her everywhere. And really fast too because faster is funner," Hattie said.

"Five years old seems awfully young to have a pony," he said.

"Not around here," Gemma said. "Caring for a horse goes hand in hand with Dick and Jane."

"Life out west certainly is different," he said stiffly.

Hattie clapped her hands. "Look. A party!"

I slowed as we neared the sprawling compound. People were milling between the main house and barn that had been turned into a temple during Vasudeva's time. A bartender dressed as a buckaroo, complete with a ten-gallon hat and six-guns, was serving refreshments at a plank set atop two wooden barrels. A similarly clad trio played music on a stage that had been erected nearby. Another costumed buckaroo waved me toward an adjoining field where vehicles were parked in rows.

"Not hard to tell the locals from the movie people," I said, gesturing at a line-up that included foreign luxury sedans and racy sports cars with California license plates next to dusty pickups.

We joined the party. Pudge spotted us and ambled over. He ruffled Hattie's hair. "Now, aren't you the prettiest filly here."

She neighed and pawed the ground with her boot.

I introduced him to F.D. Powers. As they shook hands, Pudge said, "You're a lucky man to have my son-in-law working for you. I've been trying to hire him away from the git go. He's a natural-born lawman."

Powers' expression became strained. "I am well-aware of Ranger Drake's extracurricular activities with your department, which, I must stress, are counter to Fish and Wildlife Service policy."

"Maybe so, but there's more than one bad guy no longer on the books thanks to his help. He'll probably wind up doing the same for Humboldt County sheriffs. They're trying to nail the killer of an old prospector." He turned to me, "By the way, Orville's worked his computing magic on that Nevada gold-mining company. He found something mighty interesting."

Before my boss could question him about what he meant, I asked Pudge how Amber Russell was faring.

He groaned. "I wouldn't even know where to begin." The sheriff touched the short brim of his Stetson. "Pleasure to meet you, Director Powers. Now, if you'll excuse me, there's a certain young lady I'm gonna have a glass of punch with." He took Hattie by the hand and they headed toward the refreshments.

"There's Blackpowder," I said to Gemma before Powers could ask me about Jump Diggins and Oro Holdings. "Who's he's talking to?"

"The man wearing the Mexican poncho is John Fellows. He's the director. The one with the silk scarf is his personal assistant, Tommy Briscoe. I don't know the man in the blue blazer and slacks, but the way he's dressed, I'd say he's one of the studio executives who flew in from LA on a private jet this morning."

Powers and I exchanged glances. I asked Gemma if she'd introduce us.

Her head tilted. "Why the sudden interest in moviemaking? You've never taken me to the drive-in. You don't even watch TV."

"I want to hear them say how my wife is the best-looking horse doctor Hollywood's ever seen."

"Keep spreading manure like that, hotshot, and I'll have to rope and brand you in front of your boss."

12

John Fellows was smoking a cheroot that smelled like the DC-3's tires skidding on the tarmac. A lanky man with a prominent Adam's apple, he hadn't shaved for days. Maybe it was because he'd been busy directing the movie or maybe it was a style he cultivated to go along with the poncho, swept-back hair, and rough-and-tumble looks more suited to being in front of the camera than behind it. Either way, he had an air about him that exuded confidence, entitlement, and disdain all at once.

When Gemma introduced Powers and me and described our positions with Fish and Wildlife, Fellows scowled. "I once got a script from a game warden out of Montana. He put it in a three-ring binder with a cover he'd made out of deer hide and tossed it over my wall in Malibu. I get a lot of that, but I made an exception and read his, hoping the story might be as good as the cover." He took a deep draw on the cheroot and blew a smoke ring. "It was long on bear hunting and short on sex. Poor guy. It was autobiographical."

Blackpowder chortled. "If that script had come from Nick Drake, you'd've made a movie of it 'cause it would've made your hair stand on end. He won the Heart in Vietnam and when he took up rangering here, the action didn't take forty winks."

"That a fact." Fellows squinted at me down the barrel of the cheroot now clenched between his teeth. "Putting a story on paper is one thing, but telling it on film is another. One blows away in the wind while the other lives forever. Any actor or actress will tell you being in a film is their ticket to immortality."

I asked Fellows if he believed that too. He responded, "James Dean said live fast, die young, and leave a good-looking corpse. He's been in the ground twenty years since he totaled his Porsche. I doubt his corpse has held up any, but he still looks mighty handsome in *Rebel Without a Cause*. Always will." The director puffed the cheroot to make the cherry glow brighter. "What about you? Anything ever make you believe in life everlasting?"

"The Tet Offensive," I said. "Our entire company was overrun on the first day. My squad holed up in a Buddhist temple. Casualties were high, ammo low. The cavalry wasn't coming because we were the cavalry. US Army, First Cav. It was only a matter of time before NVA regulars and VC charged to slaughter the rest of us. One of the monks told me not to fear death, that he'd already died and been reborn a bunch of times, though not always in human form."

The cheroot's cherry reflected in Fellows' eyes, but he didn't interrupt.

"When the monk said it, DJ, my radio man, was with me. Later, he said, 'Sarge, I told the boys what that hairless preacher believes. Unless he can guarantee we won't come back as roaches, we say Foxtrot that. We'd rather take our chances and shoot our way outta here right now.' "

Fellows laughed around the cheroot. "You tell a good story. You got stones. Tell you what, I got a bottle of tequila I've been saving. Let's me and you drink it and swap tales. I served in Korea where the battlefield was cold and the dying hard."

Tommy Briscoe, who was so jittery he was all but dancing in place, started waving at him. "Hullo, Mr. Fellows. Hullo! We really must be going if we are to get you prepped for the welcome speech. Miss Russell and Mr. Scott are waiting to go over their lines with you. You know how anxious they get."

The director brushed him off with a wave of his cheroot and turned to the man wearing a blue blazer and open-neck shirt who'd been introduced as the producer. "What do you say, Morty? You want to get on stage with us and tell the good folks of Harney County how much you appreciate their help?"

Morty Wassenberg had a doughy body and receding hairline beaded with perspiration. "No, no. It's your show, John. Yours, Amber's, and Garth's. Audiences don't care who put up the money. They're either looking down at their popcorn boxes when our names roll by at the start or aiming their butts at them when they roll at the end."

The director clapped him on the shoulder. "But, Morty, you know I appreciate what you do. And so do my ex-wives every time they cash their alimony checks."

The producer belly laughed, though I guessed it wasn't the first time he'd heard it. "You go ahead. I'm getting out of the sun before I pull a Wicked Witch of the West."

"I warned you to stay in Beverly Hills." The lanky director chomped the cheroot and swaggered toward the main house with his personal assistant scurrying to keep up.

Powers said, "May I join you, Mr. Wassenberg? I could use some shade myself." He loosened his necktie for emphasis.

"By all means, but call me Morty."

I took my boss's cue. "I'll catch up with you later. Gemma is going to introduce me to some people she's been working with."

Blackpowder said he needed a drink and went off in search

of the buckaroo bartender. As soon as he was out of earshot, Gemma elbowed me. "Remember talking about fool's gold the other night?"

"I suppose we could see if the hayloft is available."

"You wish." Her ponytail swished. "You know full-well what I'm talking about. Someone's trying to pull the wool over everyone's eyes. Powers flies in from DC on an impromptu visit and Morty Wassenberg jets up from LA the same day, and now they're suddenly best friends? Ha! Everybody knows his studio bankrolled Nixon's campaigns, and I remember who gave Powers his job."

She drew in so close, my nostrils filled with the scent of her shampoo. It smelled a heckuva lot better than the director's cheroot. "Come on, you can tell me. What's Powers really doing here? Delivering a personal plea to Wassenberg from the president to help keep him from being booted out of the White House?"

"I'd tell you if I could, but I can't. Not right now, anyway. I can tell you about something else though. Get this. Loq's been invited to the party by one of the actresses. It turns out they met in 'Nam."

"You're kidding. Who?"

"Dani Reyna."

"I knew Loq had a way with women, but Dani?"

"He said she was a go-go dancer for Bob Hope when they met. She was in a chopper that went down and he rode to the rescue. Loq didn't tell me which part she's playing in the movie."

"Dani always plays the bad girl, both on screen and off. In this one, she's a dancehall girl who falls in love with the gunslinger, Garth Scott, only to lose him to Amber Russell's character. Come on, let's go look for them. When you meet her, you'll see what I mean."

We began walking, but didn't get very far before we were

intercepted by Blaine Harney, Gemma's ex-husband and owner of the largest cattle ranch in the county. He touched the brim of his straw cowboy hat and said hello.

"I'm surprised you took time off from work to gawk at movie stars," Gemma teased.

Blaine was a big man, and when he grinned good-naturedly at her jab, it made me think of a bear in one of the children's books I read to Hattie.

"I am working here," he said. "A fella with the film crew came out to the Rocking H yesterday to see if it'd work out as a location for a scene they have in mind. Told me they'd rent my herd and pay my hands to help drive cattle."

"A roundup?" Gemma said.

Blaine nodded. "He asked if my boys knew how to lasso cows. I told him we called it heading and heeling in these parts, but, if they're paying, we'll say it any which way they want."

"We? You mean, you're going to be in the scene too?"

"I never turn down an opportunity to saddle a horse instead of a desk chair. Worse part of ranching is herding the paperwork."

"Have they given you a firm date for the shoot?"

"Tomorrow."

"The production scheduler should've told me. She knows since there will be horses involved, I need to be there too."

"Great. You can ride with us. I know how much you like driving cattle. I'll saddle this new filly I bought from Lyle Rides Alone. Best cutting horse I've had in a long time."

"Better than my Sarah?"

" 'Course not." Blaine turned to me. "You should join us tomorrow. Can't have too many good riders when it comes to a cattle drive." He touched the brim of his hat and moseyed off.

Another rancher stopped us to ask Gemma what he should

do about his prized bull who was showing symptoms of having contracted trichomoniasis.

Concern etched Gemma's face. She asked him a number of questions. How old was the bull? Was he isolated? When was the last time he serviced a cow? How many cows miscarried their fetuses in the spring? "I'll get over as soon as I can," she said. "Let's hope for the best."

When he'd gone, she said, "In case you didn't know, trich is a venereal disease. There's no cure. Cows will usually clear the infection on their own, but a bull over four years old usually has it permanently. If he does, he can't be used for breeding anymore. He'll have to be put down. I'd do it tomorrow, but with the movie and now having to be at the Rocking H tomorrow, it'll have to wait."

We found Pudge throwing horseshoes with an actor Gemma said played the movie's bad guy. His toupee was as shiny as some of the fancy cars parked out front. A crowd had gathered to watch the competition. Every time Pudge threw, Hattie shouted "Ringer!"

Orville Nelson spotted us from the other side of the horse-shoe pit and wheeled over in his customized chair whose sporty frame and oversized rear wheels made it resemble a dragster.

Gemma asked if his wife was at the party. They'd gotten married after the deputy finally admitted to himself that the physical therapist saw more in him than being her patient.

"Lucy went to get some punch," he said, "but I think she is really after autographs."

"I can help her with those." Gemma turned to me. "Give a holler when you find Loq. I'll come rescue you."

We watched her go. Orville said, "What did she mean by that?"

"Loq knows an actress working here and Gemma described her as a bit of a hellion."

"You must mean Dani Reyna. She is quite the character."

"Sounds like it. Pudge told me you have some information about the Nevada gold mine."

"I do, but I am afraid it resembles a set of Russian nesting dolls. Oro Holdings Limited is registered in Las Vegas and licensed to operate mines throughout Nevada, but it does not have a physical headquarters in the state. I traced Oro to a parent company that is registered in New York City. It is called Au Inc."

His eyes shined. "Did you know the Latin word for 'gold' comes from the Latin *arum*, which means 'shining dawn'? Aurora was the Roman goddess of the dawn. It is the reason the symbol for gold on the periodic table is A U."

"Fascinating, Orville. You're becoming more like one of your computers every day. Careful you don't stuff too much knowledge into that head of yours. Your deputy's hat won't fit."

"And you are starting to use more colloquialisms than your father-in-law." He adjusted the shoulder rig he used to carry his service weapon. "Au Inc. does not have a physical corporate headquarters either, not unless you count a post office box. I was able to trace it to a Panamanian law firm that offers accounting and financial services to international businesses, but then I ran into a dead-end. Privacy laws there are quite different than here. I called a friend at the FBI and he told me Panama is an offshore tax haven and law firms there help international corporations and business enterprises create shell companies in order to shelter profits and avoid paying taxes. They also hide the identity of the parent companies."

I was watching Orville closely as he described what he'd found. When I first met him, he was a recent college graduate interning at Harney County sheriff's while waiting to turn twenty-three, the minimum age to apply to the FBI. The bullet to his back cut short his dream of becoming a G-man, but it didn't diminish his affection for *Star Trek* or a steadfast belief that technology could help solve crimes.

"You're holding something back," I said.

The young deputy started bobbing up and down with excitement, making his wheelchair rock back and forth. "Your power of observation has grown even keener since you took up pen-and-ink drawing."

"What'd you find?"

"Not a what, a who. John Smith."

"Is that like a John Doe?"

"You have no recollection of the name? It was a few years ago when you and I were both new to Harney County?"

I sighed. "Orville, how old is your little boy Kirk now? One, two?"

"Eighteen months."

"And since he was born, how much sleep are you getting?"

"The same as always. Four hours maximum, usually three. You know I follow Thomas Edison's theory that sleep is a holdover from our caveman days."

"I should've remembered that, but ever since Hattie was born, I'm getting less sleep, and as a result, remembering a lot less. So, no, I don't remember a John Smith."

"It was the name of the Las Vegas-based lawyer who represented the company that purchased the ranch in Catlow Valley used by the drug traffickers who were smuggling heroin aboard Air Force cargo planes."

The memory jolted me. I pictured speeding to the remote ranch with Pudge Warbler, only to find a dead drug dealer with a bullet to the back of his head and a twin-engine Beechcraft with his executioner onboard taking off from the ranch's airstrip. The identity numbers on the plane's tail were later traced to Las Vegas.

"The mob," I said. "They silenced their own. Pudge said it

wouldn't be the last we'd see of organized crime from our neigh-
boring state. How does that John Smith fit in with the gold
mine?"

"It is the name of the lawyer who filed the papers to register
Oro Holdings Limited as a business entity." His tone grew
excited. "I looked him up on the State Bar of Nevada's register."

"It's a pretty common name."

"Actually, the register lists fifteen licensed attorneys in
Nevada with the last name of Smith. There are two Johns, but
only one has a Las Vegas address." He gave the arm of his wheelchair a victory slap. "I checked. It is the same address as the John
Smith who represented the buyer of the Catlow property."

I could all but hear a burro braying. "That's better intel than
we ever got from CIA spooks."

The young deputy beamed. "This new database of historical
crimes I have been working on is really paying off. I have been
sending my files to the FBI on floppy disks and they have been
inputting them into their mainframe computer system. In
return, they run searches for me. I could do a deeper check into
John Smith, Oro Holdings, and Au Inc. Who knows what we
might discover."

"What does Pudge think about you spending time on that?"

"I will do it at night when Lucy and Kirk are asleep."

"A chip off the old Edison block," I said.

Reverb from a loudspeaker interrupted us. "Hullo. Hullo!
May I *please* have everyone's attention," Tommy Briscoe's amplified voice rang out. The director's assistant was waving from the
stage where the trio had been playing music. It appeared he'd
tied on a new polka-dot neckerchief.

"Oh, thank you. Thank you. You are most kind. Hullo. My
name is Tommy Briscoe and it is my distinct honor and great
privilege to introduce to you the host of these festivities, winner
of Academy Awards for both best director and best picture to go

along with his two Golden Globes and three Directors Guild of America Awards. I give you the one and only John Fellows."

Tommy raised his hands and started clapping at the audience, but he needn't have bothered. Folks from No Mountain didn't require prompting to show their neighborliness to an out-of-town visitor.

Fellows hopped onto the stage and brushed off the applause. "Much obliged. While I've made a lot of films and been on lots of locations, this place here, Harney County, is special. It's not only because of the beautiful landscape and endless sky, which makes my job of capturing it in widescreen pretty easy, but you all. You're helping give this story we're telling authenticity, and that, my friends, is what makes the difference between a B movie and a great movie. Now, I know who you really want to hear from and so here they are. Amber and Garth, get on up here and give the fans a big Hollywood hello."

The two stars climbed the steps and, with fixed smiles, strolled arm in arm across the stage as the applause grew louder. Several people gave loud whistles, the kind cowpunchers used on cattle drives. Amber Russell was statuesque and a honey blonde. She wore a white summer dress and enormous sunglasses. Her teeth gleamed between red lips. Garth Scott wore a pearl-button denim shirt and an easy smile beneath a white cowboy hat that had neither a sweat stain nor speck of dust on it. He had a slight build and was no taller than his co-star, even with the hat on. The pair waved as cameras clicked. I recognized the photographer for the *Burns Herald*. Bonnie LaRue was all but pushing him in the back to get a close-up.

Gemma found me in the crowd. She had Hattie by the hand and hoisted her onto my shoulders so she could see over the crowd.

"The actor who plays the heroic gunfighter isn't very tall," I said.

"Male romantic leads never are," Gemma said. "They have to be the same height as the women so they'll both be in the frame when they kiss. When Alan Ladd and Sophia Loren were in a movie together, the crew had to dig a ditch for her to walk in so she wouldn't dwarf him. He was only five-six. Of course, around here, Alan Ladd is better known for playing the title role in *Shane*."

"And you say you haven't gone Hollywood."

"Look, Daddy!" Hattie called from atop my shoulders. "Here comes Uncle Loq and he's riding a painted pony."

Loq was bare-chested and astride a bareback brown-and-white pinto. The horse had a yellow circle around one eye and red handprints on his haunches. The mohawked Klamath was gripping the ends of a knotted rope he'd made from torn strips of his khaki uniform shirt looped around the pinto's neck. A woman with flowing black hair was sitting close behind him with her arms wrapped tightly around his waist.

When they neared the edge of the crowd, the pinto whinnied and started snorting and tossing his head. Loq leaned forward and whispered into his mount's ear. That allowed me to see the woman's face. She was the dancehall girl who'd called to me in a Mae West drawl. Now I remembered where I'd heard the name Dani before. The actress imitating Betty Boop had called her that.

A man with thick bushy hair pushed through the crowd. "What d'ya think you're doing on my horse? Get off before I yank you off."

"Uh oh. That's Wyatt Clark," Gemma said.

"The lead stuntman?" I said.

"One and the same. He looks loaded for bear."

I quickly handed her Hattie and fast-stepped after him.

"Don't touch the pony," Loq warned him. "He told me he doesn't like you because you mistreat him. It's why he ran away."

"Run off, hell! You stole him. He's studio property and I'm in charge of him." The stuntman grabbed for the shirt rope.

I snatched his arm before he reached it and spun him around. "Hear Loq out."

"Who the hell are you!" He cocked his fist.

Loq grabbed him by his bushy hair before he could throw a punch and pulled him straight up. Wyatt swore and locked his hands around Loq's wrists while his boots kicked air.

"Put him down," I said. "We can straighten this out."

The Klamath was having none of it. He touched the pinto's flanks with his heels and the spotted pony reared and then started side-stepping with Wyatt kicking and yelling alongside. I hurried after them. Loq finally let go and the stuntman dropped to the ground. Before he could make another run at horse and rider, I pinned his arms behind his back.

"Simmer down. Loq's no thief. Look at the rope. It's his shirt. He found the pinto and brought him back."

"Bullshit. There's a reason we always kill off the thieving Injuns in the movies."

"Big mistake." I pushed his right arm higher.

The stuntman tried stomping me with his heels, but I was a step ahead of him and kicked the inside of his boots so that he was all but doing the splits.

He raged and then cursed at Dani. "You little Mexican whore. You're gonna get yours once and for all."

13

Loq threw his leg over the pinto's head and drew a skinning knife from a beaded sheath on his belt. He grabbed Wyatt Clark's shirtfront and brandished the blade. "I'm going to cut out your tongue and feed it to the dogs."

As the stuntman quailed, I said, "Not in front of Hattie and the other children. Everyone is watching."

And they were. The commotion had prompted people to turn their attention from the stars on the stage to us. I glanced at Dani Reyna. She'd scooched up on the painted pinto's back and now held the khaki shirt reins. When she noticed the audience looking our way, excitement danced in her eyes.

"He's not worth it," I said to Loq.

The Klamath touched the tip of the knife to the stuntman's lips. "Speak to her again and I'll take these too."

Dani flashed teeth and patted the horse's back. "Come, Loq. We ride."

He vaulted onto the pinto behind her. She clicked her tongue and the horse took off. "*¡Nosotros montamos!*" she shouted. Loq responded with a *Maklak* war whoop.

Silence hung over the stunned crowd as they watched the

pair gallop away. But then the amplified voice of John Fellows boomed.

"How about that, folks? Give a big hand for our actors there. If you thought that little scene had you on the edge of your seats, wait 'til you see our movie when it comes out. It'll be the best entertainment a two-dollar ticket can buy."

Hands started clapping and cowpuncher whistles pieced the air again.

I released Wyatt. "Lucky for you, your director acts fast on his feet. Take a bow. Now's your chance to be a real star."

Hattie was squealing with delight when I rejoined her and Gemma. "You and Uncle Loq are in the movie!"

"It was only this one time for the party," I said.

Gemma's eyebrows rose. "Now do you see what I mean about Dani?"

"She certainly knows how to make an entrance."

"And steal all the attention away from Amber Russell."

"Pudge got called to the set yesterday because Amber fired a pistol. I wonder if it was at Dani?"

"Amber has been queen of the rodeo for a long time and I'm sure she's had to defend her crown from an up and comer like Dani before, but shooting her sounds a bit extreme."

"Blackpowder told me actors are more competitive than bull riders."

"And barrel riders too. I remember when I was competing, there were girls who tried all sorts of dirty tricks trying to cheat me out of winning a blue ribbon."

"The dozens you've tacked to the stable walls tells me they didn't always succeed."

"A few girls did in the beginning, but after that, well, it wasn't my first rodeo anymore."

"I can't believe Loq agreed to be part of a setup."

"If it was one, I doubt he even noticed. Loq seems pretty bewitched by Dani."

"Maybe, but finding a runaway horse, whispering to it, and showing respect by painting symbols on it so it would let him ride it, and then standing up to a foul-mouthed bully? It's what Loq's always done. It's who he is."

"*Semper fidelis*," Gemma said and squeezed my arm. "It's the same with you. Protect and defend. You waded right into that tussle without taking a breath."

She was right. Loq and I'd both learned stopping to take a breath in the middle of a firefight could mean taking your last.

I searched the crowd for F.D. Powers to see if he'd watched his two employees mix it up with a member of the movie crew. Luckily, he was nowhere to be seen.

"I should go look for my boss. Are you two okay on your own?"

Gemma nudged Hattie. "We're big girls who can take care of ourselves. We might even find a pony of our own and take a ride."

Hattie's eyes lit up. "Maybe one of the dogs can go with us. Maybe all three."

A few people congratulated me on my performance as I walked through the crowd. Blackpowder touched the corner of his eye. "Told you method acting was the real deal."

I found Powers and Morty Wassenberg inside the main house sitting at a table in a room off the kitchen with a pitcher of ice tea between them.

"Impeccable timing," my boss said. "We were just wrapping up."

The producer rattled ice cubes in a tall glass and issued a Cheshire cat grin. "F.D. assures me you can round up a bald eagle for the president."

"I've had taller orders."

"Atta boy."

"Does this mean the visit is a go?"

Powers clicked his ballpoint pen. "Assessments remain to be analyzed and schedules to coordinate, but I would venture to say our reconnaissance is shaping up in a most encouraging fashion. Would you agree, Morty?"

"You bet, F.D. We get the green light from Haig, first call I make is to Sinatra. Sure, Frank was a lifelong Democrat, but in seventy-two I convinced him McGovern was a pantywaist and he went all in on Nixon. Ol' Blue Eyes is a huge supporter now. I'll fly him up from Palm Springs to croon. Maybe get Nancy to come with him. Imagine father and daughter singing 'These Boots Are Made for Walking' here in Cowtown USA. That'll get air time around the globe."

"Mr. Wassenberg has invited me to fly back to Los Angeles on his plane tonight," Powers said. "His driver will take us to the Burns airfield. We will finalize details in the morning and then I will fly to Washington to hand-deliver my report to General Haig."

"How long do you think it will take him to make a decision?" I said.

"Seventy-two hours is a reasonable assumption, although it being Washington, it could take a day or two longer. Whatever the timing, we must proceed as if the order will be issued at any moment. Once I have confirmation, I will call. In the meantime, I have a special assignment for you. I am attaching you to the film production activities to be my eyes and ears while I am in Washington. Mr. Wassenberg has informed me that the personal behavior of certain individuals on a film location can be . . ."

The producer cut him off with a rattle of his iced tea. "What F.D.'s trying to say is, there's always some hanky-panky and musical beds being played no matter where a movie's being shot. We got to put a lid on it in advance of the president's arrival. The press is already making his life hell. We don't want him to walk into a real-life soap opera."

"Quite right," Powers said. "If you detect any behavior that could cast President Nixon in a negative light, I need to know about it immediately. General Haig has been quite clear about this. The last thing we need to do is offend the Silent Majority's sense of propriety."

Before I could protest, Powers said, "I have not spoken to Loq yet, but in case I miss him, please pass on my instructions that he is to man the telephone at the local field office while you are at the filming locations. I could call at any hour with news. Loq is to alert you immediately and you are to call me right back. I will also need you to assist the Secret Service advance team when they arrive to assess the Malheur refuge for that portion of the visit." He dismissed me with a click of his ballpoint pen.

As soon as I was back outside, I took a deep breath. I'd rather try to radio collar a porcupine than serve as the equivalent of a high school dance monitor. The idea of working alongside the Secret Service was no bonus either. I knew from experience the professionals sworn to protect the president with their lives had little regard for local law enforcement. When I was in Vietnam, LBJ paid a visit to Cam Ranh Bay in December 1967 to rally the troops and meet with General Westmoreland. His Secret Service detail behaved like none of us four hundred thousand GIs in country were capable of protecting him. I wasn't the only soldier risking my life every day who took it as a giant middle finger.

As bad as both of those assignments were, even worse was having to tell Loq that Powers wanted him to sit inside the lineman's shack and play telephone operator. I could already hear him respond in English, *Maklak*, and US Marine.

One of the many things Loq and I held in common was a vow never to work behind a desk. We'd become conditioned to being outdoors during our military service and years working on wildlife refuges where everything around us was always in constant motion, from the millions of migrating birds to the land that tremored from earthquakes to the tumbleweeds that broke free from their roots and rode the wind to spread their seeds.

The shadow of a passing cloud prompted me to look up. Movement was always in the sky too, the same sky that Jump Diggins and his trusty burro had lived beneath for decades until a killer had stolen their freedom to wander across the desert prospecting for gold and camping beneath the stars. The answers to why they'd been killed and who was responsible were slipping away with each passing cloud. I decided not to wait for Chief Deputy Manning Dobbs to call me with a status report. I'd check in with him to see if he'd made any progress.

I went in search of Gemma. She and Hattie weren't with the crowd lined up at the grills manned by costumed buckaroos dishing out barbecued ribs and roasted ears of corn. Thinking they might've made good on their pledge to go for a ride, I headed to the ranch's corral and stables where the horses used in the movie were kept.

Voices carried from the other side of the tack room as I rounded the corner. Pudge Warbler was sitting beside Amber Russell on a shaded bench. He was patting the top of her hand and muttering, "Now, now."

The old lawman noticed me before I could back up. I couldn't tell by his expression whether he was embarrassed or relieved to see me. The movie star followed his gaze. Her eyes were startlingly blue. She flushed with anger.

"You!" she cried. "You're on Dani's side. I saw you. Why did you do that to me? It was so cruel."

"Now, now," Pudge said again. "This here is Nick Drake. I guarantee you he's not in cahoots with Miss Reyna."

"I don't believe it. Not only didn't he try to stop Dani and her Indian from stealing my scene, he prevented Wyatt from stopping them! Wyatt is on my side. He always looks out for me."

"I can personally vouch for Drake," Pudge said. "He's my little granddaughter's daddy. Him and Loq work together, so it's only natural they step up for each other, but the way I see it, Loq was returning a runaway horse. The fact him and Dani may be in a chummy way, well, I don't see how that's got anything to do with you. You're still the star of this show. Look at all the people who turned out to get a gander at you."

Amber sniffed. "There were quite a few, weren't there? I mean, not like what I see at one of my premiers or on the red carpet walking up to the Dorothy Chandler Pavilion like at last year's Oscars."

She gasped dramatically and her red lips fashioned a pout. "Oh, my God, an Indian ruined that too! Brando wins Best Actor for *The Godfather* and instead of showing his gratitude to the Academy members and fans, he sends some girl up there to make a speech about the mistreatment of Indians. I felt so sorry for Liza who won for *Cabaret* because she was absolutely brilliant, but the only thing people could talk about at the afterparties and in the press was the beautiful girl with the long black hair wearing a white fringe dress with all those beads."

Amber leaned into Pudge's shoulder. "Do you know how hard I've worked to get where I am? What I have to do to stay here? It's never been easy being a woman in this business, and it's all but impossible once you reach a certain age, not that I'm even close to it. There's always some new it girl like Dani out to steal your role."

The actress pushed away from the sheriff. "Guess how old Garth is? He's over forty, closer to fifty. He's thoroughly ancient and wears a girdle to keep his stomach in, but he gets all the scripts he wants."

Pudge's expression was what I imagined Jump Diggins looked like when he was floundering in the mudhole. I threw him a lifeline. "Have you seen Gemma and Hattie?"

"Why, anything wrong?"

"No, I was inside talking to my boss and lost sight of them is all. I want to see if they're ready to eat."

"Last I saw, they were over at the corral petting the horses."

Amber said, "The veterinarian is your wife?"

"She is."

"I should've guessed it. Knowing my luck, John will put her in the movie and I'll have another pretty young thing stealing scenes away from me."

"I better go find them," I said. "Nice meeting you, Miss Russell."

I hadn't taken five steps before Pudge called out, "Wait a second."

The sheriff put his arm around me, keeping us so our backs were to the actress. "Here, take this, but don't let her see," he whispered. "It's the pocket pistol I took off her yesterday. She takes a shot at Dani again, she might not miss."

"She tried to kill her?"

"Scare her off more than anything, but I'm learning these actor types tend to overreact."

I glanced at the gun. It was a .25-caliber Beretta Jetfire that was hardly bigger than a pack of cards.

"Careful," he said. "The chamber's empty but the magazine's full. Eight rounds."

I slipped the gun in the front pocket of my jeans. "I'll see you back at the ranch. Maybe at breakfast you can tell me the rest of the story about how you stopped Reggie Dobbs and his gang."

He glanced back at Amber before responding. "I'll try, son, but no guarantees."

14

Dawn was newly broken when Gemma and I got out of bed and set to work. It promised to be a long day, starting with attaching the horse trailer to the back of her Jeep, loading Sarah and Wovoka, and driving to the Rocking H in time for the filming of the roundup scene. Never having been on a film set before, I had no idea what would happen once John Fellows ordered "Action."

On my way to the kitchen, I glanced out the window. Pudge's rig wasn't parked in front. I pushed open the swinging door and found November on the other side pouring oatmeal into a pot of boiling water. My heart sunk. "I didn't hear you come in last night. Does this mean Tuhudda made the journey?"

"Not all lives are long and not all deaths are short," she said. "Tuhudda has lived a long time and his death is taking a long time also. He has much to relive if he is to carry all his memories with him. Nagah will come get me here when it is time to be there."

The smell of freshly brewed coffee made me feel better. Though the old healer didn't drink it—she only drank tea made from plants she picked and dried herself—her coffee was the best I'd ever tasted. I poured a mug and savored it.

"Where are you going?" November asked while she stirred the oatmeal.

"The Rocking H. They're filming a cattle drive today. Gemma needs to make sure the horses don't get injured and we'll both help Blaine Harney and his hands with the herding."

"What about Girl Fell from Sky?"

"We didn't think you'd be home and so we were going to take Hattie with us, but it would be better if she stayed here. Is that okay?"

"Of course. She still has much to teach me."

"You mean the other way around. She'll be fluent in *Numu* like Gemma is because of you."

Her tsk was sharp. "Girl Fell from Sky teaches me to remember surprise. Each day and everything that happens that day is new for her. It can be the same for us old ones as long as we do not fear to look at each day as a new day and in a new way." November lifted the wooden spoon. "She is awake now and getting out of bed."

A few seconds later I heard the sound of feet running in the front room. "Mama, Daddy. A lady is outside."

"Wait, Hattie," I said. "Wait for me."

But it was too late. She'd already opened the door and was flying across the front porch and down the steps toward an unfamiliar vehicle. The driver was pulling something from the front seat, something wrapped in a bloody blanket.

"I need the vet," the woman shouted as she wrestled with the bundle. "I'm the dog trainer with the movie. He's cut. Cut real bad."

Hattie let loose with an ear-piercing cry. "Daddy, help her."

The woman finally got her arms around the bundle and stumbled toward me. "Here," I said. "Let me take him."

I was surprised by the animal's weight. He was seventy pounds easy, closer to eighty. The dog's head flopped outside the blanket and his tongue lolled to the side. I immediately flashed on Jump Diggins when Manning Dobbs and I had turned him over.

"Hattie, hold the door open," I said.

Gemma was coming from our bedroom. "Put him on the dining table," she said as calmly as if asking me to pass her the salt and pepper. "I'll need hot water. Clean towels too."

"I'll get them," Hattie said and skittered toward the kitchen.

I laid the dog down as gently as I could. He'd yet to open his eyes or make a whimper.

The trainer gasped for breath. "It's Jake. I heard a howl. From the stable. I went to see . . . His leg. I used . . . used my belt as a tourniquet. Wrapped him in a saddle blanket. Drove fast. Don't know . . . don't know if fast enough. Please, doctor. Don't let him die."

Gemma took hold of a corner of the sodden blanket and began to unwrap it. The dog's eyes opened.

"Hello, Jake. You remember me. Good boy. What a good boy you are. Let me take a look."

A belt was cinched tight around the upper part of Jake's right foreleg. The skin above it was puffed up, the fur below drenched with blood. Hattie ran in with an armful of towels. "Here, Mama. *Mua's* bringing water."

"Put them on the table, then turn a chair around, push it next to the table, and stand on it. Hold onto the back of the chair. You can watch and help me."

Gemma turned to me. "I already put my medical kit in the Jeep. I also need the case with IV bags and the collapsible stand. It's the black one."

When I returned with them, Gemma was cleaning the dog's leg with a towel dampened in a bowl of hot water that

November had brought. The old healer stood at Gemma's side. Dogs were special to the Paiute. They had pulled their travoises when they moved from camp to camp in the old days, guarded their wickiups from coyotes, and sounded the alarm when enemies approached.

"I have to loosen the tourniquet," Gemma said. "It stopped the bleeding and saved his life, but I want to try and save the leg too. There's going to be a lot of blood, Hattie, but remember, a body can make more."

"I'm not a scaredy-cat," she said.

"Good girl."

The trainer swallowed. "Oh, Jake."

Gemma gloved up and her hands became a blur as she worked on the big dog. She administered a syringe filled with a sedative and then used an electric clipper to shave the matted fur. The exposed skin was white as an uncooked drumstick except for the red slash that ran from his shoulder to above his paw. Gemma loosened the belt. Blood spurted from a couple of spots and streamed from others. She dabbed. She compressed. She fastened hemostats. I handed her surgical tools when she called for them by name.

I'd seen wounds like it before in combat. It wasn't a deep hole made by a sharpened pungi stick or a fixed bayonet. It was a slash made from an arcing blade—a very sharp blade that had been honed to a razor's edge.

"Talk to Jake," Gemma said to Hattie. "Tell him what a good boy he is while I suture him. Tell him you're going to be his nurse while he heals. That you'll pet him and check his bandages. That you'll give him food and water."

"I can do that?" Hattie said.

"You can do anything—anything you put your mind to. Never let anybody tell you otherwise."

November started chanting as Gemma stitched the wound. I

lost track of the number of times the curved needle went into flesh and out as well as all the knots she tied. Hattie told Jake all the places that she was going to show him when he was up and running around. The chicken coop where she collected fresh eggs every morning. The corral and stable where Sarah and Wovoka lived. The dirt airstrip where her mama took off and landed her airplane.

"You can go flying with us," she said. "It'll be so fun. You can see the mountains and the lakes and, best of all, the tops of clouds."

An hour later Jake was lying on a clean blanket at the foot of Hattie's bed while she sat next to him singing a nursery rhyme about a dog named Bingo.

"He's pumped full of antibiotics, painkillers, and fluids," Gemma said as we stood in the doorway watching. "Only time will tell if he suffered any lasting damage to his nerves and tendons. That, rest, and love is all he needs now."

"What do you want to do about the film shoot?" I said.

"Go, of course. The trainer has already left to pick up the other dogs. She's got a job to do. So do I. So do you." I'd already told her about Nixon's possible visit and F.D. Power's orders for me to keep an eye on the movie crew.

"I'll load the horses," I said.

"I'll restock my medical bag," she said.

While high-spirited by nature, Sarah and Wovoka didn't balk at being led into the horse trailer. The pair of cutting horses always seemed to know an adventure awaited them at the end of the road. I checked that all our tack was onboard. Gemma came out carrying her gear.

"I left fresh bandages and painkillers for Jake in case he needs them," she said. "Between November and Hattie, he couldn't be in better hands."

Gemma got in the passenger seat and I took the wheel. We

thumped over the cattle guard and onto the blacktop and drove south.

She held up a sheaf of papers. "These are the notes about the scene they're shooting today and the horses they're going to use. The production scheduler gave them to me at the barbecue. I'm sure there'll be a new version by the time we get there. The script will get updated throughout the day. That's the way it's been so far. Sometimes it feels like John Fellows is making it up as he goes."

"That's because he's an auteur director."

"What's that?"

We were passing through No Mountain. I hooked a thumb at the dry-goods store and tavern. "Blackpowder told me about it. He's been reading books on acting. An auteur director puts his own signature on a film. Vision, camerawork, style, the whole shooting match. A bunch of French directors started doing it that way and it caught on. Alfred Hitchcock? Bigtime auteur."

"Listen to you. Next you're going to tell me you're looking forward to being on camera today."

"I saw a movie he made once. Hitchcock. They were showing it at the PX when I was at basic. It was about these birds pecking people to death. It made an impression. When I took the job out here and witnessed my first migration darkening the sky over the Malheur, I ducked every time a bird flew close."

Gemma laughed. She had the best laugh, the kind of laugh that made me feel good no matter how bad the rest of my day was going.

We were nearing the road that would take us to the Rocking H when I asked her how she thought Jake got cut.

Gemma lowered the pages of notes. "I assumed he'd run into a harrow or scythe or some other kind of sharp tool the cult had left behind, but after I shaved him and saw how straight the wound was, I decided he must've jumped up on a window and the pane broke."

"Did you find any glass in it?"

"No, and I was looking for shards too. I didn't want to close him up and leave something behind that could cause an infection."

I mulled that over. "Maybe it wasn't glass. There are three dogs and they do different things like Garth Scott's stunt doubles do, right?"

"Uh huh. One is used for close-ups because he can make different expressions on command. Sad, happy, a smile, a frown. Another dog is used for tricks like fetching and spinning in circles. And then there's Jake. He's trained to do the fight scenes. Charging bad guys, knocking them down, grabbing them by the leg. His special trick is taking a weapon out of their hand."

"Maybe that's what happened."

"What do you mean?"

"Jake tried to take a knife away from someone. The wound sure looked like it was made by one."

Gemma scoffed. "Nobody staying at the Crossed Bars would hurt Jake. Everyone knows him. He's an actor, a member of the company."

"Maybe it wasn't someone who knew him, like a thief who snuck into the Crossed Bars in the middle of the night trying to steal something. Movie cameras must be worth a lot of money. Jake heard a noise and went to take a look. The thief got scared and pulled a knife. Jake's training kicked in and tried to take it from him, only the thief wasn't an actor and the knife wasn't made of rubber."

"That's pretty far-fetched, but I don't have any other explanation for why the wound looks the way it does. But it didn't happen in the middle of the night. If it had, Jake would've bled to death. He got the cut early this morning. The trainer said she heard him howl. It must've been right then."

"Then it's lucky whoever did it ran off or the trainer might've been knifed too. We need to tell Pudge. Try him on the radio."

"We're almost at the Rocking H. We can tell him in person because I bet he'll be there."

15

We'd been driving across miles of fields belonging to the Rocking H when we turned down a long gravel drive that ended in front of a sprawling ranch house. An assortment of trailers and motorhomes were circled like covered wagons in a pasture near the corral.

"This place is too well-kept to be in an Old West Western," I said.

"They're using it as a staging area for equipment trucks and the cast's trailers," Gemma said. "The shoot is taking place nearby where Blaine has stationed three hundred head. It's all in the notes." She fanned the pages.

"Why aren't we going there now?"

"According to this schedule, John will give us last-minute instructions here. The way it usually goes, he announces some big change. We can mount up and ride over after that."

"You can't wait to get in the saddle, can you?"

"You'll find out if you'd hurry up and park."

I pulled in behind a bobtail truck. Its roll-up door was open and revealed coils of electrical cable, aluminum foot lockers, and dollies.

"That's the gaffer's truck," Gemma said. "He's the head electrician and supervises the grips who move equipment around. The cinematographer is responsible for all the camera work. His name is Lubik. Just the one name, like Cher. He's Eastern European and very temperamental. How the film looks is supposed to be his responsibility, but John is always telling him what to do. Your auteur director thing. Lubik bristles every time."

Gemma started ticking off other jobs as we walked to the ranch house. "Let's see, John has two assistant directors along with his personal assistant, Tommy. Under Lubik there are the camera operators. Then there's the sound engineer and his team, the lighting director and crew. There's an art director and her assistants. Makeup and wardrobe each have a leader plus a team. I don't know how many set builders there are. One woman's job is to be in charge of the clapperboard which has the scene and take written on it. She holds it up and reads it in front of the camera. It's like a bookmark for when they view the dailies and later when they do the editing. The list goes on. It takes dozens of people working behind the camera to make a single scene and that doesn't even count all the actors and stuntmen in front of it."

"Don't forget the head veterinarian," I said.

Gemma smiled. "I'm hoping the animals cooperate today so I can do what I really want to do, and that's drive cattle."

We joined a crowd on the far side of the ranch house. Blaine was leaning against the corral with a few cowhands gathered in a semicircle. Wearing their own hats, chaps, and boots, they looked like they'd ridden straight out of the last century. The broad-shouldered rancher beckoned to us.

"I was telling the boys the instructions I got last night," he said. "We're to go about our business like it's any other day, only no looking directly into the camera and no cussing. The movie's aiming for a PG rating. They get an R, they'll lose money. I asked the director if it'd be okay if we whistled and whooped. He said if that's what real cowboys do, then go right ahead. I told him the only kind of cowboying we do on the Rocking H is the real kind."

"Don't forget cowgirling too," Gemma said.

Blaine grinned. "Those of you who haven't ridden with Gemma before, tie your hat on and grab the saddle horn if you aim to keep up when she gets her Sarah cutting and heading. Both of them have more cow sense than a cow."

Loq was standing across the yard. "I didn't know you were going to be here," I said.

"Now you do. How come you're here?"

"Blaine needed some extra hands with the roundup. Is Dani here? I didn't get a chance to say hello yesterday."

Loq chinned at the circle of trailers. "She's getting in costume."

"Is she in the roundup too?"

"The part where the cattle bust loose. She gets swept up in them while she's being chased on horseback by the rancher who's fighting with the homesteaders. The stuntman playing him, that is."

"Wyatt Clark?"

Loq nodded.

"Who does Dani's stunts?"

"She does. Riding, shooting, fighting, dancing."

"The notes Gemma has don't say anything about a stampede."

"The new ones will."

"Did Dani tell you that?"

"The director did when he asked me to be in the movie."

"Wait. What?"

"Fellows tracked me down after the barbecue and said he

wanted me to do the same thing today. Make an entrance on a horse and cause the herd to stampede."

"I thought this wasn't a cowboy and Indian movie."

"What kind of Western would it be without showing the people who've lived here the longest and whose land was stolen by ranchers and homesteaders?"

"Do you have to wear a costume and makeup?"

Loq looked down his high cheekbones at me. "I paint myself. The pony too."

"The pinto with the yellow rings around its eyes and your red handprints on him. You didn't return him to the Crossed Bars stable?"

"He doesn't like it there."

"Where's he now?"

"Here. I trailered him to the Rocking H last night and picketed him in a pasture near the barn. I slept beside him so he wouldn't be scared anymore."

A stocky man wearing a black leather jacket and black-rimmed glasses with tinted gray lenses approached us. He had a soul patch and was pinching an unfiltered cigarette between his thumb and forefinger. "I am Lubik. Cinematographer," he said, his accent heavy. "You made Wyatt look like asshole."

"He did that all on his own," I said. "We only kept him from making a bigger one out of himself than he already had."

Lubik snorted and smoke came out of his nostrils. "That funny. What you name?"

"I'm Nick Drake and this is Loq. We're Fish and Wildlife rangers."

"Yes? Real American hero." He turned to Loq. "You real Indian?"

"I'm *Maklak*, of the Klamath Nation."

"Ah, so. I am Slavic, of Hungarian Nation." More smoke came out of his nostrils. "All the best cinematographers Hungarian. Me, Vilmos Zsigmond, Lásló Kovács." He pointed his cigarette at Loq's beaded sheath. "I give you advice, real Indian. Next time, no cut Wyatt with words. Use knife. He pig. Where I come from, we put pig on spit. Not all get apple in mouth."

A trail of smoke followed him as he walked away and joined a group that included Amber Russell, Garth Scott, and the actor who played the villainous land baron. All were in costume. All were listening to Amber.

"What did Lubik want?" a woman said from behind us.

It was Dani Reyna. She was carrying a riding crop and dressed in an embroidered jacket and tight britches. Her thick long hair cascaded beneath a flat-brim hat. Stage makeup accentuated her naturally dramatic look.

"He said I should scalp the stuntman," Loq said.

Dani blew him a kiss and then said to me, "You're Nick. Loq told me about you."

"Pleased to meet you, Miss Reyna."

"It's Dani. I understand you're married to the veterinarian."

"That's right."

"And her father is the county sheriff."

"Pudge Warbler."

"So he said when he questioned me after Amber tried to shoot me." Dani tilted her chin. "Did you hear about that?"

That reminded me I'd put the movie star's Berretta in the Jeep's glovebox when we left the barbecue with the intention of giving it back to Pudge in the morning. The pocket gun was still there.

"I heard something about a gun going off."

"It was no accident. Amber's a bad shot is all." Dani gave it a couple of beats. "Unlike me."

"Nobody should be shooting at anybody here unless they're using props."

"That's not what Loq told me when we were in Vietnam."

Her eyes started dancing like they did when she was astride the painted pony. "I shot as many men as I could."

"That was the rule of war."

"Here's a rule you should tell your father-in-law. Never believe anything Amber tells you. He needs to learn that before he does something he'll regret."

"I'm sure Pudge can decide that on his own."

"He won't be able to. Amber is a skilled actress. She's very good at spinning tales that are actually spiderwebs. When the sheriff thinks he's doing the right thing, it'll turn out to be the most wrong thing he's ever done."

"What sort of thing is that?"

Dani's eyes danced some more. "Whatever Amber needs doing that helps her get what she wants even if it means destroying everyone around her. She's very dangerous, especially when she's desperate."

"The sheriff has dealt with plenty of desperados before. They all made the mistake of underestimating him."

"Amber's not like other people. The sheriff shouldn't trust her. Nor should you."

Loq looked on without saying a word. His expression didn't give anything away.

I asked Dani why Amber fired a gun at her.

"Because her fame is sinking and she needs to be seen as a bigger star than me or she'll wind up selling Clairol on television. In our world, the only thing worse than bad publicity is no publicity at all."

"Does that mean you're dangerous too?"

"I'm Zapotec. Our gods are rain and light. We descended from the clouds and ruled the three valleys of Oaxaca. We built the mighty stone temple of Monte Albán, created a writing system before the Maya, and outlasted the Aztecs. When the Spaniards invaded, they tried to destroy us with their steel, sicknesses, and sperm. But still we Cloud People survived. Am I dangerous? Ask Amber why she fears me. Ask why she's trying to deceive your father-in-law into killing me."

Tommy Briscoe's voice chirped through a megaphone, calling everyone to gather.

"Let's go hear how John is going to change our lives," Dani said. "The ones we have on camera and the ones we have off."

16

J ohn Fellows was wearing the same poncho as the day before and smoking a cheroot. The only difference in his appearance was the addition of a Spaghetti Western cowboy hat and a viewfinder hanging from a lanyard around his neck. He stood in front of us with hills rising behind the corral to form a Technicolor backdrop.

"We're going to do something different today," he said. "Something new, something bold, something that will make this film be talked about forever. It starts with me turning up the heat. This cattle drive is not going to be a leisurely stroll through the park. Cows are going to spook. Cows are going to stampede. Riders are going to gallop. Dust is going to fly. Stuntmen will spill. Blood too, and not all of it will be corn syrup and food coloring."

Fellows dared someone to challenge him. No one said a word.

"I'm going to film an action sequence the likes that have never been seen before. Everyone talks about *The Wild Bunch*, how Peckinpah revolutionized filmmaking with his multicamera angles and quick cuts and slow-motion. Now, Sam is brilliant,

I'll hand him that. And he's certainly an artist. He also happens to be a drinking buddy of mine. But today, I'm going to out-Sam Sam."

He chomped his cheroot. "We're going to film multiple views simultaneously as the action unfolds. Some cameras will be on cranes. Some on tracks. Some will be handheld by cameramen on horseback. They'll be so close that horse snot will splatter the lenses. Some of the actors will be wearing mikes. Some of the cows and horses too. I'm going to capture every sound— pounding hoofs, snorting horses, bawling cows, and screaming men."

The glow of Fellows' cheroot reflected in his glare. "Once everyone's in position and I call for action, there's no stopping until we run out of film. And I've got miles of it with a budget that allows me to shoot it all. It's either go big or go home with our tails between our legs, and I for one don't plan on doing that. Not now. Not ever."

He blew a chain of smoke rings. "Like these," he said, jabbing the cheroot through the circles. "The best shots we get today will be linked together in the editing room. One right after another. The action will be so seamless the audience will get saddle-sore writhing in their seats watching it. Their hands will ache from grabbing the armrests and clutching their dates. It's going to be wild. It's going to be dangerous. And it's going to be spectacular."

The director glared some more. "Anybody scared, anybody thinks it won't work, anybody doesn't want to be part of cinematic history, step aside."

Nobody moved. Fellows sent more smoke toward the heavens. "That's what I thought. That's why I chose each of you personally. You got more than talent. You got guts. And today, you're going to need them. When we finish, drinks are on me. A lot of drinks. No one's going to be working tomorrow. Hell, you won't even be able to get up off the floor."

Wyatt Clark led a cheer. Other stuntmen joined in. The rest of the actors and film crew soon followed.

Blaine and his cowhands looked at each other. "I don't get the fuss," the big rancher drawled. "A stampede? Heck. That's as regular around here as lightning. Come on, let's saddle up and show these tinsel towners how we cowboy in Harney County."

They whistled and whooped. Gemma did too. Their cheers were louder than anyone else's.

I returned to the horse trailer to get Sarah and Wovoka. Fellows approached.

"Good-looking horses," he said. "Especially the buckskin with the matching socks. I see he's not gelded."

"He and the mare have had one foal already. Their next one will be our daughter's first horse. She's already named it."

"I still got that bottle of tequila. Tonight will be the night you and me crack it."

"Then here's to you getting what you need today."

"I will. I always do." Fellows squinted at me. "When we spoke yesterday, I wasn't aware Loq also served in Vietnam and now you work together rangering."

"Loq told me you asked him to be in the movie. He's a very skilled rider."

"He's more than that. He's got that special something that a camera can't get enough of. Audiences either."

"What's that?"

"People see in him what they want in themselves. Competence. Courage. Fierceness. Freedom. Strength. Sex appeal. Whatever they don't have, whatever they wish they had. All the great actors have it. You can't teach it. You can't learn it. You either got it or you don't. Loq's got it and then some."

"If you say so."

"But you know what Loq doesn't got?"

"What's that?"

"Sense enough to stay away from Dani. She'll eat him alive." Fellows waited for me to say something. When I didn't, he said, "Make it real out there today, soldier. Make it count. Don't be afraid to get hurt."

"I never am."

His squint tightened. "Maybe Loq's not the only one who's got it."

I led the two cutting horses to the corral where the other riders were mounting up. Gemma was talking to Pudge. The sheriff eyed the horses and me. "Looks like you've all been lassoed by Hollywood."

Gemma harrumphed. "I'm not acting, I'm riding."

"You already sound like you're delivering lines from a script. Next thing I know, I'm gonna have to drive down to Los Angeles every time I want to visit my granddaughter."

"Fat chance."

Gemma put her boot in the stirrup and swung onto Sarah's back. The mare nickered. Horse and rider joined the line of Rocking H cowboys trotting away. Wovoka shook his mane and pawed the ground, eager to join them.

"Did Gemma tell you about the dog she had to stitch up?" I said.

"She told me you thought someone took a knife to him," Pudge said.

"He didn't step on a nail or jump through a window."

"That may be, but I need someone who saw it happen to come forward or the person who did it to confess. That is unless the dog has been trained to speak." He sucked his teeth. "What I will do is keep my eyes and ears open along with talking with the trainer to make sure she keeps watch over the other two."

"Fair enough. By the way, I talked to Dani Reyna a little bit ago."

"That firecracker and Loq sure put on a show. Interrupted my horseshoe game. I was a ringer shy of twenty-one points for the win. Turns out the actor who plays the villain has tossed more than a few in his day."

"Dani said I should tell you not to believe Amber, that she's spinning a web to trap you into doing something you'll regret. Namely, killing Dani."

"She did, did she?" The old lawman's eyes narrowed beneath the short brim of his Stetson. "Son, I expect you mean well telling me that, but you're not telling me anything I don't already know. Despite what you and Gemma might think, I'm working here. Have been all along. On what and how I go about doing it is my business."

"Understood, and if you need any help, let me know." I sat Wovoka. The buckskin snorted. "You know that gun you took off Amber and gave to me for safekeeping? It's in Gemma's Jeep. The glovebox."

The old lawman hitched his gun belt. He looked across the yard at the movie star. "Seeing as I'm in no rush to give it back, might as well leave it be."

I leaned forward and whispered to Wovoka, "Catch 'em boy." It was all the eager stallion needed. He bolted into a lope without so much as a bootheel from me.

We caught up to Gemma and Sarah on the top of a rise that overlooked a swath of high desert that was etched with gulches and dry washes and dotted with clumps of wild grass and sagebrush that grew around boulders and thickets of junipers. Cumulus clouds moseyed across an endless sky.

"They didn't need a set designer to dress this up," Gemma said.

"Beautiful, you bet, but it'll make for tricky riding when we have to turn the stampede and get the cattle to circle and stop. If it's danger and action Fellows wants, he's going to get it."

"Look, they're setting up the cameras now. There's one on a crane over there and another on a track. I see Lubik. He's running around like a madman shouting instructions."

"I met him earlier when I was with Loq. Lubik told him he should stab Wyatt next time instead of warning him."

"I'm sure he was joking."

"He sounded pretty convincing to me."

"Lubik works with actors. He dresses and talks like he's a heavy in some kind of East German spy movie. Speaking of Wyatt, there he is now. See him? He's stunt doubling for the evil land baron in this scene. He'll be chasing Dani's character."

"I thought she was playing a dancehall girl. What's she doing way out here away from Blackpowder's saloon?"

"She rides over to tell the rancher his wife is cheating on him with Garth's gunslinger character."

"Isn't she supposed to be in love with the gunslinger too?"

"She is, but she's also crazy jealous. If Dani's character can't have him, she doesn't want anyone to. She hopes the land baron will kill his wife when she tells him. What she doesn't plan on is he tries to rape her. Dani escapes and he chases her. Wyatt has his work cut out for him today. He'll also be doing stunts for Garth's character."

"Aren't there other stuntmen who could do that?"

"Yes, but as the lead stunt double, Wyatt gets his choice. He always picks the most difficult ones. His motto is, 'Ride fast, fall hard.' It's the reason he's the highest paid in the business."

"He must've worked with Amber before. She told Pudge and me that he's always looked out for her."

"He can't say no to her. That's because she's a movie star and he's only a stuntman. They may work on the same film, but they live in different worlds. Amber is the queen of the rodeo and Wyatt is the clown in the barrel."

Blaine rode up on a muscular gray. "They're about to blow the whistle. You all set?"

Gemma said, "Give me a sec to get in costume." She took off her hat, pinned up her pony tail, and slapped her hat back on. "If I have to play a man, I better look the part."

Blaine glanced at me. "Are you going to tell her or should I?"

"Tell me what?" Gemma said.

"That even a fake moustache couldn't mask your beauty," I said.

"Men!" she scoffed, but couldn't conceal a smile.

Blaine laughed. "They gave us new instructions. We're to start off like it's a regular drive, but somewhere down the line, something spooks the beeves. They won't tell me what because they want us to be surprised for real. We'll let the herd run and give Fellows his show, but cameras or no cameras, we need to turn them before they reach Bone Ravine." He pointed east. "We'll have twenty acres of open ground near the edge to get them circling back on themselves. That should be enough."

"Should be or will be?" Gemma said. "I don't want go over the side and add my bones to the ones already at the bottom."

"I don't aim to add mine either."

The minutes dragged by. Finally, the director's amplified voice rolled across the high lonesome. "And, Action!"

17

It was Blaine's ranch and his cattle. He'd grown up on the Rocking H like his father and grandfather before him, and knew the lay of the land better than anyone. The honor to be the point rider was his. He wielded a stock whip, making the leather tip snap and pop. Right behind him was the herd leader, a strong, calm cow that had earned the respect of the rest of the cattle. Blaine led us around the base of the rise and into view of the cameras.

We kept the herd moving in a spearhead formation. Gemma and I were the flank and swing riders respectively on the left side while a pair of veteran cowboys rode the same positions on the right. The two greenest members of the team rode drag and sucked dust. Now and then, a couple of steers would try and peel off, but they were no match for us and we easily pushed them back into line.

An outcropping pinched the trail in one spot. A calf balked, lost his footing, and went down. I reined Wovoka into the herd to block the cattle coming from behind so they wouldn't trample him. They streamed past on either side. The calf bawled as he struggled to his feet. His mother heard him, broke rank, and tried to circle back. Gemma was on her in a flash and wheeled Sarah to head her off. I got the calf moving again. With Gemma chasing down the mother, I moved up to the flank position.

"Hyah, hyah," I yelled.

A volley of rifle fire answered back. The bangs spooked the herd leader. She bellowed and surged. Blaine cursed loudly and snapped his stock whip, but couldn't keep her from making a headlong rush. The herd followed instinctively. Loq was astride the painted pinto on the top of a low hill. He was bare-chested and wearing buckskin leggings like the ones Searcher's bundle had been wrapped in. The *Maklak's* cheeks were slashed with red paint and he brandished a lever-action rifle.

Loq fired again and urged the pinto into a gallop to keep pace with the stampeding herd. He put the reins between his teeth and shot another volley as he rode. The cattle ran faster. Loq brought the pinto to a shuddering stop and made him rear. It was a movie poster pose and I only had a moment to wonder if maybe his days as a wildlife ranger were over before I was forced to turn Wovoka away to keep from being caught in the crush of panicky cows.

Chasing after the calf's errant mother had taken Gemma away from the herd, but now the beeves that had been bringing up the rear were swarming around her. She deftly danced her high-spirited mare through them. I pushed through and joined her.

Gemma's face was flushed, her teeth gleamed as she grinned. "If the cameras catch me having fun, I'll end up on the cutting room floor. Let's race alongside and help tire out the herd. It'll make it easier to turn and circle them before Bone Ravine."

"Roger that," I shouted back. "There's a dry wash up ahead. I'll take it and drive out any strays."

Sarah leapt forward. Wovoka did too. We galloped across the desert, careening around junipers and jumping sagebrush.

Sparks flashed from horseshoes striking rocks. The rush of air in my face felt good. There were no chains in it, no rules to it, no obligations of any kind, only freedom.

The mouth of the dry wash opened and I rode into it. Roostertails of sand flew up from Wovoka's pounding hoofs. I slowed him when two heifers appeared up ahead. The year-old cows stopped, turned, and stared straight at us.

"Come on girls, time to rejoin your friends. There's fresh graze waiting for you at the end of the trail. Hyah! Hyah!"

They snorted and bumped into each other as they clumsily turned around. Both raised their tails and squirted liquid grass. I held Wovoka back. "Best not get too close."

The pair crow-hopped over bushes and scrambled up a crumbling embankment and out of the wash. "Go," I said. The buckskin vaulted and we sailed up and out. The stampede was a hundred yards ahead and the two wayward heifers were chasing after it. Wovoka accelerated to a full gallop to catch up.

I was leaning low and had my head slightly tilted to guard against grit shooting into my eyes when I saw another rider galloping in on my left. Dani was whipping a white filly with the crop. She wasn't afraid to ride fast over uneven terrain. More gunshots banged, but they weren't coming from where Loq had been; they came from behind Dani. A man chasing her on a black stallion was firing a six-shooter.

My reflexes kicked in and I reined Wovoka to the left to head him off. I reached for my holster. As I drew my gun, something black loomed on the other side of the two riders. It was a camera mounted on a crane with the cameraman strapped in a bucket seat behind it. For a moment I'd forgotten it was all a show. The gunman was Wyatt. I holstered my gun and eased Wovoka off, hoping I was out of camera range. I didn't want to hear what Fellows would say if I wasn't.

Dani galloped straight into the stampede and was soon

swept away. Wyatt kept firing his gun, but then suddenly horse and rider separated. The horse kept chasing after Dani while the stuntman flew through the air still in the saddle, his feet still in the stirrups. It was an amazing trick and I was trying to figure out how he'd done it when the saddle dropped away and Wyatt somersaulted and crashed back to earth. He bounced. Once. Twice. Three times. And then his head smacked against a rock. I could hear a pumpkin thunk and see a gout of blood spit like a lunger hawking phlegm.

Camera or no camera—that's what Blaine had said—and so I rode fast to Wyatt, jumped off my horse, and knelt beside him. One look at the blood streaming from his cracked skull told me it wasn't fake. The stuntman had ridden fast and fallen hard. Too hard.

Someone yelled. A man was waving a clipboard at me. "Get out of the shot." A woman holding a walkie-talkie chimed in. "Get out of the shot."

"He's dead," I yelled back. "For real."

The pair looked at each other and then hurried over. Clipboard man stared at the body and promptly vomited on his clipboard.

Walkie-talkie woman gasped, "Oh, no." She made a slashing gesture across her throat at the cameraman. "Kill it." Her face was ashen. "This is my fourth production. Nothing like this has ever happened before."

"A stunt gone wrong?" I said.

"There wasn't supposed to be a stunt. The script didn't call for one."

"You need to radio for help."

"What do you mean?"

"Call someone. Call Fellows. Tell him his lead stuntman is dead."

"I can't. He'll fire me."

"Give me your walkie-talkie." She did. I clicked it. "Emergency. Emergency."

"Hullo!" Tommy chirped in a hushed voice. "We're supposed to be maintaining radio silence."

"A man's been killed."

"Who is this?"

"Nick Drake. Wyatt Clark took a bad fall. He's dead."

"What do you mean dead?"

"Dead. As in dead. Tell Fellows."

"I can't do that. The cows are coming. He won't leave the shot."

Static buzzed in my ear. Tommy had turned off his radio. I blew air and looked at the ground. The saddle had landed upside down. The stirrups were flopped on either side like broken wings. So were both ends of the cinch that were still attached to the saddle with leather billets, but the middle had torn apart. Without the cinch strapped around the horse's girth, the saddle would slide off, or, in Wyatt's case, fly off. I took the torn ends and matched the two edges. While part of it was torn, the other part was sliced clean through.

I walked a short distance to be out of earshot of walkie-talkie woman. The handheld radio had multiple channels. I changed to a new one. "Calling Sheriff Warbler. Emergency." No response. I changed channels and tried again. Still no response. I changed channels a third time. It was a charm.

"This is Deputy Nelson. I read you. Over."

"Orville, it's Nick. Are you at the Rocking H?"

"I am. The sheriff wanted me to help with crowd control. The word got out they were filming here today and the public has shown up."

"I need you to change channels. Use the number of months your son is old." I clicked off and switched to channel 18. Orville came back on.

"Why the need for a secure channel?" he asked.

"We need to keep this hushed. Get Pudge out here right away. Someone fell off a horse." I gave him directions and landmarks.

"I will call for an ambulance."

"Call the coroner instead. And, Orville, bring your evidence kit."

A few minutes later Pudge's pickup with the sheriff's gold star on the door bounced along the same trail that Wyatt and Dani had galloped on. Orville's rig was close behind. The old lawman pulled to a stop several yards away and surveyed the scene before joining me. The young deputy followed, his arms pumping as he maneuvered his wheelchair over rocks and through sand. Pudge glanced at the dead stuntman.

"Someone gets thrown from a horse and you don't call for a first aid kit but an evidence kit, I got to think you got yourself involved in another killing." His short-brim Stetson waggled back and forth. "You making up for lost time after taking the past four years off?"

"I was flushing strays out of a wash and on my way back to help turn the stampede when I saw Wyatt chasing Dani. He was riding hellbent for leather when he and his saddle went airborne. I thought it was a stunt. It wasn't."

"Says who?"

"Her." I nodded at walkie-talkie woman. "She said the script didn't call for one. And then there's that." I redirected my nod at the saddle. "I haven't said anything about it to the film crew."

The sheriff bent down and studied it before picking up the middle ends of the cinch and putting the two edges together like I'd done. "Like trying to time a lit fuse on a stick of dynamite," he said in a low voice so only Orville and I could hear. "You got to know how much to leave so it blows up when you want it to."

"You'd think a professional stuntman would've doublechecked his tack before galloping off."

"Whoever did this, dirtied it to cover their tracks. It must've slipped Clark's eye. Either that or someone else saddled his horse for him and told him it was jake. I'll need to check on that."

"Something else you'll want to look at is what's inside the camera's film pack. They didn't stop shooting until after he landed."

"That a fact?" He ran his thumb along the edge of the doctored cinch. "A clean slice equals a sharp blade."

Tires crunching over rocks signaled an approaching vehicle. A distant drumbeat of hooves also sounded.

Pudge picked up the saddle and put it on Orville's lap. "This is evidence. Nobody looks at it but us. Secure it in your rig.

"Yes, sir," Orville said and wheeled away.

Fellows slid his lanky frame from behind the wheel of a doorless World War II–vintage Jeep. Tommy got out too. The director scowled at the stuntman's body.

"Of all days, it had to be this day he takes a header. Did his horse stumble or go down?"

"Neither," Pudge said. "The cinch broke. The saddle flew off and Clark rode the Pegasus."

"Never heard that term before. Paints a picture. I'll give it to my screenwriter." He looked around. "I don't see the horse or saddle? Where'd they end up?"

"The saddle's been secured. Protocol. The horse?" Pudge turned to me.

"He kept chasing after Dani and the stampede," I said.

Fellows motioned to walkie-talkie woman. "Was the camera rolling?"

"Of course. We only turned it off when . . ." She couldn't say the words.

"What about footage of the chase? Is there anything I can use?"

"I'm sure there is. We were tracking Dani with a jib shot as soon as she left her mark. First with a close-up and then we widened so we got Wyatt charging behind her. Oh, John. It was thrilling. The action. The landscape. They were riding so fast, we couldn't breathe. When Wyatt tumbled through the air, our hearts stopped."

"It was that real?"

"It was, John. It was like we were tumbling with him. And we got it all on camera."

Pudge cut her off. "Show a little respect here. There's a man here who lost his life. Someone's about to get a knock on the door and learn he's not coming home. Not today. Not tomorrow. Not ever."

"And the best way to honor him is to make sure he lives on in film," Fellows said. "He would've wanted nothing less. His family too, if he's got one. I don't know that he does. All I know is Wyatt Clark was a legend. If there were Oscars awarded to stuntmen, he'd have a shelfful. Since there aren't, I'll do the next best thing and dedicate this film to him. It'll say so right in the closing credits."

18

Loq and Dani rode up. The Klamath was leading the saddleless black stallion. They looked down at the dead stuntman. The dark-eyed actress's lips curled. "*El esta muerto pero no lo siento.*"

"How dare you not be sorry he's dead!" walkie-talkie woman cried.

"Why should I be? Yes, I despised him, but he died doing what he loved. We should all be so lucky to meet death while in love."

Loq threw his leg over the painted pony. He didn't hand the reins to anyone, but the pony didn't budge. He whispered in the black stallion's ear and then dropped his reins too. The horse stayed put. Loq crouched beside the dead stuntman and raised his hands toward the sky and sang. He took his skinning knife from the beaded sheath and slashed the air above Wyatt's face.

Pudge stepped forward. "Hold on there, Loq."

"He was my enemy, but now he's dead. It was not my kill and so I ask his spirit to forgive me for letting him die without a warrior's honor." Loq resumed slashing the air.

Fellows twirled his finger at the cameraman. The

cameraman got behind the Panavision and aimed the lens at Loq and the dead stuntman. Another Jeep skidded to a stop and Lubik jumped out. He took it all in and then scrambled behind the cameraman, leaning in so close that the two men's heads were conjoined. "Tight," he said. "More tight. Fill frame with real Indian face."

Loq finally stood and picked up the reins to the pinto and Wyatt's horse. The camera stopped rolling too.

Lubik clapped the cameraman on the back. He came over to Loq. "I told you, real Indian, use knife on pig, not words. But, okay, pig is dead."

"What the Sam Hill?" Pudge said.

The cinematographer pushed up the black frame glasses with the gray-tinted lenses that had slipped down his nose. "I no like pig. I no like Wyatt."

Pudge looked at Dani. "You and the stuntman, you saddled up at the same place, the same time?"

Dani's long black hair flounced. "Yes. They brought the horses on a trailer and took some close-ups of me in the saddle." The actress tilted her head as if posing for a camera. "Then I rode to my mark and when I was cued . . ." She whipped the air with the leather crop. "I like to do it fast."

"Did you saddle your own mount or check it before getting onboard?"

"There are people who do that."

"What about Clark? He saddle his own and check it himself?"

Dani hesitated. "I don't remember."

"Why not?"

"Because I was already in character. His character had just tried to rape me. I was fleeing him. I'm happy he fell off and died."

"You mean his character, don't you?"

Dani's teeth flashed. "You're asking about our saddles, but what you should be asking is, why did Wyatt fire real bullets at me."

"What are you talking about?"

"His gun had live rounds. I heard them whistle past my ear. Wyatt was trying to kill me."

"You can tell the difference between bullets and blanks by their sound?"

"Also the difference between bullets striking bone and bullets striking organs. If you don't believe me, ask Loq about our time in Vietnam. I can still hear it. Crack is bone. Thud is organ. Crack. Thud. Thud."

The sheriff looked down at the stuntman. His holster was empty. So were his hands. I replayed the scene. Maybe the reason my reflexes had kicked in and I drew my own weapon was because I'd heard live fire too.

I searched the ground for Wyatt's gun by circling his body and widening my rings. When I reached Fellows' Jeep, I crouched and looked under it. The gun was there. I pulled it out. It was a single-action, six-shot Colt Peacemaker. Some called the .45 the gun that won the West. It was an original, by the look of it, or a very well-made replica. I checked the cylinder and removed a spent casing. The tip didn't have the tell-tale crimps of a blank. I checked the others and then put them back.

Pudge came over. I handed him the pistol. "Dani's right. They were all live. He didn't use a cowboy load either." A cowboy load left the chamber opposite the hammer with its built-in firing pin empty to guard against an accidental strike.

"Clark was a stuntman. He was hooked on risk." The sheriff spun the cylinder beneath his nose. "Orville," he shouted. The young deputy quickly wheeled over. "Take this back to the office. It's evidence. To exactly what, I'm not sure, but we'll find out."

Pudge thrust his jowls at the lanky director. "Who's in charge of weaponry?"

Fellows pointed at the body. "Wyatt. He did it all. Lead stuntman, head wrangler, chief armorer."

"He's the one who handed out guns and made sure they were full of blanks?"

"We don't always use cold guns. For sound purposes, we record firing live rounds into trees, walls, sandbags, the ground. Then we dub it in. Peckinpah did that on *The Wild Bunch*. The final scene where William Holden is firing a belt-fed Browning machine gun at the Mexican Army, you feel it right here more than you hear it." He punched himself in the stomach.

"Here's something you need to hear as well as feel," Pudge said. "I need a looksee at every piece of ammo, live or dummy, you got before you do any more filming with guns involved. I don't care how many rounds it is. And I'm also gonna need to see what's in that camera over there and the one where Clark and Miss Reyna were getting on their horses."

"Impossible!" Fellows said. "It's proprietary. No filmmaker would allow his unedited work to be viewed by a nonprofessional."

"Let's me and you get something straight right here and now," the old lawman said. "You may be a bigshot down in Hollywood, but up here, I'm the law and what I say goes. It wouldn't change anything if you were Anthony Mann or John Ford. A woman has accused a man of shooting at her for real. That man is now lying dead at our boots. I don't know if his death was an accident or intentional. Until I find out, this is my show."

Fellows glared.

The sheriff continued. "From here on out, no one, and I mean no one, involved in this movie leaves Harney County. I'm also ordering that no one in your company talks to anyone about what happened here today. The people in my department will do the same. The last thing any of us needs is the press to get ahold of this and make it into something it ain't before we know what it is."

"Agreed," the director said.

"As for now, the story is there's been an accident and we're investigating it and the name of the victim is being withheld pending notification. End of story. How fast can you get me that film and ammo?"

Lubik answered before Fellows could. "Film must be developed. We do tonight. Show dailies tomorrow."

Fellows said, "I'll need to call Morty Wassenberg and tell him what happened. He's the producer and your orders are going to slow down our production schedule. That means a lot of money. His money."

"Call away." Pudge motioned to Loq. "Take Clark's horse back to the Rocking H and secure it there. I'm gonna want to take a look at him later."

Loq and Dani got back on their mounts and rode off with the black stallion in tow.

Pudge curled a finger at Lubik and Tommy. "Come on, help me and Drake load Clark into the back of my deputy's rig. He's got a date with the coroner."

The cinematographer came right over, but Tommy started swaying. "I can't. I've never touched a dead person before. I'm going to be sick."

"Ah, don't get your silk neckerchief all in a knot."

"I'll do it," Fellows said. "I carried plenty of corpses in Korea. Most of the time they were frozen stiff."

I got back on Wovoka and rode to Bone Ravine where Gemma and the cowboys were overseeing spent cattle grazing in an open field.

"Hey, slowpoke, where have you been?" she said. "You missed all the fun."

"Long story. I need to get back to town. You ready to go?"

Gemma eyed me suspiciously, but said she was and so we bid farewell to the Rocking H rancher and his hands, trailered Wovoka and Sarah, and headed home.

"What happened back there?" she said. "I saw John roar off in his Jeep with Lubik right behind. After we stopped the stampede, someone was supposed to come over and tell us whether they needed any more shots, but no one did."

"Wyatt was killed. He flew off his horse. The cinch appears to have been cut."

"Are you sure it didn't come undone from the billets."

"It was sliced halfway through in the middle. Pudge saw it the same way. Him, Orville, me, and whoever cut it are the only ones who know about that part. Now you do too. It's going down as an accident until Pudge is ready to say otherwise."

"Loq doesn't know?"

"It's always hard to tell with him. He showed up with Dani and held a ceremony over the body with his knife, but said it wasn't his kill. That's not to say Pudge won't be questioning him later because of the riff he had with Wyatt at the barbecue."

"What a day. First Jake the dog and then a stampede and now Wyatt. I'm ready for this movie stuff to be over and all these people gone so we can get back to our real lives."

We arrived home. Before getting out, Gemma opened the glovebox and saw the Beretta Jetfire. "What's this doing in here?"

I told her about it and how Pudge gave it to me for safekeeping.

"You can't leave it in here. Hattie could find it. Lock it up in Pudge's gun case."

"I'll take it to the lineman's shack right now. I have to call F.D.

Powers and tell him what happened today. It could scotch President Nixon's visit."

I was putting the little gun in my pickup's glovebox when Hattie came running out.

"Mama, Daddy. Come look. Jake's awake."

She ran back into the house. Gemma and I followed and found the big dog lying on Hattie's bed, not on a blanket on the floor like we'd left him. Jake didn't raise his head, but thumped his tail at us.

"Can we keep him?" Hattie said. "Can we? Please? Please?"

Gemma gave me a what-are-we-going-to-do-now look. I said, "You're taking very good care of him, Hattie, but you have to remember Jake belongs to someone else."

"But Daddy!"

"I got to go to work. We can talk about it later."

No Mountain's main street was empty as I passed through. I pulled up to the lineman's shack and checked the Code-a-Phone. There was only one message, but it wasn't from my boss. It was from Chief Deputy Manning Dobbs.

"Uh, hello Nick, it's Manning. I hope you get this. I wanted to let you know there's been a development in the Jump Diggins case. As a matter of fact, we've arrested the killer. Actually, Bull Hammond did. A citizen's arrest. It was like he thought. An Indian at Summit Lake did it. He confessed and is in jail here. Thanks again for your help."

I replayed the message and then dialed the sheriff's office in Winnemucca. I had to wait a few minutes before getting transferred to Dobbs.

"It's Nick Drake. I got your message. What's Hammond doing making an arrest and who is it?"

"You asked me to tell you and now I have. I'm busy. I got to go."

"Wait. Can you at least give me some details?"

"It's like my message said. Bull's theory panned out. He spoke to some of the miners who recalled seeing an Indian cutting across Quartz Creek Road around the time and day of the murder. The coroner pinpointed it. The miners didn't think anything of it at the time except for the fact that the Indian was naked."

I felt hit by an electrical cattle prod. "What did you say?"

"He wasn't wearing any clothes. Why they remembered him. Bull drove out to the Summit Lake reservation and asked around. This naked Indian was camping near there. Bull saw him and the Indian took off. Bull caught him. The Indian confessed. Now he's in my jail awaiting a hearing."

"Did he give you his name?"

"He's not talking. Not to me anyway, but Bull knew him from before. He's called Searcher."

I breathed in, breathed out. "Listen to me, Manning. Listen very carefully. I know Searcher. He didn't do it. He couldn't have. I can alibi him."

"But Bull says . . ."

The line clicked and a woman's voice came on. "Excuse me. This is the operator breaking in. I have a very important call from Washington DC. I need the Harney County, Oregon, party to remain on the line and the Nevada party to hang up."

"Manning, I'll call you back."

The line was clicking when I said it. I don't know if he'd already been disconnected.

"Ranger Drake, is that you?" It was F.D. Powers.

"Yes, sir. I was in the middle of an important call."

"Surely, not as important as this one is going to be."

"I was going to call you as soon as that one was over. I assume you heard the news."

"Indeed. Morty Wassenberg called me. I must say the information about a fatal accident on the film location is cause for concern. Were you there?"

Either Fellows didn't tell the producer everything or Wassenberg chose not to tell Powers.

"I was doing as you ordered, keeping an eye on the movie crew. I was invited to help drive cattle for a scene. The man who died was riding in front of me when he went off his horse. He was killed instantly."

"Saving grace, that, I should say. Morty said the sheriff is managing the process, but protocol calls for delaying production while he completes the paperwork."

"Among other things. Will you be informing General Haig?"

Power's ballpoint pen was getting a workout. "Of course. He is the president's chief of staff. He needs to know even the minutest detail. I must say this incident could well prove to be an impediment to our plans. Washington is in a political upheaval the likes that have not been seen since President Andrew Johnson. I will keep you apprised of developments. In the meantime, carry on as if he is coming."

"Yes sir."

I redialed the sheriff's office in Winnemucca to resume telling Dobbs why he was dead wrong about Searcher and that it had to be a frame job by Bull Hammond. The dispatcher told me he'd left for the day and would return first thing in the morning. I hung up, knowing I'd be standing in front of his desk when he got there.

19

D arkness came late to Harney County during the summer months and dying light was still purpling the sky as I left the Warbler ranch and drove to the Will camp. The Wills didn't have a telephone and I needed to ask Nagah if he'd mind manning the Code-a-Phone while I was in Nevada. Once again, November, a pot of soup, and a hand-woven basket of cornbread rode with me. The old healer had insisted on coming when she learned where I was going.

I had another reason for making the drive across Harney Basin. I wanted to say goodbye to Tuhudda in case he died while I was away. Thinking of my old friend slumped in his sick bed launched a cavalcade of the departed marching through my thoughts: my parents, the squad mates I'd led into an ambush, enemies I'd killed in combat, and murder victims I'd discovered. Jump Diggins and Wyatt Clark brought up the rear.

November and I'd been driving in silence. Feeling the need to say something, I began recounting my conversation with John Fellows about the respective beliefs of actors and Buddhist monks when it came to immortality. I asked her how those squared with her own. The *Numu* elder tugged the striped

Pendleton blanket wrapped around her and stared mutely at the road ahead. She finally responded when we reached the spot where we'd seen the Paiutes from Summit Lake ferrying Donna Has Many's body to Lyle Rides Alone's ranch.

"*Mu naa'a*, Wolf, the great creator, gives power to everything," she said. "From the rocks on the ground to the stars above. Some have more *puha* than others. Some can change shape, others cannot. But a rock that turns itself into dust still has its *puha*. A star that lets go of the sky still has its *puha* when it becomes night fire."

"What about *Numu?* When you journey to the spirit world, do you stay there forever or can you come back as someone or something else?"

"You ask me that question, but you are really asking what will become of Tuhudda. His *puha* is strong no matter what or where he is."

"You sound as if you're certain he's going to die."

The thin shoulders beneath the striped wool blanket shrugged. "Yes, Tuhudda will die. I will die. You will die. How can there be life with no death and death with no life?"

"Loq told me Tuhudda's lessons will only end if I let them."

"Loq is smart for a *Maklak* and *Maklak* are mostly known for being brave and stubborn."

"I looked into Buddhism after I made it out of that temple in Vietnam," I said. "I'd gotten the monk wrong. Reincarnation isn't what he was after. It was something called Nirvana. Enlightenment. When he achieved that, then, kaput, no more having to be reincarnated and endure all the suffering that comes with being alive, whether as a human or a cockroach."

"Our Tlingit brothers and sisters also believe when the body turns to dust, the soul leaves and forms another body. Di'neh believe they have two souls. One remains in the afterworld while the other forms again. They are called Those Made Again."

"Di'neh, the Navajo people wrongly called Apache in the movie Pudge was watching when he fell asleep," I said.

November tsked. "I do not understand a people who believe a movie makes them live forever."

I thought of Amber Russell and her obsession with Dani Reyna. "They want to believe it because they're terrified of growing old and being replaced. See, if they're in a movie, then they're still the age they were in the film no matter how many years later when someone watches it."

November's tsk was sharper this time. "A people who fear growing old are selfish. How can a people survive if there are no old ones to teach the young? No mothers to show daughters how to bear babies and gather wada root and grass seeds. No fathers to help their sons become warriors. A people who do not grow old are no people at all."

I took the turnoff to the Will camp and pulled up in front of Tuhudda's single-wide. Nagah was sitting on the front stoop, reading a book in the dimming light. Since starting the path to manhood, he'd let his hair grow long. It was now tied in a single braid that fell past his shoulders.

He jumped up when he saw November in the passenger seat and rushed to help her out. "Good evening, Girl Born in Snow," he said in *Numu*.

"I have brought healing soup and cornbread for your grandfather," she said. "There is some for you too."

"Thank you, but I do not need any. Whatever Grandfather doesn't eat now, I will save for him to eat later."

I spotted the smile tugging at the corners of the old woman's lips when Nagah passed her test. Others before self was the Paiute way. It's what helped them survive for thousands of years in one of the harshest environments on Earth.

I asked Nagah if his grandfather was awake.

"It's becoming harder to tell. Sometimes he speaks with his

eyes closed and sometimes they are open without him speaking." Nagah spoke matter-of-factly. Though he'd grown accustomed to seeing illness and death among animals while working with Gemma, I knew it had to be difficult when it came to watching the man who'd raised him.

"I'll grab the soup pot if you take the cornbread," I said.

We followed November into the trailer. Tuhudda appeared not to have moved since I saw him last. His cheeks were drawn and mouth puckered. He rasped when he breathed and the sweet smoke from a braid of sage smoldering in a bowl next to his bed couldn't mask a smell that reminded me of a waterhole shaded by very old willows.

"Hello my old friend," I said.

"Nick Drake," he mumbled without opening his eyes.

"You knew I was coming before I left," I said, finishing his favorite saying for him.

"This is so."

"I've come to see you before I leave for Nevada in the morning."

"What is there?"

"Unfinished business."

"Ah, the worst kind."

"I found a man who'd been shot and killed. His burro too. He was an old prospector. Blackpowder Smith knew him. The lawman in charge is young and inexperienced. He's also afraid of the man he replaced as chief deputy. That man convinced the young lawman that Searcher killed the prospector. Now Searcher is in jail for a crime he didn't commit. I am going back to set things right."

I thought he hadn't heard me, but then he mumbled, "But you are not afraid of the old chief deputy. You do not fear anyone but yourself because you are a warrior. First in the green world. Now in the brown world."

"The young deputy reminds me of a soldier who was under my command. I failed to protect him and he was killed. I don't want that to happen again."

Tuhudda coughed up phlegm. "You did not kill that soldier. His enemy did. A warrior who dies in battle has honor, not shame. Do not take away his honor by blaming yourself. If you can help the young lawman find his honor, then you must."

The breath it took to speak so many words set off a coughing fit. The Paiute's chest rose and fell. Sputum frothed his lips. Nagah wiped his grandfather's chin with a cloth. November, standing off to the side, rocked back and forth and started humming.

"I'm sorry, my old friend," I said. "I didn't mean to burden you with my story. I only wanted to say hello."

"It is never a burden to help someone, only an honor," he rasped. "Who are we if we do not honor each other?"

Tuhudda became so still it appeared he fell asleep. I knelt next to him and took his hand. Despite the fever that had sapped his strength, it was cold to the touch. His fingers were gnarled from holding the reins of a pony, lashing twine woven from rolled sagebrush bark around tree limbs to build a wickiup, clutching a walking stick as he climbed Steens Mountain, carving figurines out of soapstone for a rainmaking ceremony, caressing his wife, cradling his children, pulling back a bowstring to teach his grandson how to shoot an arrow straight and true.

"You did not come to say hello but goodbye," he mumbled, the words whistling through missing teeth.

"You speak the truth, but my heart is too heavy to say it."

"That is because you believe goodbye is an end. But we will talk again. And laugh. And walk together."

I swallowed the lump rising in my throat and choked back tears. "And drink coffee. Whenever I make some, I'll pour two cups. Yours will always have lots of sugar in it. Sweeter is always better. It's what you always say."

"This is so."

Tuhudda lapsed into silence again. I couldn't hear his breathing over November's humming. I looked at Nagah. His face was still, his eyes wide open, but I knew he was seeing all the times he'd spent with his grandfather and the lessons he'd learned. How to protect sheep from coyotes and cougars. How to make fire with two rocks. Find water in a sea of sagebrush and sand. Ride a pony. Learn to read and write. Tap his inner courage to ask a veterinarian for a job and teach him how to fly an airplane.

The old man suddenly gripped my hand and raised his head a few inches off the pillow. His eyes blinked open. "I heard the forever feet on the path that has no end."

I glanced at November. Was this it? Was the next breath to be his last? But her eyes were unseeing as her humming turned into chanting. I looked at Nagah. His eyes were also unseeing of the moment. It was as if he were a boy back in a grassy meadow beneath a yellow sun watching over the Will family's sheep while playing a flute his grandfather had carved for him.

"It's okay, Tuhudda," I said. "Your family and friends are all there to welcome you."

His eyes turned fierce, burning away the rheum. "No! I saw the Forever Walkers in my dream. I saw you in a camp below Big Mountain. I heard them as you did. Saw them as you did."

The Forever Walkers. November had described them as a band of Paiute from long ago who left everything behind as they tried to outrun a fever. That I'd heard them while camped above Jump Diggins and Ruby was one thing, but that Tuhudda had dreamed he saw me with them was quite another. I'd lived long enough in the high lonesome to know many things were inexplicable, that it was always better to accept them than be a river that breaks itself against the rocks trying to forge a new course.

"You're right, my old friend," I said. "I saw them, heard them."

"That is what makes you a warrior. You have not closed yourself off to believing things that you were told as a child cannot be. Your medicine is strong. Medicine is *puha*. Power."

"I didn't speak to them. Did you?"

One eye fluttered and then shut. The other remained fixed. "I told them I was Tuhudda, named for Deer. The Forever Walkers said 'Blessings son of Tooonugwetsedu, named for Cougar, grandson of Padooa, named for Bear. Have you come to join us?' I told them you would return and need their help. They said, 'Then we will give it.' "

"How will I find them again?"

"They will find you."

"And what do I say to them?"

"Ask Searcher."

"Why would he know?"

"Because Searcher walks with them when he wants to." The pupil in his eye started constricting and his head lowered back on the pillow.

"But Searcher is in jail."

"If this is so, then it is because he wants it to be so. When Searcher no longer wants it to be so, it will no longer be."

Tuhudda's chest heaved and he started wheezing. It sounded like a coarse rasp shaping a piece of wood.

I squeezed his hand. "Take care, my old friend."

Tuhudda's breathing grew shallower.

I turned to November. "Did he mean Searcher is a Forever Walker?"

"No. Searcher walks with them when he wants to, but he is not one of them. He is of another band, but he is the last."

"What do you mean, the last?"

"The rest of his band has left this world. Only Searcher remains. Many *Numu* bands are no more forever because of the wars against us, both those fought with bullets of lead and those with bullets of disease. It is the same with other tribes. A Yahi man came out of the wilderness in California many years after the rest of his people had died. A white man asked him his name, but he could not answer because his people's way forbid him to say his own name out loud until another Yahi introduced him by name first. The white man called him Ishi. When Ishi died, the Yahi died and his true name died also."

"Maybe Searcher isn't his real name."

"Only Searcher knows that. Now go, Nick Drake. Do as Tuhudda says. Help the young lawman find his honor. Talk with Searcher. Do what he says, for he can show you what is important and what is not. I will stay with Tuhudda. You will see him again."

"In this world or the next?"

November tilted her head. "Does it matter?"

Nagah walked with me to my pickup. "Your grandfather is wise and powerful," I said.

"Yes. He will always be with me." He patted his chest.

"I wanted to ask you for a favor, but after seeing Tuhudda, I realize you can't leave his side."

"He'd be dishonored if I didn't grant you the favor. What is it?"

I told Nagah I was expecting an important call from my boss. "He'll leave a message on the Code-a-Phone to call him back. If you could swing by the lineman's shack from time to time and check the messages while I'm away, it would be a great help. If he leaves one, radio me as soon as you can so I can call him back."

"I know how to use the machine. I'll do it."

"One other thing. If you see Loq, tell him I went to Nevada and to radio me with any news." I explained what happened to Wyatt Clark. "Sheriff Warbler is investigating the murder, but Loq is hunting for the killer too."

"Because it's Loq's way."

"Yes, and also because there's a woman acting in the movie he believes needs his protection."

"What evil is she in danger from?"

"Jealousy," I said.

"A powerful enemy." He said it as a simple fact, the same as his grandfather would. I could see the wisdom of Tuhudda settling over Nagah like a ceremonial blanket passed down through the generations. Tuhudda was putting a lot of responsibility on his grandson's shoulders to keep the *Numu* culture alive, but something told me Nagah was strong enough to bear it.

On the drive home, I began mapping out a plan for Nevada. By the time I pulled up to the Warbler ranch, I knew what my first steps would be. I also knew those steps could easily be thwarted and that I'd have to improvise. It was the Bard of Scotland's rule all over again.

Pudge's pickup wasn't parked in front of the house when I got there. I found Gemma reading in bed.

"November stayed behind," I said. "It's a vigil now."

"How's Nagah taking it?"

"Like the man's he grown into."

"I'm so proud of him. I've talked to him about going to college, but he says he's getting a better education working with me. Once Tuhudda's gone, he might reconsider. I hope he does."

"We'll see."

Gemma sighed. "Sometimes I wonder what our lives would be like if we'd been able to have another baby. A son."

"Busier and with a lot less sleep," I said quickly.

"I'm being serious."

I sat on the edge of the bed and pulled off my boots. "I know you are."

"Don't you ever think about it?"

"Of course I do. But you know what I think about more? How lucky we are. We survived a plane crash and you battling a coma to give birth to our amazing daughter on a mountainside in the middle of a snowstorm. If the price we had to pay to bring Hattie into this world and for you to survive your injuries means no more pregnancies, then I accept that."

Gemma was silent for a while. I unbuttoned my shirt. She said, "You said no more pregnancies. You didn't say, no more babies. We could adopt. There are plenty of children in need of a good home."

"Then let's look into it," I said.

Gemma smiled. "What time will you leave?"

I finished undressing. "At first light."

"It's a long drive. You better get some sleep."

I gathered her in my arms and began nuzzling her neck. "Who said anything about being tired?"

20

A hot, dry wind was blowing when I pulled into Winnemucca. Strips of paper fluttered like kite tails from a peeling billboard advertising an all-you-can-eat buffet for $2.99. Heat waves rose from the parking lot in front of the Aces Wild Casino while the neon tubes outlining the spade, diamond, club, and heart on the marquee flickered dully through clouds of stinging dust. An inflatable swan bobbed drunkenly on the choppy waters of a motel pool.

Waiting at a stoplight, I glanced at the pickup's visor. Gemma had fastened a new snapshot to it before I left. She and Hattie were sitting on the top rail of the corral with Sarah and Wovoka in the background. I pulled into Fifth Street and parked across from the Humboldt County Sheriff's Department. The building was larger than the sheriff's office in Harney County, but the size reflected the law-and-order needs of a town with five casinos operating twenty-four hours a day rather than a populace that was only twice the size of Burns.

Chief Deputy Manning Dobbs looked up from his desk. "I called to let you know we caught the killer. I didn't say I needed any help."

"But you do," I said. "You know why? Because you said 'we caught the killer.' At best, Searcher's a suspect. At worst, he's Bull Hammond's fall guy."

"You don't know that."

"I know Searcher didn't kill Jump Diggins. He couldn't have. He wasn't anywhere near the murder site. I talked with him earlier that morning in Virgin Valley. He spent the night there. The night before he slept in the Pueblos on his way walking back from the Duck Valley reservation. He was miles away from where Jump was shot."

"Can you prove it?"

"Searcher told me. He had no reason to lie."

"Well, he's not speaking to anyone now."

"Then all you have to go on is Hammond's word. Ask yourself why is he so determined to catch Diggins' killer? It's not his job, it's yours. You're the chief deputy."

The young lawman raised a cautionary finger. "Don't tell me what I should or shouldn't be doing."

"Even if I have information about the mine's operator? It might change your opinion about Hammond's motive for blaming Searcher."

"Not that again. I already told you. Why would Oro Holdings have anything to do with killing a no-account prospector?"

"A Harney County deputy discovered the mine is connected to the Las Vegas mob."

Dobbs scoffed. "It sounds to me like the deputy has too much time on his hands and too much imagination."

"What he has is gumption and superb investigative skills, not to mention friends at the FBI who confirmed the connection."

"How so?"

"Oro Holdings was registered to do business in the state by a Las Vegas lawyer named John Smith who'd done legal work for what turned out to be a mob-run ring of drug smugglers a few years back. They left a trail of bodies in my part of Oregon. Oro is a shell company hiding under an even bigger shell out of New York. The real owners are hiding behind an offshore law firm in Panama that has more ways to hide profits and identities than a casino has shills and suckers."

"But it's a legitimate company. I checked," Dobbs said. "Oro Holdings had to post a legal record of its name in the newspaper like any other business. I read it myself. I called around. Oro has an excellent standing at the local bank. The mine pays its bills on time. No worker complaints have ever been filed."

Seeing the young deputy made me think of Private Danbaby again. He believed the VC would adhere to the Geneva Convention. "What about Jump Diggins? Did you find anything out about him?"

"He had an arrest record. He'd been cited for vagrancy several times and was arrested for trespassing on more than one occasion. Jump's exactly what I said he was. A good-for-nothing drifter."

"And he reminds you of your father."

Dobbs' acne reddened. "You don't know what I think about my father."

"I know what I think because I learned quite a bit from Pudge Warbler and a friend who was collateral damage to the bank heist your father pulled. Here's where it gets interesting. My friend? His name is Blackpowder Smith. He tried running off into the desert to forget the living hell your father cast him into and ended up meeting Jump Diggins. They spent months together digging for gold. Guess what? They found it. Guess where? Right where Oro Holdings is mining now."

"You're making that up."

"No, I'm not. The same as you didn't when you wrote a school paper about how you wanted to become a lawman because of what your father did."

"How do you know about that?"

"Because your teacher called Pudge to verify what you wrote. That was after your mother asked him for help getting reward money so she could raise you. Pudge wasn't able to do a thing about that, but he did send her some of his pay."

"Guilt money."

"The only thing Pudge felt guilty about was he couldn't stop your father sooner. Do you want to hear what really happened that day?"

Dobbs wavered. "I'll give you five minutes."

Five minutes turned into ten and then fifteen as I relayed the rest of the story Pudge told me early that morning over coffee and frybread after he arrived home from his office in Burns where he and Orville had been working overtime investigating Wyatt Clark's murder.

It turned out I'd guessed right that Pudge had taken the shortcut from Hines all those winters ago when he was chasing Reggie Dobbs and his gang making their getaway in Doc Wooster's blue Buick Roadmaster with the shiny grille. As the then-young deputy leadfooted down the icy dirt road and blasted through snowdrifts, he radioed dispatch and was patched through to a feed-and-grain store in No Mountain.

Jack Jericho, an old broncobuster turned store owner, answered the phone. "Whatcha need, podner?"

"It's Pudge Warbler. Have you heard the news?"

"Store's for working, not dancing. Don't got a radio. What news?"

"Is Blackpowder working today?"

"If you can call it that. He's mooning over some gal while he's loading sacks of feed for his delivery rounds. I even spied him holding a sack and dancing with it. He said he was practicing doing the waltz for his wedding. Why?"

"Go get him and put him on the phone, but stand next to him and listen in when I tell him what I got to tell him."

"That bad, huh?"

"Yep."

A few seconds later, Blackpowder Smith's voice came across Pudge's radio. "I hear you got a bee in your bonnet. You need me to pull the stinger out?"

"I don't got time to sugarcoat this, Black. I'm on the Hines shortcut in pursuit. The sheriff and the rest of the deputies are fifteen minutes behind me, maybe more. There's been a holdup at the First National in Burns. Two dead, three wounded, and, well, I'm afraid they took Connie hostage. They're making a run for Nevada in Doc Wooster's Buick. They killed him for it. They may have grabbed his wife Belinda too. Don't know for sure. They're gonna be tearing through No Mountain in about five minutes." Pudge took a breath. "You still with me?"

Blackpowder didn't answer, but Jack Jericho did. "We ain't shit our britches yet, Deputy. You want us to bushwhack these sidewinders for you? Happy to oblige."

Pudge ignored the old timer and focused on his friend. "Connie's alive. She has to be. She's no good to them otherwise."

The radio clicked and hummed, but then Blackpowder said in an eerily calm voice, "I'm goin' go stand in the road right now. Me and a thirty-ought-six Jack Jericho's been trying to sell since last deer season. When Doc's Buick comes at me, I'm goin' put one right in the driver's eye."

"Now, hang on. Connie is likely to get killed if you do that. Belinda too, if she's in there."

"Then tell me a better way 'cause that's my fiancée in the car and we both know what they'll do to her if they get clear of here. If you and the posse are behind them, that means there ain't no more lawmen between No Mountain and Nevada, and what is across the state line don't amount to nothing."

"We'll get Connie back. Belinda too, if they got her. But not in No Mountain. The killers could run into the post office or a house and take other hostages. More people could get killed. We'll do it past town. The best spot is at the Narrows before the Malheur refuge turnoff."

"You want me to get down there ahead of 'em, is that it?"

"That's right. Take a rig and stop near the end of the causeway so you're blocking the road. They can't go around you or they'd end up going over the edge and into Mud Lake. Pull the wires out so they can't start it in case they get ahold of it." Pudge didn't have to say if that happened, it meant Blackpowder and him were dead. "Stay low. They're armed. One's got a grease gun."

"Then he'll be the first one I shoot. Where'll you be?"

"Right behind them. I'll box the Buick in. We'll keep them pinned until the sheriff and the others catch up. The robbers will see there's no way out and give up."

"You say they killed Doc and two others at the bank?"

"That's right."

"Then they're not goin' give up."

"I expect not, but I don't see we got another choice but to give this a try."

"Okay, I'll do whatever it takes to get my sweetheart back."

"I'll go with ya," Jack Jericho piped up. "We'll take the two-ton flatbed. Sonsofbitches won't be able to git around her."

"No, you stay put," Pudge said quickly. The last thing he needed was the old cowboy in the way. He'd worn a patch over his right eye ever since he'd been horned by a bull during his rodeoing days; his legbones were held together with pins. "I need you in No Mountain in case the bank robbers double-back. You can alert the sheriff."

"I'll do more than that. They come back here, I'll shoot 'em dead is what I'll do."

"Then straight shooting to you," Pudge said. "Okay, Black, get going. I'll see you at the Narrows."

Blackpowder didn't answer. He'd already grabbed the .30-06 Springfield rifle and a box of cartridges and was sprinting for the flatbed truck that he'd been loading with hundred-pound sacks of grain.

Pudge didn't let up on the gas. He purposely hadn't told Blackpowder everything he knew. On his last radio call with the sheriff, he learned the men's identities and criminal records. The leader was named Reggie Dobbs. His likeness was on wanted posters throughout Nevada, Utah, and California.

The sheriff described him as having a pompadour, sleepy eyes, and a Lothario sneer. He'd served time in the Nevada State Pen for kidnap and rape. Upon release, Reggie had gone on a killing spree. His first victim was a night manager at a motel in Provo. He shot a check-out clerk and box boy to death while sticking up a grocery store in Truckee. Then he hijacked a car in the parking lot. Behind the wheel was a young mother. He raped her and then strangled her and dumped her body beside the road outside of Fernley, Nevada. In the Burns bank robbery, he shot the teller for being slow handing over the till. "Teach you for being a butterfingers," he jeered.

His two accomplices were Bud and Junior Trask, brothers from Elko who'd been in and out of reform schools and jails since they were boys. Bud was older by four years. Witnesses at First National said he wore a black fedora like the gangsters in the picture shows and had a lit cigarette dangling from his lips. He puffed on it when he fired a burst from the grease gun into the chest of the World War I pensioner who was moonlighting as the bank guard. Junior had on a newsboy cap and was the driver. His first arrest was for boosting cars when he was thirteen. That was five years prior.

Pudge hit the shortcut's junction with the main road and

picked up the pace. He raced past his ranch house and tried not to think about his wife Henrietta and little girl Gemma inside who were unaware that a carful of killers had driven by minutes before him. He forced the image of his young family from his mind. Thinking of them instead of focusing on what he had to do could cost him a valuable second in a showdown. Pudge sped into No Mountain, but braked when he saw Jack Jericho standing in front of his store waving a double-barreled shotgun.

"I seen 'em, Deputy," he shouted. "Squirrely looking kid driving the Buick. Another in the front seat smokin' a cigarette like he was on a Sunday drive. Had on a black hat."

"Anyone else in the car?"

"A man in the backseat. Wore his hair all whipped up on top. Had his arms wrapped around a blonde pulled in so close it looked like they was, well, I don't gotta spell it out for ya, do I?"

Pudge tasted bile. "That'd be Connie Barstow, Blackpowder's fiancée. Belinda's got gray hair."

"If thar was another woman, she musta been on the floor or in the trunk. It weren't like the kid driving cared if he mowed down anybody, the way he was putting the spurs to that Buick."

"Wave the sheriff straight on through when they come. He knows the drill."

Pudge stomped the accelerator again. This time he couldn't push away the thoughts of what poor Connie must be going through at the hands of Reggie Dobbs. He prayed Belinda had run off into the fields near her house and was hiding. Pudge glanced at his rearview mirror. There was still no sight of the sheriff and other deputies, but the look in his eyes gave him a jolt.

As he crested a low hill, Pudge stopped. Below ran a thin strip of elevated blacktop on the eastern shoreline of Mud Lake, the middle of three natural sumps that drained Harney Basin. Toward its end, the causeway crossed over the Narrows channel that linked it to Malheur Lake. It was full of icy gray water that was bounded on both sides by dry lakebed ribbed with snowdrifts. Jack Jericho's feed-and-grain truck was stopped above the channel and parked at a right angle to block both lanes. The hood was raised to signal a breakdown. Brake lights glowed from Doc's Roadmaster that was halted a couple hundred yards shy. No doubt the bank robbers were discussing their options.

Pudge took in the scene and wondered why the criminals had taken such a wrong turn in life. He remembered a lesson he learned when he was a boy. He and his best pal Buck Travers had run away from home after getting in trouble for playing hooky. Mad about the lickings they'd received from their fathers, they'd hitched a ride to Malheur Lake in the back of a rancher's truck and then waded across the shallows to one of the islets that ringed the shore. They spent the next couple of days playing pirates and scrounging for food, reduced to chewing on wild onion bulbs to stem their hunger. On the third day they met a young Paiute who was hunting ducks with a bow and arrow. After introducing himself as Tuhudda Will, he plucked the feathers from a fat mallard he'd shot. He made an oven out of mud, wrapped the bird in grass, and slow roasted it so the meat stayed tender and juicy.

The Paiute watched silently as Pudge and Buck devoured it. When they'd finished picking the bones clean, he said, "You eat good, but you do not feed yourself so good. If you cannot do that, how can you feed others? Go home and ask your fathers to teach you. Mine taught me as his did him. A boy becomes a man when he accepts there is no shame in learning no matter how hard the lesson or the teacher. This is so."

Pudge and Buck hiked back to No Mountain to take their medicine. They did a lot of growing up, and, years later, both enlisted and fought in World War II. Only Pudge came home. Buck served under General George S. Patton and was burned alive when his tank was hit by a Panzer. Every time Pudge thought about his boyhood friend, he pictured the duck roasting in the mud oven made by Tuhudda Will.

The Buick's brake lights blinked off. The big sedan started to back up. Pudge knew it was time to teach a lesson of his own. He mashed the gas pedal and hit the red lights and siren. Junior Trask saw the deputy's pickup bearing down. He panicked, and instead of turning around to take the sheriff's vehicle head on, threw the transmission into drive and the powerful straight eight punched the big sedan forward.

Pudge closed the distance. Junior slammed on the brakes so he wouldn't smash into the two-ton flatbed blocking the way. Pudge stopped too, but kept a gap between them. He stared over the steering wheel wondering where Blackpowder was. The passenger door of the Buick swung open and a man wearing a black fedora got out. Bud Trask clamped the grease gun to his hip as he pointed it at the pickup and pulled the trigger. Pudge threw himself flat on the bench seat as .45-caliber slugs ripped into the engine block and shattered the windshield. Ejected brass clattered on the pavement.

A louder shot rang out. Pudge looked up and saw the black fedora sailing through the air. Bud's face was a red mushroom from the high-powered round fired into the back of his skull. Blackpowder was standing up behind a pile of feed bags he'd fashioned into a bunker and worked the bolt on the Springfield to chamber another round. He didn't need to fire it. The grease gun smacked the pavement and so did Bud Trask. The black fedora was the last to land.

Pudge jumped out of his pickup as a wail erupted from the Buick and the driver's door swung wide and stayed open. Junior Trask ran to his dead brother and knelt beside him. "Buddy!" he screamed. "Buddy!" He glared at Pudge beneath the brim of his

newsboy cap, his face twisted with rage and grief. "You kilt him."
He made a move toward the grease gun.

"Touch it and you'll join him. Lay belly down on the pavement,
hands clasped behind your back. Do it now." Pudge aimed his hand-
gun, not at the teenager, but at the head of the man in the backseat of
the Buick. Blackpowder's rifle was already trained on Junior.

The rear window of the Buick rolled down. "My pistol is
stuck in the ribs of pretty Miss Connie sitting right here next to
me," Reggie Dobbs called out in a sing-song voice. "It's got a hair
trigger. You shoot Junior, I'm likely to flinch and it goes off. You
shoot me, it definitely goes off. Bye-bye pretty Connie."

Pudge kept himself from flinching when Blackpowder's
fiancée turned toward him. Her hair was mussed, her terrified
face smeared with tears and lipstick. The neckline of Connie's
dress had been ripped open and her exposed shoulders and
breasts were the color of snow.

"The sheriff and deputies are right behind me," the lawman
called back. "The only way out of this is to give yourselves up.
You don't need to die here. Junior neither."

Reggie's laugh was sing-song too. "And pretty Connie and I
aren't alone either. The not so pretty Belinda is going to get into
the front seat now and drive us out of here with me and Connie
riding in the backseat pretty as pink. Tell Farmer John to get
down from his truck. Junior's going to get in and drive it the rest
of the way across. As soon as we're over, he'll block the road
again to keep you from wasting gas following us."

Pudge's automatic didn't waver. He swapped looks with
Blackpowder to confirm the flatbed couldn't be started. He told
him with his eyes that he couldn't risk shooting Reggie. Even if
he did hit him, there was that hair trigger.

"Okay, we'll do it your way," Pudge said. "Go on, Black, climb
on down."

"I forgot to mention something," Reggie taunted before Blackpowder moved. "You and Farmer John need to toss your weapons over the side first."

"Not before Junior gets in the truck. We don't want to be sitting ducks to that grease gun."

"I'm calling the shots here, not you. And my trigger finger is starting to itch to get back touching pretty Connie in all her private places again." He made kissing noises at her.

"What about Buddy?" Junior wailed. "We can't leave him here."

"We can and we will," Reggie said. "Now move that truck, Junior. Belinda, move your skinny ass too and drive us out of here."

Pudge saw a head of gray hair pop up from the far corner of the backseat where she'd been hunched. "I don't know how to drive," she cried. "I never learned."

"Move," Reggie said to her. "Don't make me shoot pretty Connie."

"I don't know how! My husband did all the driving." Belinda's shakes were dizzying to watch.

"Change of plans then. You get my gun stuck in your skinny ribs along with all of my attentions while pretty Connie crawls over the front seat and gets behind the wheel. Go on, ladies. Be quick about it. You know what happens when you disappoint me." His sneer curled even higher.

While Belinda froze, Connie slid head first over the back of the front seat and kept on sliding, right out the door Junior had left open. She picked herself off the pavement, stumbled across the blacktop clutching the top of her torn dress, and screamed. "He's a monster!"

Junior Trask grabbed the grease gun and raised it at her. Before he could pull the trigger, Blackpowder fired. The slug from the Springfield knocked Junior Trask flat on top of his brother. Connie darted to the edge and jumped into the channel. Pudge squeezed his US Marine Corps–issued sidearm. The round pierced the rear window of the blue Buick and found its mark below Reggie Dobbs' pompadour. The killer's pistol went off as his fingers spasmed.

Blackpowder hopped from the flatbed and leapt into the icy water below. Pudge sprinted to the Buick. Belinda was shrieking hysterically from the corner of the backseat. Reggie's bullet had gone wide and slammed into the door panel.

After making sure the killer was no longer a threat and Belinda was unhurt, Pudge looked over the side and saw Blackpowder surface with his arm around Connie. He kicked and crawled for the bank. Pudge ran down the causeway and back across the dry lakebed. He yanked his sputtering friend out of the water and began giving Connie mouth to mouth. It was too late. She was gone and so was the young man Blackpowder had once been.

When I finished telling the story, Manning Dobbs steepled his palms, bowed his head, and recited the Lord's Prayer. After "Amen" he opened his eyes and said, "I'll take you to see Searcher now and then you can tell me what you know about this John Smith person and the gold mine."

21

The holding cell was dimly lit and the lidless steel toilet in dire need of plunging. A single bunk was bolted in the corner. The mattress was flapjack thin and the only blanket even thinner. Searcher was lying on top of it with his eyes fixed on the ceiling. A loincloth fashioned from a dirty towel had been duct-taped around his waist. His left ear was cauliflowered and the side of his face had bruises that were the shape of crescent moons.

"Searcher, it's Nick Drake," I called through the iron bars.

The Paiute didn't respond. He didn't even move.

"I bring greetings from Tuhudda Will and Girl Born in Snow of the *Wadadökadö* band."

Still, he didn't react.

I turned to the young chief deputy and said through gritted teeth, "Bull Hammond worked him over. Look at those bruises. His elbow's swollen twice its size. It could be broken from being wrenched behind his back. Has he seen a doctor?"

"The prisoner refused to be examined."

"How do you know that? You said Searcher hasn't spoken since you locked him up."

"The doctor came, but the prisoner faced the wall. The doctor said without his permission, there was nothing he could do."

"Did you bind that towel on him? The tape's too tight. It's making it hard for him to breathe."

"Bull did before he brought him in. He said he didn't want a dirty Indian's bare butt touching his car seat."

My teeth gritted harder. "Did Searcher have a weapon when Hammond confronted him?"

"Bull didn't mention any. All he said was the Indian took off running and it was either chase him or shoot him. When he caught him, the Indian confessed."

"But you didn't hear him confess."

"No, but Bull said the Indian came right out and said it. He told him he shot the donkey for meat and then shot Jump to cover it up."

"Where's the rifle that did all this killing?"

"The Indian said he threw it in Summit Lake."

"When did Searcher do all this talking, after Hammond blackjacked his brains in or when he was wrenching his elbow?"

Dobbs flushed. "I don't know."

"Unlock the cell and let me in."

"I can't do that. It's against policy. You need to speak to the prisoner through the bars."

"You're more than the chief deputy now. You're the acting sheriff. You get to make the policies. Let me in."

"All right, but you have to leave your gun out here. Knife too, if you have one."

I unbuckled my holster and fished the clasp knife out of my pocket. Dobbs opened a drawer in a desk shoved against the opposite wall, took a key from it, and motioned me to put my weapons in the drawer. He closed it and then unlocked the cell with the key from the drawer. I went in. Dobbs locked it behind me.

Searcher's chest rose and fell ever so slightly. I crouched next to him and checked his eyes. Humans blink fifteen to twenty times a minute. An owl ten times. Searcher was blinking half that. Hammond had likely fractured his skull and left him concussed.

"It's Nick Drake," I said again. "You need medicine."

Searcher exhaled and then turned his head toward me. "You saw the lights and heard the noises," he said softly. "Did you learn what is behind them?"

The only surprise of his sudden return to consciousness and continuation of our last conversation was that it didn't shock me. "I've started to, but I don't know everything yet."

"To search and understand is *puha*."

"Power," I said.

"To act upon it takes *puha* also."

"I already see that bad men are behind the gold mine. Learning who they are is one thing, stopping them is another."

"You will need help."

"From who, the Forever Walkers? I heard them the night I found the prospector's body, saw them walking. Tuhudda Will said he spoke with them in a dream. He said you could help me find them."

"If you want it to be so, it will be so."

"I need to get you some help first and that starts with getting you out of here. When you and I spoke at the hot springs in Virgin Valley, you said you had spent the night there and the night before in the Pueblo Mountains."

"Yes, on my way from Duck Valley."

"And when we both went our separate ways, I found the bodies of a prospector and his burro who'd been killed the day before in a gully below Big Mountain, near the gold mine. Where did you go?"

"To the place white men call Blowout Mountain."

"I thought you were taking medicine to the Fish Eaters at Summit Lake."

"And so I did after I went to Blowout Mountain and spent the night there."

"Why did you go there first?"

"As I was walking to Summit Lake, a hawk told me a bighorn sheep was on top of the mountain. I went to tell her you were looking for her. I slept there to be closer to the stars so my dreams would not have so far to travel."

"My sheep? The one with a collar around her neck?"

"She told me she does not like to wear it."

"Did you take it off her?"

"No. It was not mine to take."

"When you left Blowout Mountain, did you walk on Quartz Creek Road to Summit Lake?"

"White men's roads are not my way. I cannot feel Mother Earth beneath my feet. The roads lead to death for *Nuwuddu* who try to cross them."

"Did you shoot the prospector and his burro?"

"Why would I and with what? My journeys are without fear and so I have no need for a weapon."

"Did you tell the man who beat you and brought you here that you shot the prospector?"

"I did not speak to him because he is the kind of man who is deaf to all things that are true, the song of birds and the song of wind in the trees. He cannot hear truth because he cannot speak it. He only hears the lies he tells to himself and tells to those who lie to themselves that he is speaking truth."

I turned to Dobbs who was chewing his bottom lip. "Searcher is innocent. He has no weapon, no reason to kill Jump

Diggins. Bull Hammond had every reason to blame Searcher. To protect the gold mine, his job, and himself."

"I don't know," he mumbled. "I don't know."

"Sure you do."

"But I've already booked him. The other deputies know he's here. The papers have been sent to the judge for a hearing. I can't unlock the cell and let him walk out of here. I need to think about how to do it properly so he won't get picked up again. He might get more than a beating next time. He might get shot."

"By Bull Hammond," I said. I put my hand on Searcher's arm. "I'm going to help the deputy get you safely released. I'll be back."

Searcher returned to staring at the ceiling and Dobbs let me out of the cell. We returned to his office and took our seats at his desk. I told him everything I knew about John Smith, Oro Holdings, the connections to organized crime, and why I was convinced Hammond was covering up the murder of Jump Diggins.

Dobbs listened and then picked up the telephone and dialed. I assumed he was calling the judge to have the request for a hearing rescinded and the papers drawn to release Searcher. As it rang, he said, "I had this instructor at the police academy who started off as a patrolman with Las Vegas PD but is now a detective with their Organized Crime Task Force. He might be able to provide some insights. I must warn you, his language can be pretty salty."

A voice on the other end of the line said loud enough for me to hear, "Garzas."

"Detective, it's Manning Dobbs. Remember me? You were one of my instructors at the academy. I'm now the chief deputy at Humboldt County Sheriff's."

The exchange of pleasantries was brief. Dobbs got right down to business and told the detective about Jump Diggins, the proximity of Oro Holdings to the murder site, and the connection to John Smith. Garzas said something I couldn't hear. Dobbs said, "I'm going to put you on speaker. The man who discovered my victim is here with me."

The deputy pushed a button and set the receiver back in its cradle. "Ron Garzas meet Nick Drake. He's a ranger with the US Fish and Wildlife Service."

"Pleasure," Garzas said. "As I was saying, John Smith's name pops up at OCTF briefings from time to time. We even got a nickname for him. The Paperboy. Real estate deals, business licenses, slot machine registrations, whatever takes paperwork, he writes and files it."

"For what type of clients?" Dobbs said.

"Smith has a few legit ones, mainly low-rent storefront types, but his bread and butter are businesses that connect to OC in one way or another."

"He sounds fairly low level."

"He is. The Paperboy wields a pen, not a tommy gun."

"Have you linked him to any organized group in particular?" I asked.

The detective paused. "How much do you know about the history of the mob in Vegas?"

Before I could answer, Dobbs said, "Nick's from Harney County. That's in Oregon."

"You don't say? I've driven through there. Emptier than my savings account." He chuckled. "They call Highway 50 in Nevada the loneliest highway in America, but the two-lanes up there get even less traffic. I remember driving into Burns the first time. It was getting on dark and there were no casinos with neon marquees and revolving searchlights lighting up the sky like down here. Vegas? You see it coming a hundred miles away."

"I call that light litter," I said. "It blocks out all the stars."

"That'd be a tough sell convincing Nevada to change its don't litter signs to Keep Heaven Beautiful. People come to Vegas to sin on purpose." Garzas gave a short laugh. "Okay, I got one for you. Free of charge. A down and dirty history lesson of the mob in Vegas. You ready?"

"All ears."

"It started in the nineteen forties when a hit man who founded Murder Inc. came to town. Name of Bugsy Siegel. Ring a bell?"

"Of course."

"Handle like that, who hasn't heard of him? Bugsy had this dream of running a new kind of hotel casino. He was an associate of Lucky Luciano who'd organized the Mafia into a national crime syndicate. Bugsy sweet-talked Lucky into putting up the cash to build his dream palace. It was called the Flamingo, but it opened on a dark and stormy night, like the title of the book Snoopy is always trying to write while sitting on top of his doghouse."

He paused. "You know, in the *Peanuts* comic strip? My wife, she loves *Peanuts*. Reads it every day. That's because her name is Lucy and she's like the girl in the comics, always yanking my football away at the last moment." Garzas issued a short laugh again.

"Nobody, and I mean nobody who's anybody, showed up for the Flamingo's opening," he continued. "Talk about a Broadway show bombing. Eventually an old pal from Bugsy's early gang-land days by name of Meyer Lansky came to town to make the trains run on time. Bim, bam, boom. The joint took off and a cash cow with a built-in tax dodge was born. See, the mob invented and then perfected skimming the casino take in Vegas."

"How did it work?"

"Lot of different ways. Simplest was having two sets of books, one for the revenooers, one for the mob. Then there was the old switcherooski. Money goes down to the counting room and half of it gets put in a suitcase and winds up in the trunk of a Caddy. They even rigged scales used to weigh currency, like a butcher putting a thumb on it when you're buying steaks. The ballsiest skim was a casino that arranged the robbery of its own cash being transported by an armored truck. They wrote it off as a loss and got an insurance payout for it. Gives new meaning to a double take."

"Somebody must've been paid to look the other way," I said.

"No doubt about it. Gambling was legalized in Nevada in thirty-one, but casino licenses and fees were handled at the local level. Lots of yokels were getting their palms greased. The state finally took over regulating in forty-five, forty-six. In addition to collecting fees, they also slapped a tax on the gross. That along with federal taxes meant higher overhead for casino owners."

"And a bigger incentive to skim."

"You catch on fast. The mob was raking in cash by the truckful, so naturally they guarded the skim with their lives. More to the point, other people's lives. Look what happened to Bugsy Siegel. Six months after the Flamingo opened, he's sitting in his girlfriend's living room in Beverly Hills reading the *LA Times* when a sniper opens fire through the window with a .30-caliber M1 carbine, the same gun my old man used to mow down Nazis in France. Bugsy takes four slugs to the head and lungs. A marble statue took a fifth. It survived. Bugsy didn't. The gunman got away and the murder weapon was never found."

Garzas exhaled. "That carbine has taken on a life of its own. Mobsters, both real ones and wannabes, consider it some kind of holy relic. There must be a half dozen different M1s in circulation touted as the real deal. People pay big money for them. I've heard as much as five grand. You ever seen that Humphrey Bogart movie, the one with the statue of a falcon everybody's conniving and killing for? Bugsy's rifle is the same thing. Stuff that dreams are made of."

I asked the detective why Bugsy was killed.

"The mob believed he was skimming the skim and it was their way of teaching others what happens if you do. Not only does the gambling take get skimmed, but so does everything else connected to a casino. Labor and construction costs are big ticket items. Bills get padded after they're paid. Even the B-girls picking up Johns get their tips skimmed."

"Did Lucky Luciano order the hit?"

"If he did, then he made the call from Italy because he'd already been deported. My money has always been on Meyer Lansky. Gambling and friendships mix as well as grappa and motor oil. With his old pal out of the way, he was top of the pecking order at the Flamingo. More casinos started sprouting up and down the Strip. Stardust, Tropicana, Riviera. Gaudy names and men wearing gaudy suits running them. So much money was being made that Vegas became an open city for the mob with two dozen Mafia families working side by side, all happy as clams."

"Is that still the way it is?"

"Nah, a lot's changed. JFK got elected and made his brother attorney general. Bobby had a hard-on for the mob and wanted to make a name for himself for the day he'd run for president. He believed gambling was their lifeblood and went after the casinos to cut it off. His big plan included unleashing an army of state gaming agents using wiretaps. Bobby thought people would flip, but they didn't. They were more scared of the mob than the Justice Department."

"Tell him about Howard Hughes," Dobbs said.

"I was getting to that. What Bobby couldn't do, a crazier than a bedbug billionaire could. Three years after JFK was assassinated, Howard Hughes pulled into Vegas in a private train and was whisked up to a room on the top floor of the Desert Inn. He taped the curtains shut, stripped off his clothes, and over the next four years bought up nearly all of the mob-run properties without ever leaving his room. He started with the Desert Inn and followed with the Sands, Frontier, and Silver Slipper. Them along with buying thousands of acres of undeveloped land, not to mention an airport. When Howard needed gaming licenses, he had the governor fetch them for him."

"Former governor," Dobbs said.

The way Garzas said, "Right," I knew he was rolling his eyes. "Howard spent more money than the Mafia ever did and the politicians viewed him as a legit businessman who would drive the mob out along with their habit of planting bodies in the desert. See, the pols believed more money and less murder would give old Sin City a new reputation as a family vacation joint, complete with restaurants and shopping for the wives and swimming pools for the kiddies. That made for a bigger checkout tab at the front desk and more tax revenue for the state. With everybody starting to use credit cards like Diners Club and BankAmericard to pay their hotel tabs, it made it harder to run a skim."

I asked what happened to Howard Hughes.

"He was good at buying casinos but lousy at running them. Most of the mob bosses took his buyouts and lit out for Miami, but their middle managers stayed behind and weren't about to forget how to skim just because some old guy wearing only his skivvies was signing their paychecks. By the time Howard wised up, he'd been taken for fifty mil. That was his cue to cut and run too, which he did on Thanksgiving Day four years ago. His people carried him down the Desert Inn's fire escape in a stretcher and flew him out of the country in a private jet. They say he never let in housekeeping the whole time he was holed up in there." Garzas snorted. "Must've had to fumigate the friggin' room."

"If the mob left Las Vegas, how come Las Vegas PD still needs a special force for organized crime?"

"I said most, not all. You know what they say about a power vacuum?"

"According to Aristotle, nature abhors one."

"College boy, huh? Well, your Greek pal's got nothing on the Mafia. Soon after Howard Hughes bugged out, a Chicago mob called the Outfit saw an opening and decided to fill it. They sent a soldier gunning to be made a *capo* down to Vegas. Anthony Spilotro, nicknamed Tony the Ant. He stands only five foot two. My Lucy's got him by three inches easy." This time the detective's laugh made the telephone's speaker reverberate.

"The Ant assembled a crew and tried to muscle his way into the casino business. When the Nevada gaming commission wouldn't be bought off like the old days, he resorted to the mob tried and true. Extortion, protection, fencing. Burglary is Tony's main game. The *Las Vegas Review-Journal* dubbed him and his boys the Hole in the Wall Gang because they tunnel through exterior walls and ceilings to get into banks, homes, and jewelry stores."

"After the name of the gang in the Butch Cassidy and Sundance Kid movie that came out a few years ago," Dobbs said. "I went to see it the night before I boarded the bus for basic training."

Garzas started singing. "Raindrops keep falling on my head, but that doesn't mean my eyes are turning red." He said, "Hole in the Wall is an actual pass in Wyoming. I liked the movie too, but look how it turned out for them? I mean the real outlaws Newman and Redford were playing. Butch Cassidy, Sundance Kid, Flat Nose Curry, and the rest, either all shot dead or thrown in jail to rot. Mark my words. We've come close to catching Tony the Ant in the act and it's only a matter of time 'til we do. When that happens, he'll meet the same fate, a slug or a cell."

"Breaking and entering seems a long way off from financing and operating a gold mine behind the cover of a Panamanian shell company," I said.

"I agree it's a stretch. If Tony the Ant is part of it, maybe his role is to keep me and the rest of the OC squad busy chasing him so the dons can do their thing. His gang isn't the only one that fits our definition of organized crime. We got an interstate gang of car thieves who boost autos out of hotel parking lots and run them to chop shops in LA and Dallas. Multiple crews are smuggling in pot, cocaine, heroin, and young girls from south of the border. And a ring of so-called businessmen fly in from the Far East to attend conventions but what they're really doing is passing very hard-to-detect counterfeit money by buying diamond rings and watches at all the jewelry stores that have popped up inside the hotels."

I asked the detective if he had any thoughts of why an organized group of criminals would go to the trouble and expense of licensing and operating a gold mine.

"Money, what else. It's always about the money. And, more importantly, coming up with a scheme not to pay taxes on it. OC treats them like they're the clap."

"You mean it's another skimming operation?" Dobbs said.

"I'm thinking money laundering. Casinos were always big-time laundromats for the mob. They washed money from bank robberies, fenced stolen goods, and drug sales for a fee. It worked like this. Say a guy has five hundred G's of dirty money. He brings it to the casino, exchanges it for gambling chips with a wink, wink, and a nod, gambles it away until he loses the prescribed cut, and then takes the remaining chips and exchanges them for clean cash. The dirty cash gets washed when the tourists exchange their chips at the end of their stay. Hard to trace that dirty money when the bills go back to a thousand different bumpkin towns all across America."

Garzas took a breath. "If your gold mine is laundering international dirty money, then where it came from and who they're doing it for is way above my paygrade. That's something the feds will have a better handle on."

"The FBI?"

"To do the busting, sure, but the Treasury Department has the authority and means to track down money coming into the country and going out, whether it's greenbacks, gold bars, or wire transfers to secret Swiss bank accounts. Remember, it was Treasury agents who brought down Al Capone. Heck, Nick, you work for the feds. You don't got a buddy over there who can help out?"

"DC is a long way from Harney County, but I do know a deputy in Burns who's a whiz at tracking down info. He's the one who found the connections between John Smith, Oro Holdings, and Panama."

"If he finds anything else, I'd appreciate him giving me a call." The speaker went silent for a second. "Speaking of sharing info. Manning, you want to fill me in on your homicide victim?"

"There isn't much to tell. I haven't gotten very far in the investigation outside of the fact he was an old prospector and shot in the back from a distance. Two rounds fired from a high-powered rifle." Dobbs went on to describe the murder scene. He left out the fact that he had Searcher in jail.

"Nevada has more unsolved killings than lonely highways," Garzas said. "Yours sounds similar to a couple down our way. Two men were both shot in the back by a rifle a week apart, one near a new housing development going up in Summerlin and another between a casino in Henderson and Hoover Dam. Both victims were found about a hundred yards from the nearest dirt road. The footprints in the dirt and the way they fell suggest they were trying to make a run for it when they got hit. The killer didn't bother to bury them. It's like he wanted them found."

"What caliber of weapon?" Dobbs asked.

"I don't know. OCTF isn't in charge of the investigations since neither victim was a known affiliate of Tony the Ant or any of the other gangs we chase. Robbery Homicide is handling the case. You want, I can ask someone to get in touch."

"I'd appreciate it."

"Fair enough. Look, I got to jump. Hope this helps. Good talking to you, Nick. If you're ever in Vegas, drop by the shop and say hello. Manning, congrats on making chief deputy. Remember, kiss lots of babies. You're going to need to butter up the voters when it's your turn to run for sheriff."

Dobbs pushed the disconnect button. We'd been staring at the speakerphone as if Detective Garzas was in the room with us, but now our eyes met. The deputy was looking at me expectantly, like Private Danbaby used to do waiting for me to issue an order or lead the way.

"How much does Winnemucca resemble Las Vegas when it comes to organized crime?" I said.

"Not much. Las Vegas has nearly one hundred times our population and that doesn't even account for all of the visitors. They got eight and a half million last year and the number is growing by about a million a year. That's not to say all our casinos have always been on the up and up. Or still are."

"Like the place where someone threw a barstool at you?"

"That was at the Aces Wild. Their slogan is where the action never stops. The owner is flashy and likes being the big shot in town. Paul Waiterock. He hosts the county commissioners after all of their meetings and boasts that he's on a first name with the governor and Nevada's congressman and senators. Framed pictures of him shaking hands with politicians and entertainers hang in the lobby. Waiterock owns a big spread on the outskirts of town and hosts charity events. The pediatric ward at the hospital is named after him."

"But . . ."

"But what?"

"You're suspicious of him. I can hear it in your voice."

"Waiterock is the subject of a lot of gossip. The few times his casino has been cited for gaming violations, the charges always get dropped. People talk about the kind of visitors who come to have private meetings with him. They don't look and act like local ranchers or tourists."

"Any proof he's connected to the mob?"

The deputy sighed. "The department is undermanned, underpaid, and busy trying to keep the peace. Even if we wanted to investigate Paul Waiterock, we don't have the time or budget." He did the bowing his head as if receiving communion thing again. "If I launched one on my own, I'd be out of a job the next day."

"Sheriff Coons would fire you?"

"If not him, then everybody from the state attorney general down to the mayor of Winnemucca. Waiterock carries a lot of weight in this town. Financial and political. All of northern Nevada, for that matter."

"Sometimes you have to rock the boat to be able to live with yourself. Have you ever had a run-in with him?"

"Not a run-in, more like a one-sided conversation. It was after I was named chief deputy. Waiterock told me he'd always been very supportive of law enforcement and to let him know if there was anything I wanted or needed."

"Sounds like he was offering you a bribe."

"He didn't come right out and say it, he's too slick for that, but he let me know that my predecessor and him had what he called a quote unquote very friendly and productive working relationship."

"Any proof that Bull Hammond was on the take?"

"Nothing concrete, only a feeling."

I mulled that over. "You said Hammond told you that Searcher threw the murder weapon in Summit Lake. What happened to the slugs in Jump Diggins?"

"The coroner bagged them as evidence. The best he could do was approximate the caliber size. He said it was somewhere in the thirty to thirty-five caliber range."

"That covers a lot of weapons, everything from an M1 carbine like the one Detective Garzas said killed Bugsy Siegel to a .358 Winchester."

"Without the casings, that's as good as he can do with the equipment we have. We're not the FBI or some big-city police department."

"Mind if I take a look at them?"

"That's pretty irregular."

"I got pretty good at identifying live and spent ammo when I was in Vietnam. We needed to know what weapons were being used against us as part of our job stopping supplies coming down the Ho Chi Minh Trail. The VC were hauling in everything from Chinese-made carbines to AK-47s from the Soviet Union. Even M49 machine guns made in Yugoslavia. The intel we gathered was passed on to the spooks and then to the State Department, which used it in negotiations with those countries."

Dobbs thought about it. "I suppose it'd be okay, but we need to go downstairs."

"Is that where the coroner's office is?"

"Yes, but the slugs are in the evidence room next door. We boxed them up along with Diggins' clothes. The packsaddle and other stuff too."

I pictured Ruby and the spilled pinto beans. "Lead the way."

22

W e took a flight of stairs rather than the freight elevator. The lower we went, the stronger the smell of formaldehyde grew. The stairway opened onto a hallway that was plenty wide for gurneys wheeling bodies in and out. Ballasts of fluorescent lights cast a bloodless hue.

"That's the coroner's office," Dobbs said as we passed closed double doors with "Medical Examiner" lettered across them. "He's not here today. He only comes in when he has a customer. That's what he calls the dead. The other deputies call him the croaker. They got in the habit when Bull was chief deputy. I've tried to get them to stop, but . . ." He squared his shoulders and kept walking.

We passed a couple of more doors. "Here's the evidence room."

Dobbs took a key ring from his utility belt, found the one he was looking for, and inserted it into the lock. The hinges creaked as he opened the door. The smell of formaldehyde had seeped in and mingled with an odor akin to the smell of cyanide leaking from the gold mine's wastewater pond. The room's stench made me long to be outside in the high lonesome with its clean desert air, sweetened by the fragrance of sagebrush.

The deputy switched on the lights. They were less harsh than those in the hallway. He signed his name on a clipboard, checked his wristwatch, and jotted down the time. The room was lined with overflowing shelves. Dust particles danced in a narrow beam of sunlight that streamed from a transom window at the top of a wall. Since we were in the basement, that meant the window well was below ground level. Snow must've collected in it during the winters because old water stains on the wall dripped from the corners of the sill. They resembled the shapes of Africa and South America.

A wooden-framed packsaddle was on a middle shelf. It was made of two crosses connected to the ends of short planks. A cardboard box next to it had a series of letters and numbers written on it in black marker that were a combination of day, month, year, and what I assumed was a case number.

Dobbs retrieved the box and placed it on a table. He began removing the contents. The first thing to come out was the old prospector's faded brown hat with the turned-up brim and band made of jackrabbit fur. Next was a clear plastic bag that contained his frayed shirt. It was folded so that the two gunshot holes were visible. Another plastic bag held his patched jeans and the wide leather belt.

His frown grew as the deputy dug deeper into the box. A clasp knife, blue bandana handkerchief, and a drawstring pouch containing a rabbit's foot and box of matches joined the other items. The scuffed calf-high boots with worn-down heels were the final items.

He looked up sheepishly. "It's not in here. The evidence bag with the slugs. I witnessed the coroner put it in the box. I placed it on the shelf myself." Dobbs reached for the clipboard. His lips moved as he silently read the log. He held it up. "See? Here's our signatures and the date and time. No one signed in after that until I did right now."

I asked him if Hammond turned in his keys with his badge and gun when he retired and went to work at the gold mine.

"I don't know. If he did, he would've handed them over to Sheriff Coons, not me. I wasn't appointed as his replacement until after he was gone."

"What did Hammond do after he brought in Searcher and you went to book him?"

Dobbs shrugged. "I imagine he either went back to the gold mine or home. He's got a place in town."

"But he could've come down here. He could still have his keys. No one would've seen him."

He started to speak but the words died on his lips.

"Where's all the gear that was strapped to the packsaddle? Maybe a slug got stuck in something."

"It wouldn't fit on the shelf, so we unloaded everything and went through it. We didn't find any slugs. We put the gear in a gunny sack, except for the food. We tossed that out so it wouldn't rot and make the room stink any worse than it already does."

Dobbs pulled the packsaddle from the shelf and placed it next to the evidence box. Then he retrieved the gunny sack that was in a back corner where other bulky items were stored. He unloaded a shovel, pick, pan, bedroll, and canteen. Every item was worn, well-used, and ordinary.

The deputy went back to examining the packsaddle's frame. He pointed to the top of one of the crosses. "Look, the wood here is splintered. Maybe a bullet did that." Dobbs turned the frame over. The bottom was darker than the top, a result of rubbing against a saddle blanket for decades.

I asked what happened to the canvas tarp that was used to cover the load.

"I chucked it along with the food," Dobbs said. "It was filthy and reeked of donkey and woodsmoke."

"Where did you throw it?"

"In a dumpster out back. Why?"

"Has the building's garbage been picked up?"

"Not until Friday."

"It could still be there."

"But it's canvas. A slug wouldn't have stuck to it."

"Maybe it got caught in a fold. It's worth a look. I'll go check."

"All right. I'll box everything up and meet you there."

I hurried up the stairs and through the lobby and out the front door. It was good to breathe fresh air again and feel sunlight on my skin. I circled the building but pulled up short. A trio of identical metal dumpsters were lined up in a row.

"Three-card monte," I muttered.

A corporal in my squad was always luring other soldiers to bet cigarettes that they could guess the Queen of Hearts among the two black jacks he placed face down and slid around. They never stood a chance against his sleight-of-hand. I'd seen him make a Ka-Bar appear out of thin air once during a close-quarters fight. He'd run out of ammo and a guerrilla tried to take him prisoner. The NVA would pay rewards for turning in American GIs. The guerrilla never saw the seven-inch blade the corporal plunged into his heart.

I marched to the middle dumpster and raised the lid. It was half-full of green garbage bags fastened with twist ties. I lifted a bag and tore a hole. Balls of crumpled paper, used Styrofoam coffee cups, and cigarette butts spilled out. I tore open another and found more deskside trashcan jetsam. I lifted the lid on the left-side dumpster. A waft of woodsmoke and burro let me know I'd picked the Queen of Hearts. I pushed two green bags aside to reveal a bunched-up, sun-bleached canvas tarp.

Leaning halfway into the dumpster, I grabbed the tarp with

both hands, pulled it out, and unfolded it on the pavement. The canvas covering was about the size of the quilt that covered Gemma's and my bed. Looking at its stains and streaks of dirt, I wondered if they told a tale of Jump Diggins' life like the quilt's patches did of Gemma's great-grandmother. She'd stitched them together after she and her husband traveled the Oregon Trail in a covered wagon and settled in Harney County where they built a cabin, had a family, and raised cattle.

The centerpiece of the quilt was a star-shaped patch from the first bolt of fabric she'd bought from a mail-order catalogue. She used it to make shirts and blouses for her children and curtains for the cabin's window. Her husband used to joke that it was a good thing she finally ran out of material before sewing seat covers for the chairs he'd made or he might've sat on his kids by mistake. A white square was from her wedding dress that she'd been saving for her daughter. Before she could pass it on, she had to tear it into strips to bind the bleeding stumps of her son's arms whose hands had been cut off in a thresher. The faded blue triangle of denim was from her husband's favorite work shirt.

Gemma told me the stories on nights when we held each other tight after making love in the moonlight shining through our bedroom window. As I listened, I wondered if her great-grandmother relived each event while sewing the patches together. Did her heart pound like it did the day she wore her wedding dress? Did she feel her husband's arms around her as she cut the square from his shirt? Did she gasp like she had the first time she opened the cabin's curtains to witness the miracle of the sun rising over Steens Mountain and shining on her new life? Would I live long enough to know my own grandchildren and hear Gemma telling them about their great-great-grand-mother's quilt?

Looking at the canvas tarp's tableau, I picked out a stain that resembled a mudhole. Did seeing it make Jump Diggins relive how close he and Ruby had come to dying if not for Black-powder Smith happening along? Did the rust-colored circle give him the same jolt of excitement as it did when he'd set down the prospecting pan that made the mark and saw gold nuggets flashing among a slurry of water and gravel for the first time? How many campfires had blown smoke into the canvas as he traveled through the high lonesome? Thousands? Tens of thousands? Could he hear all the songs he'd played on his harmonica to the accompaniment of coyote howls? Could he count all the shivering stars above him as he slept alone in his bedroll?

I pictured those scenes the same way as I had imagined the ones I'd sketched of him and Ruby the night I spent above their bodies, the time I heard the Forever Walkers. The dirty and worn canvas was a touchstone to Jump Diggins' past, and while it didn't hold any solid evidence like a bullet that could be used to identify his killer, I was reluctant to bunch it up and toss it back in the dumpster. It deserved more respect than that. He deserved more respect than that. And so I began folding the tarp in the same manner as the stars and stripes to be presented to a fallen comrade's family.

As I snapped the folds lengthwise, creased the edges, and began forming a tight triangle, a stain caught my eye. I studied it more closely. Smudges began to take on the appearance of a landscape and the lines seemed to have a purpose. I'd come across plenty of petroglyphs carved in stone by ancient *Numu* to recognize a directional and other symbols. One mark was a ridgeline punctuated by a mountain peak. Another an arrow pointing to the ground. Still another a creek. I spotted an X toward the top and then a tiny R drawn at the bottom. Black-powder's words screamed in my head. X was a wild goose chase. R marked the spot.

It was a map, all right, but to what and where, I could only guess. I glanced around for Manning Dobbs, but he'd yet to leave the building. I unfolded my knife and cut out a square from the tarp. Both map and knife went back into my pocket.

I placed the remains of the canvas into the dumpster and covered it with two green garbage bags. They weren't sod and the dumpster wasn't a crypt, but it was the best I could do under the circumstances. I closed the lid and went to look for Dobbs to prod him into getting a move on and release Searcher.

I found him in his office. He was standing next to his desk and on the phone again. His face was tense. "Okay, I'll be right over." It was only after he'd hung up that he saw me.

"Trouble?" I said.

"A family matter. Did you find the tarp?"

"It was in the dumpster, but no bullets. There is another possibility for finding a slug."

"How so?"

"In Ruby. She took a couple of rounds."

His Adam's apple rose and fell as he swallowed disgust. "The buzzards would've been at her by now. Coyotes too. They'll have dragged whatever's left of her up and down the gully."

"Probably, but it's worth a try." I studied Dobbs' face. He was clearly rattled. "This family matter, can I help?"

"No. Well . . ." He wavered. "That was my mother. She called to tell me . . . She said Bull Hammond came to the house."

"What?"

"There's something I should've told you, but I got to get over there right away. Searcher is going to have to wait. You can ride with me. That is, if you still want to help."

23

Dobbs kept his mouth shut, eyes straight ahead, and both hands on the wheel of the white Jimmy with "SHERIFF" painted in big green letters on the side. When we turned onto an overpass that spanned a dry riverbed, I wondered if he was thinking about the causeway where his father had died during the gun battle with Pudge and Blackpowder.

He might have been, because as soon as we crossed, the young chief deputy said, "My mom tried real hard to put my father behind her, but she never could because of me. She was still a teenager when I was born and never finished high school. I lost count of the different places where she worked to support us. Waiting tables at cafes, serving drinks at bars, cleaning motel rooms."

The pavement was growing more potholed and the high desert more windblown the further from downtown we got. The air of a boomtown gone bust hovered over scattered subdivisions where sunbaked empty lots bristling with tumbleweeds outnumbered modest tract homes three to one.

"Mom had boyfriends, but none of them stuck for long," he

continued. "They didn't want to take on the added responsibility of raising me. There was also my father's reputation. Some men ran when they learned who she'd been married to. Others were attracted by it. You know, the ultimate bad girl. A minister thought he could save us. He baptized me and then took her out on dates. Eventually he gave up on us." Dobbs dipped his head. "God never has."

The stoplights ended and traffic was so sparse that some drivers treated stop signs as optional. The deputy obeyed every single one.

"Bull started coming around when I was thirteen. I know I should've told you earlier." He gulped. "They met when my mom was working at the Aces Wild. He'd bring a bottle to the house after she got off work and if I was still up I'd be sent to my room. Bull always wore his uniform. Mom told me she couldn't stand him, but if she said no, he'd make her life a living hell."

Dobbs slowed as we turned onto a street marked with a yellow "Dead End" sign. It was riddled with bullet holes of various sizes. He braked in front of a squat, camel-colored stucco house with a cement front stoop. A dirty sedan with a lopsided back bumper and dented rear quarter panel sat in the driveway. Parked between it and the garage was a Harley-Davidson. It had a raked front fork with shiny chrome tubes and a stitched black leather saddle riding low behind a gas tank painted with jagged flames.

"The bike belongs to Stu," the deputy said. "He and Mom started living together when I was in the MPs. He owned a motorcycle shop in town and rode with a bunch of guys. They weren't a chartered Hell's Angels chapter, but they acted like it. I met Stu for the first time after I got out of the service. He was paying all the bills and Mom didn't have to work anymore. She was plain worn out from years of being on her feet all day. Last year he got in a really bad wreck that left him with a broken back and shattered pelvis. His friends rebuilt his chopper for him, but he can't ride it anymore. He sold his shop and they live off what he got for it along with his disability pay."

I asked him if this was the house he grew up in.

"We moved here when I was eight. It was in foreclosure like a lot of the houses that were built out here. Mom bought it for next to nothing. I lived here until I enlisted. When I came back to Winnemucca, I rented an apartment in town not far from the sheriff's office."

"Did Hammond help you get the job?"

His acne reddened. "I've prayed a lot on this, but, yes, he did. Bull thought it would convince my mom to kick out Stu and they'd go back to the way it used to be."

"How did she break it off with him in the first place?"

"She found out Bull was married and told his wife."

Dobbs took his foot off the brake and we eased past the house. He made a U-turn at the dead end and parked in front of the camel-colored house aiming back the way we came. I didn't ask if he was expecting we'd have to make a hasty exit.

Before we got out, he said, "Bull hasn't been to the house since Stu moved in. The fact that he showed up now, well, it can't be a coincidence to Jump Diggins' murder, can it?"

"Not likely," I said.

Strips of dirt lined the cracked walkway that led to the front stoop. They might have been planted with flowers at one time, but only weeds grew in them now. A western fence lizard eyed us from a perch atop a flat rock that was the color of the moon and just as lifeless. He blinked but didn't run.

Dobbs rapped on the front door while turning the knob. A waft of cool air greeted us as we stepped into a semi-dark living room that had all the curtains pulled. A pall of cigarette smoke drifted above a brown recliner set in front of a wheezing air conditioner that protruded from the wall. Condensation from the front grille dripped into a Tupperware bowl. A television was on.

The woman sitting in the recliner was thin like Dobbs and wore a flowered housecoat that hung on her like a bedspread draped over a coat rack. The rosebuds on her frayed bedroom slippers were a dirty pink.

"Who's your friend, Manny?" Her voice was raspy.

"Nick. He's helping me with something." Dobbs turned to me. "This is my mom, Bobbie."

"Pleased to meet you, ma'am," I said.

"Well, aren't you polite." Bobbie took a drag on her cigarette. Smoking and living in a dry desert climate hadn't been kind to her skin. I did the math and realized she was barely forty but looked fifteen years older.

"Where's Stu?" Dobbs said.

His mother waved the cigarette toward the hallway. "Taking a nap."

I glanced at the TV. A woman and man were clenched in a tight embrace as dramatic music swelled. When they finally broke off their kiss, the camera zeroed in on them. The actress was Amber Russell. I didn't recognize the actor, but he resembled Pudge Warbler.

Bobbie noticed me watching. "I've seen this one a couple times. It's like all her movies. She's the beauty with two men fighting over her. In this one, she throws off the younger guy for the older one because he's seen it all and done it all and treats her like a queen." She shook her head. "The thing of it is, he's nowhere near as rich or sexy."

Dobbs crouched next to the recliner. "What did Bull want?"

"I didn't know you was bringing company when I called."

"It's okay, Mom. Nick's met Bull. He knows what he's like."

"Poor you," Bobbie said to me. She exhaled smoke. "Bull told me he's making lots of money at the gold mine, Manny. More than he ever did with the sheriff's. You should fill out a job application."

"Is that what Bull told you I should do?"

"I'm only thinking about what's best for you. Can't a mother do that?"

She picked up a tall glass set on the floor next to the recliner and took a drink. Her eyes watered when she swallowed.

Dobbs asked her again why Bull came by. Bobbie stubbed her cigarette out in an overflowing ashtray. "Okay, smarty pants. He told me you'd gotten yourself into something way over your head about some desert tramp who was killed by an Indian out by the gold mine and I need to tell you to stick it to the Indian. If you don't, you could get hurt. You need to do what Bull says. I'm being serious."

"Did Bull tell you what proof he has the Indian did it?"

She shook her head. Her hair could use a shampoo. "Only that you should believe him and convince the judge too. Bull said if you do that, he'll get you a job working security at the gold mine and finally make some real money."

"Did Bull talk to Stu when he was here?"

Bobbie nodded. "It was the same old BS. New evidence has come to light with those assault-and-battery charges from a couple of years back. Blah, blah, blah. Bull can make them go away if you do what he says about the Indian."

Dobbs turned to me. "Before Stu had his accident, he and some friends were at a bar and got in a fight with a gang of bikers from Reno. Stu was released after a couple of days. The judge dismissed the whole thing."

Bobbie lit another cigarette and blew smoke in my direction. "Bull's still hassling him to get back at me. It drives him crazy knowing Stu can't use his legs no more but he's still twice the man he is."

Dobbs asked her what Stu told Bull.

"He said he wasn't a cop no more and stop hassling us. You included."

The deputy sighed. "I can take care of myself, Mom."

"I doubt it."

I said, "Excuse me, ma'am, would it be okay if I used the bathroom?"

"Your mother sure taught you some manners. She must not have had to hold down two jobs at once to put food on the table because her husband went out and got himself killed robbing a bank." When I didn't react to that, she took another drink. "It's down the hall. Go ahead and flush. It won't wake Stu. He couldn't hear a tidal wave."

The hallway was dimly lit and the carpet a minefield of dirty clothes. The first door on the left was open. It was a small bedroom with a single bed and scuffed dresser. A line of model cars rode a shelf above a school desk. The next door was open too. It was the bathroom. I passed it by and opened the door at the end of the hall, stepped inside, and shut it behind me.

A bearded man was lying on top of the bed covers. His curly shoulder-length hair spilled onto the pillows. He wore a white sleeveless undershirt. Winged tattoos blued both shoulders and his forearms were sleeves of inked images that included skulls, buxom women, and hearts shedding tears. Bandy legs stuck out from a pair of gray boxers. A pair of white crew socks covered his motionless feet.

His eyes snapped open. "Who the hell are you?"

"I'm a friend of Manning's. He's talking to his mom."

"She went crying to him because that fat ass Bull Hammond was here? Thought I couldn't take care of him myself, that it?"

"Bobbie said you told him to stuff it. She's trying to talk Manning into taking a job at the gold mine."

"Kid does that, he'll wind up under a pile of rocks. He's soft. Always has been despite being an MP and now wearing a tin star. Just so you know, he's not mine. If he was, I'd've raised him not to be a punching bag for fat asses like Bull."

"That your twelve hundred cc panhead in the driveway? It looks like a sixty-five, the last year Harley made that engine before switching over to the shovelhead. Those bikes take off like a scared rabbit but leak more oil than an offshore rig."

Stu looked me up and down. "It ain't oil, it's blood. Panhead's got more heart than most men. You see the forks on it? I milled those tubes myself. I mean, the original ones. These are modeled after them. I used to have my own shop, but then got sideswiped coming home one night and had to lay it down. Damned if the driver didn't turn around and run back over it. A hit and split. I ever catch the bastard, he's gonna get a chain ride behind a Harley pushing the red line." He made a spitting noise. "You ride?"

"Triumph Bonneville."

"A Desert Sled, huh? You're into racing, not cruising down the long open road."

"Speed's always been my need," I said.

Stu grinned. He was no dentist's regular. "Same for every biker. Either when you're trying to get someplace you want to be in a hurry, like a bar or a hot mama's crib, and even more so when you gotta split fast."

"Truer words have never been spoken."

Stu nodded approvingly. "My boys rebuilt mine when I was laid up in the hospital. When they learnt I couldn't straddle it no more, they said they'd build me a trike. I told them what they could do to themselves. Three-wheelers are for old farts and pretenders."

I glanced at the nightstand. It was crammed with pill bottles. Stu followed my gaze.

"Downers, mostly. Reds and yellow jackets. The black beauties are to wake me up. I need the whole freakin' rainbow to deal with the pains in my legs even though I can't move them no more. My back, don't get me started. If you're in need, help yourself. I got Medicaid. It pays for everything."

"No thanks. Smack nearly did me in a few years ago. I can't go back there. Ever."

Stu studied me some more. "If you're not after my stash or foxy old lady, then what? I can't ride it no more, but the bike's not for sale. Not ever. It's still part of me, savvy?"

"I figure if there's anybody around here who can tell it to me straight about Bull Hammond, it's the dude who owns a Harley panhead. Riding that beast takes guts, and Manning and I need help from someone who has plenty to spare."

"Is Bull hassling the kid again to try and get Bobbie back in the sack?"

"He's got something to do with a murder out by the gold mine Manning's investigating. I'm helping him out. What's Hammond's game?"

"I told you. He's got the hots for my old lady. Always has. Next time he comes sniffing around . . ." The biker reached under his pillow and drew a snub-nosed .38. "Here's the whole truth, Judge, nothing but. I woke up to find a strange man strapping a gun standing at the foot of my bed. I shot him before he could shoot me. Man's home is his castle, right? Even a cripple." He grinned.

"I meant, what's his game at the gold mine."

"Making easy money, same as always. When he was with sheriff's, he was badging and cadging nonstop. Free coffee and donuts, no charge for dry cleaning his uniform, car washes for his personal wheels. Whatever he could get from storeowners who were either too chickenshit or didn't want to make trouble. He's never paid for a drink or lap dance in his life."

"Does that include at the Aces Wild?"

"Especially there. My old lady used to cocktail there."

"The owner doesn't sound like the kind of man whose frightened of anybody or gives anything away for free unless there's something in it for him."

"And there's nothing wrong with your hearing either. Bull? He's Paul Waiterock's go-to guy. An out-of-towner has a fit over a blackjack dealer miscounting a stack of chips, the casino's security guards—a couple of real Mutt and Jeffs—have a word with him. If that doesn't shut him up, then Bull appears with some bogus story about his car being hit in the parking lot. When they go outside to take a look, Bull tells him the facts of life with this leather pouch of silver dollars he keeps in his back pocket."

"Do you speak from experience?"

When Stu shrugged, the angel-wing tattoos on his broad shoulders took flight. "He uppercuts it into your nuts and when you drop your hands to cup them, he roundhouses it across the side of your dome." He fingered his head. "Leaves dents you can read *e pluribus unum* in." I pictured the crescent moon bruises on Searcher.

"Is Waiterock connected to the gold mine?"

"There's nothing around here he doesn't have his fingers shoved into past the knuckles. Anything new comes to town, he wants a piece of it and always gets it too. A new business opens? A developer builds a new housing tract? Waiterock gets his cut."

I asked Stu why he thought Dobbs would get killed if he went to work at the mine.

"Because he's a punk, that's why. He'd step on the wrong toes without even knowing he was doing it. That place attracts Triple A hard cases."

"Doesn't toughness go along with the job?"

"Sure, miners gotta be, blowing up stuff, crushing rock, and pouring acid. But I'm talking about the ones in suits."

"How's that?"

"My buddy drove truck there, the ones that got tires twice as tall as a man. You're in a brawl, you want him swinging a chain with you, not at you. The other day his shift's over and he's driving down the hill. The road's narrow and he needs a six-pack in the worst way. A car comes driving up the hill. He doesn't pull over to let it pass. It doesn't pull over either. It's a Mexican stand-off. He rolls down his window and tells the driver to back up. Two dudes in shiny suits hop out. The driver's holding an automatic, the other a rifle. 'I didn't hear you,' the driver says. 'Say again?' "

Stu jabbed his snub-nosed .38 in the air as he acted out the scene. "My buddy thinks about it for maybe a whole second and then backs up the hill into a pullout. When the car passes, the driver points his piece at him and says, 'Next time, tappity tap tap. One in each eye.' The passenger, the one with the rifle, laughs. Not howling like a hyena, more like a dog panting. My buddy said that weird laugh gave him the creeps more than the piece stuck in his face. I asked him why he pussied out. You know what he said? 'I know a professional hitter when I see one, and I saw two.' "

"Is your friend at the mine now?"

"Nah. He never went back. He took a job working construction somewhere in Utah." Stu slipped the revolver back under the pillow. "Hey, I gotta take a leak. Hand me that pisspot over there and then take a hike. Tell Bobbie there's a cleanup on Aisle Five."

His chuckle followed me down the hall.

24

The inflatable white swan was still bobbing in the swimming pool when I pulled into the motel's parking lot. I stayed behind the wheel and tried to talk myself into getting a room. I wasn't a fan of motels. The beds were lumpy, the showers tepid, and the walls too thin to mute the sounds of amorous couples next door. On road trips, I usually camped or slept in my pickup. But staying in a Winnemucca motel would save having to drive out into the desert and then back again in the morning. In addition to searching for a spent slug in Ruby's remains, I planned to look for the R drawn on Jump Diggins' tarp. A topographical map of northern Nevada would help narrow down possible locations, but the only place to get one was at the local Bureau of Land Management office and it was closed for the day.

When Dobbs and I split up after the visit to his mother's, he told me he was going back to his office and work on getting Searcher released. In the morning he planned to go through Sheriff Coon's personnel records to see if he'd ever written up Hammond and to look for any reports the sheriff might have on Paul Waiterock. Then he was going to call the Robbery and

Homicide division at the Las Vegas PD and ask about the rifle used to kill the two men Ron Garzas had mentioned.

I reached for the glovebox to retrieve my wallet. Beneath it was Amber Russell's pocket gun. I'd forgotten to leave it at the lineman's shack for safekeeping. It was another reminder of how fatherhood and lack of sleep wasn't helping with the memory department. There was nothing I could do about the movie star's Beretta now, and so I left it and went to the front office.

The woman behind the front desk had teased hair and a blouse with pink poodles on it. "Single or double?"

I asked her which one had the most comfortable bed.

"Depends on what you need it for."

"Sleeping, what else?"

"Honey, in case you hadn't noticed, you're in Nevada." When I didn't laugh, she said, "Take the double. Bigger room, bigger bed. It'll cost you an extra three dollars, but it comes with a coupon that'll save you that much if you eat dinner next door."

"At the Aces Wild?"

"They have an all-you-can-eat buffet or you can order off the menu. The meatloaf made German-style is my favorite. Comes with a side of mashed potatoes and gravy. I advise customers to stay away from the chili. It's hard on the plumbing." She winked. "Both the motel's and their own."

I forked over fifteen bucks and she handed me a key attached to a gold plastic fob with the motel's name on it.

"Number thirteen is a ground-floor unit. You can park right in front. The AC is already on and it's close to the ice machine. Checkout is ten a.m. Here's your dinner coupon, and, no, you can't use it on cocktails, gambling chips, or the girls who work the bar."

I re-parked my pickup, checked that the rack holding my two long guns was locked, and grabbed my gear. The air in Room 13 was cool and the bed looked freshly made. I peeled off my clothes and turned on the shower. The pipes must have been exposed to the sun all day because the water was instantly hot. I let it wash away the smell of formaldehyde, dumpsters, and cigarettes.

As I stood under the spray, I reviewed what I'd learned so far. It wasn't much. Organized crime and the gold mine were obviously connected. Paul Waiterock was linked to both in one way or another. And Bull Hammond was definitely trying to interfere with the murder investigation. But there was still no answer to who killed Jump Diggins and why.

The hot water started to run out. I turned off the shower, put on a clean shirt, and made a beeline for the Aces Wild. I hadn't eaten anything since the breakfast I'd shared with Pudge more than twelve hours earlier.

The restaurant was strategically placed at the rear of the casino. The safest bet in the house was no diner could reach it without stopping to feed the gauntlet of one-armed bandits that lined the way. Since the buffet reminded me of too many chow lines, I informed the hostess I preferred to order from the menu and asked for a table in a quiet corner.

"Would you like a cocktail?" she said. "I can place a drink order for you now."

"Water's fine."

"If you change your mind, flash me the high sign."

The menu played up the restaurant's location. There was a Full House Salad, Ace of Clubs Sandwich, and Jackpot Roast. The waitress brought a pitcher of ice water and filled my glass. She had a nice smile that went along with her girl-next-door demeanor that made me think she went to Manning Dobbs' church.

"Can I get a regular steak or does it have to be the High Stakes Steak?" I said.

"The names are kind of silly, aren't they? I'll ask the cook to grill you a ribeye with a baked potato on the side." She winked conspiratorially. "It'll be our little secret."

"Perfect. I'll take it rare."

"Do you want any steak sauce?"

"No thanks. Never use it."

"I'll put a rush on your meal." She smiled again and whisked the menu away.

I opened a book I'd brought along for company. Newly published and titled *Pilgrim at Tinker Creek*, it was written by an author new to me by the name of Annie Dillard. Gemma gave it to me, saying I was in for a surprise. It only took a few pages before I knew what she meant.

The writer's year-long chronicle of the creatures that inhabited the woods outside her Virginia back door read like my own thoughts had been put into words. She saw good and evil, peace and violence in nature the same way I did at the wildlife refuges. For her, it was the delicate beauty of a wave of monarch butterflies juxtaposed with the savagery of a giant water bug sucking a frog dry of blood. For me, it was a V of tundra swans touching down on Malheur Lake versus a cougar disemboweling a spotted fawn. Her observations were scientifically insightful and unabashedly spiritual, and I knew from my own experience she'd witnessed more than insects, plants, and animals on her explorations: she'd been in the presence of the Divine.

As hard as I tried to lose myself in the power, grace, and beauty of Annie Dillard's word symphony, I couldn't tune out the racket of whirring slot machines and the whoops and groans of gamblers surrounding a craps table. The noise grew even louder when the hostess led six men in my direction. Four sat down at the table next to mine. The two who'd been trailing them split up and sat alone at tables with direct sight lines of the four men, the entrance to the restaurant, and the door to the kitchen. I made the pair as the casino's private security officers who Stu had described as a Mutt and Jeff team.

"This calls for champagne," said a tan and trim man who was groomed and dressed in the manner of a magazine advertisement hawking expensive watches modeled on the wrists of famous athletes. I recognized him from the photos hanging in the lobby. It was Paul Waiterock.

"I'll see to it right away, sir," the hostess said. She spun on the toes of her high heels and all but sprinted to the horseshoe-shaped bar that dominated the middle of the casino.

"I took the liberty of ordering a celebratory dinner for us," Waiterock said. "Surf and turf. Fresh lobsters flown in from Maine. Angus beef fattened in Montana."

"That's nice, Paul. Real nice," said the man sitting next to him whose neck spilled over the collar of a white-knit sport shirt worn under a brown leather blazer as shiny as vinyl. "Mikey and me, we appreciate the gesture. Don't we Mikey?"

"Hundred percent appreciate, Ray. Hundred percent," the twitchy man seated next to him said in a rapid-fire way. "Makes us feel right at home." Mikey wore a dark burgundy suit, black shirt, and gold chain.

The hostess came back with a bartender in tow who was carrying a champagne bucket. A busboy set out four champagne glasses. The cork was popped, the glasses filled.

Waiterock raised his. "To new partnerships. To new friends. To business. To profit."

"Back atcha," said Ray.

"Hundred percent back atcha," said Mikey.

"Health and wealth," said the fourth man who was sitting with his back to me. "Not necessarily in that order." He heh-heh-hehed. I thought of Stu and his description of a gunman's laugh that sounded like a panting dog.

The bartender still held the bottle. He quickly refilled the glasses. Waiterock gave him a subtle nod and he went off to fetch another.

Ray held up his glass. "You know why this ain't like no other wine glass? How it got this shape? Goes all the way back to France hundred years ago. The Frogs, they invented champagne, see, and they made a special glass to drink it from modeled after Marie Antoinette's right tit. She was the queen but wound up getting her head chopped off. Her husband Louis the fourteenth or some other teenager number did too. True story."

"Hundred percent true, Ray. Hundred percent," Mikey said, bobbing up and down. "But better if they'd used Marilyn Monroe's, rest in peace. Wouldn't have to keep filling our glasses so often."

Ray laughed. The other man dog-panted heh-heh-heh again.

Waiterock said, "I also took the liberty of arranging for some private entertainment after dinner. You'll find there won't be a Marie Antoinette among them."

Ray slapped the table. "Right at home, Paulie. Mind if I call you Paulie? That's the way I feel. Like I never left Chicago. You built a good organization up here, I can see that. Mikey and me, we're glad we made the trip up from Vegas to seal the deal."

"Hundred percent glad," Mikey said. "Hundred percent."

The waitress arrived with my meal. I put *Pilgrim at Tinker Creek* to the side as she put the plate down and laid a large wooden-handled steak knife next to the cutlery that had already been set.

"Can I get you anything else?" she said.

"No, I'm good," I said. "Thanks."

"Bon appétit."

As she turned to leave, Ray leaned over and snatched her wrist. "You hear that, Paulie? This sweet young thing speaks Frog. Reminds me how Napoleon got his last name. One night

Marie Antoinette invites him up to her bedroom for some boom-boom. You know, the way the Frogs like to do it. She drops her dress, but poor Napoleon, he takes one look at her tiny tits and his bone falls apart."

The waitress blushed and buried her eyes in the floor. Ray held onto her wrist as he waved his champagne glass. Mikey said one hundred percent true and the other man heh-heh-hehed.

I nodded at Ray's grip on the waitress's wrist, "Let her go."

The men at the table went silent. Ray looked me, his eyes narrowing behind a flattened nose. "What d'ya say?"

"Let the waitress go."

"What's it to you?"

I glanced down at my plate and then back at him. "I asked her to bring me some A1. I don't want my steak to get cold."

Heh-heh man turned around in his seat. He had dead eyes and a pencil moustache that formed an upside down V under his nose. He started to push out of his chair, but Ray backed him off with a look and dropped the waitress's wrist.

"No problem. Wouldn't want to get between a man and his meat."

Ray laughed and Mikey said hundred percent true and heh-heh man heh-heh-hehed without taking his dead eyes off me.

The waitress ran to the kitchen. I looked over at Waiterock and gave him a hard stare. He didn't react and turned back to his guests. I refocused my attention on the steak and baked potato. I'd only taken a few bites when Mutt and Jeff approached. The tall one stood while the short one sat down across from me.

Mutt leaned forward and said in a low voice, "We got a nice table on the other side of the restaurant set up for you. The busboy'll bring your plate. Follow me. I'll show it to you."

"That's okay. This one's fine," I said.

Mutt frowned. "The thing of it is, this is a reserved section.

The hostess made a mistake seating you here. Management is asking you to switch. They'll comp your dinner. Dessert too. Come on, I'll get you all squared away. You wanna nice red wine to go with that steak? On the house."

"Tell Mr. Waiterock, thanks, but no thanks." I started carving another piece off the steak.

Mutt's frown grew. He leaned on his elbows to get closer and without moving his lips said, "Listen, pal. I'm asking nice. As a courtesy to you. You wanna take it, the courtesy. Know what I mean?"

"I'm going to finish my supper right here." I pointed the steak knife at him. "Know what I mean?"

Mutt started breathing heavily. Jeff pulled his jacket aside to reveal a holstered pistol clipped to his belt.

"Really? Do you think your boss's new business partners are going to act kindly to him after they're pulled in as material witnesses to a shooting?"

Jeff quickly closed his jacket. Mutt looked at the steak knife and then back at me. "You shoulda taken the courtesy."

The pair walked back to their seats. On the way, Mutt gave Waiterock a questioning look. The casino owner shook his head and went back to talking with Ray, Mikey, and heh-heh man.

I took my time eating. When I was finished, the hostess, not the waitress, brought my check. Complimentary had been stamped on it in blue. I put a ten-dollar bill down and got up. Mutt and Jeff eyed me, but didn't leave their seats. Waiterock didn't look my way at all.

As I crossed the casino, I tuned out all the flashing lights and noisy gamblers and kept my senses focused like I was back walking point on patrol. No one followed me. I exited the casino and waited outside, but Mutt and Jeff were no shows. Bull Hammond didn't appear swinging a leather pouch either. No one was lingering between the parked cars as I walked back to my motel room.

I paused outside the door to number 13 with the key on the gold plastic fob in my hand. Something didn't feel right. I reached for my service weapon, but then remembered I'd put the .357 in the night stand drawer before taking a shower.

I kept my eyes on the door and walked backward to my pickup and took Amber's pocket Beretta from the glovebox. The semi-automatic had a tip-up barrel. I opened it and checked the chamber. It was empty. Pudge had told me the eight-shot magazine was full. It was. I chambered a round and gripped the butt. It disappeared in my palm and the barrel barely extended beyond my curled trigger finger. I returned to number 13, stepped to the side, unlocked the door, and pushed it open.

I counted to five. No one started shooting. No one moved inside. I followed the little .25 caliber into the room. It was empty. I exhaled and locked the door behind me. It wasn't the first time my gut had been wrong. I stuck the gun in the pocket of my jeans before getting undressed so I wouldn't forget it again when I left in the morning.

As I got into bed and drifted off to sleep, I hoped the human equivalent of the evil and savagery Annie Dillard and I witnessed in nature wouldn't inhabit my dreams. Or my tomorrows either.

25

First thing in the morning, even before a cup of coffee, I called the sheriff's office. The gravelly voiced dispatcher put me through to Manning Dobbs. When the young chief deputy answered, he yawned and sounded groggy.

"Didn't you get any sleep last night?" I said.

"I worked late and never left. I must've dozed off at my desk."

"What's the latest on Searcher?"

My question was met with a long silence. "He's gone."

"What do you mean, gone?"

"I checked on him when I got back from my mom's. He was lying on his bed and I told him I was still working on his release."

"What did he say?"

"Nothing. He didn't acknowledge me. The judge's office is upstairs, but he doesn't like drop-ins and so I went to my desk and called him to make sure he'd gotten my request for a release. His assistant answered and said he had and was going to sign it and she'd bring it to me as soon as he did. I started looking through Sheriff Coon's files and lost track of time. When

I realized I still hadn't gotten the release, I went up to the judge's office, but they'd already left for the day."

I asked Dobbs what he did next.

"I went to the holding cell to tell Searcher what happened and that he'd be released in the morning." He took a deep breath. "When I got there, the cell door was open and Searcher was gone. I must not have locked it when I let you out."

"Did anyone see him leave?"

"If they did, they didn't raise an alarm or tell me."

"Do you think the judge had his assistant let Searcher go after he signed the release?"

"No, he's strictly by the book. Plus, the duct-tape and towel were on the floor. The judge and his assistant wouldn't have let him walk out naked."

"It really doesn't matter, does it? You were going to release him in the morning anyway."

"I suppose you're right, but where did he go and how was he going to get there?"

"His own two feet will carry him," I said, borrowing an oft-spoken phrase from November. "Listen, I need to tell you about who I saw at dinner at the Aces Wild last night. Paul Waiterock was at the table next to mine. Him and three men from Chicago by way of Las Vegas."

"How do you know that?"

"They said so." I described Ray. "He's the boss. The twitchy one named Mikey is his yes-man. I didn't hear a name for the third man, but he has a pencil moustache and when he laughs, he pants like a dog. He fits the description of a professional gunman Stu told me about."

"When did you talk to Stu?"

"At your mother's when I went to the bathroom. Stu said a friend of his was working at the gold mine and had a roadside encounter with two gunmen."

Dobbs sighed. "What else did you find out at dinner?"

"They were celebrating some kind of new partnership. I didn't get any last names, but the way they looked, talked, and acted, maybe Garzas can ID them. He might even know why they came to your jurisdiction."

"I'll ask him when I call Robbery Homicide about the caliber of the bullets used on their two victims."

We agreed to keep in touch throughout the day. I checked out of the motel and drove to the BLM's Winnemucca District office. It was on the east side of town between a used-car lot and trailer park. When I introduced myself to the clerk working the desk and asked for topographical maps, his brow furrowed.

"You're going to need to be a tad more specific, Ranger. The state covers seventy million acres border to border and we manage forty-eight million of them. Do you know how many topographical quadrangle maps the United States Geological Survey has drawn for Nevada?"

"I imagine a fair number."

"Try one thousand seven hundred eighty-five on for size. If you can't be a tad more specific, I hope you have a trailer parked out front to haul them all."

I expected him to slap his knee and start hee-hawing, but when he didn't, I began rethinking my strategy. Blackpowder had pulled Jump Diggins out of a mudhole in the Carson Sink, the center of an ancient lake that was forty times the size of nearby Lake Tahoe back when woolly mammoths roamed. It was more than one hundred miles from where I stood. One hundred miles in the other direction was where he and Black-powder found gold. Even if I used those two as search area endpoints, I'd need hundreds of topo quads. That still left every-where else in Nevada that Diggins had been picking and shov-eling during his lifetime.

"The BLM office in Harney County carries lots of different

kinds of maps," I said. "There are recreational maps showing campgrounds, hiking trails, and fishing and hunting zones. Even the management areas for wild horses and burros are on BLM maps. What about this office?"

"We have those along with maps showing mining claims. BLM manages upward of two hundred thousand active claims in Nevada. Another million have been filed, but most of those are either abandoned or have never been mined. We map them because the state is riddled with old shafts, glory holes, ditches, and rusty stamp mills. You have to watch where you step in this state."

"Your district encompasses the Sheldon Wildlife Refuge, doesn't it?"

"Yes. It extends west to California and north to Oregon and south to the Carson City district. Eleven million acres."

"Does the Carson City district cover the Carson Sink?"

"It does."

"Okay, I'll take all the different recreation maps you have for both districts. I'll also take any maps that show the location of mining claims, both active and abandoned, especially those that are anywhere near the Sheldon refuge."

"Now that's what I call a tad specific."

I walked out with a large stack of folding maps and put them in the pickup's glovebox so they wouldn't slide off the front seat when I was bumping along dirt roads. That left no room for the little semi-automatic that was still in my pocket and so I left it where it was.

Leaving town, I headed north on Highway 95, and then took the Highway 140 turnoff. I was only on it a short distance before I exited onto a dirt road signed Leonard Creek that would eventually lead west to the Summit Lake Indian Reservation. I thought about Searcher and wondered if he'd struck out for there when he let himself out of the holding cell or if he'd decided to walk to any of the other thirty Paiute reservations in the Great Basin.

An hour later, the pickup's radio burped. "Go ahead," I answered.

"Where are you now?" Dobbs asked.

"I'm about to turn onto Quartz Creek Road and then up the Sagebrush Creek track. What did you find out?"

"Ron Garzas knew about two of the men you saw. Ray Guzik and Michael Stazek, aka Mikey Staz. They're associated with a long-time Polish-American mob in Chicago that dates back to Prohibition days. It was organized by a bootlegger named Joseph Saltis, better known as Polack Joe. For a time they were aligned with the mob called the Outfit. That's the one that sent Tony the Ant to Las Vegas. Ron said the two groups had a falling out over the casino business. Ray Guzik's group wanted a piece of the action on the Strip and the Outfit wouldn't agree to it. Ron doesn't know the third man, but said he's likely an enforcer."

"It sounds like the trio came to Winnemucca to work out a deal with Waiterock because they hit a roadblock in Las Vegas. Maybe it's more than casino action they want in on. Maybe it's the gold mine too."

Ruts grabbed my front wheels and I dropped the mike as I wrestled the steering wheel to keep from bottoming out. I reeled in the cord. "Sorry, lost you there for a second. Did Robbery Homicide have any info on the caliber of the rifle?"

"I didn't need to ask them because Ron already had the answer. It turns out both victims were shot by a .30 caliber."

"A Bugsy Siegel rifle," I said.

"That's exactly what Ron said. He's giving the two victims a closer look to see if maybe they're connected to organized crime given the location of the shootings. One was near a casino associated with Tony the Ant and the other a new subdivision that's going up. Ron said the money that goes along with construction is a soft target for a mob protection racket."

"Let me know what he finds out."

"Wait, one other thing." Dobbs took a deep breath. "Bull called me a few minutes ago. He spoke to my mom. She told him I wasn't going to quit the sheriff's or go along with him about Jump Diggins' murder. Bull said if I didn't, it wouldn't only be bad for me, my mom, and Stu, it'd also blow back on him."

"You know you have sufficient grounds to arrest him for interfering with a murder investigation."

The radio was silent except for static. "I know, but I can't do that."

"Why not?"

"Because of who he is. No other deputy would back me up. The DA wouldn't prosecute him. Bull would turn the entire thing back on me and get me fired."

I didn't press it.

"Bull knows you're in Winnemucca," Dobbs continued. "My mom told him you came to the house with me. He said you'd gotten way out of your lane and I should order you to leave the county and go look for your bighorn sheep in Oregon before you get hurt. How did he know about the bighorn? My mom didn't know, so she couldn't have told him."

"I did when I confronted him about the poisoned buck."

"Do you think he knows you were at the Aces Wild last night?"

"Probably. Waiterock's private security guards were there. Stu told me they used Hammond for special jobs they couldn't do themselves."

"How did they know who you were?"

"They asked me to move to another table."

"Did you?"

"Backing down leaves a bad taste in my mouth. I didn't want to ruin my steak dinner."

Dobbs let static speak for a bit. "That still doesn't explain how they got your name."

"They probably saw my Fish and Wildlife pickup parked at the motel and badgered the desk clerk for it."

"Maybe you should go home."

When I didn't reply, Dobbs said, "And you won't, like you didn't change tables. Okay, I get it. But you can't go to the gold mine. Bull was there when he called. He has a bad temper. I've seen it."

"I'm turning onto the Sagebrush Creek track now. I'll be off radio when I'm searching the gully. I'll give you a call later and let you know if I find anything."

"Did you hear me? Stay away from the gold mine."

I turned off the radio without saying "over and out."

My tire tracks were still visible from the time I'd camped above the gully and kept vigil over Jump Diggins and Ruby. I parked and got out. The odds of finding a spent slug were worse than any game of chance at the Aces Wild. Ruby's death was life for other animals, everything from coyotes to turkey vultures to ants would feed on her carcass. Such was nature's law.

The burro had been shot in the hindquarters and neck. No scavenger would've taken the time to chew around or spit out any of the .30 caliber slugs that I now believed she'd been shot with. I'd read wildlife biology reports about how eating lead bullets was pushing California condors to the brink of extinction. They weren't the only birds at risk from lead poisoning. If President Nixon did end up visiting the Malheur refuge and TV cameras were able to catch a bald eagle winging overhead, I'd try to tell him about it. Maybe he'd add regulating lead ammo to his environmental protection agenda.

After climbing down the gully, I quickly found the spot

where Ruby had breathed her last. The remains of her halter were still attached to her skull that had been stripped of hide, eyes, ears, and brains. The lower jaw was missing and the upper teeth that remained were locked in a permanent bray.

I hiked to Quartz Creek Road, but didn't find any more parts of her carcass. I turned around, retraced my steps, and kept walking. Her right hip was two hundred yards past her skull. A short length of vertebrate and a femur lay nearby. I knelt next to the hip bone and examined it. A black spot showed. It wasn't a hole, but an embedded slug. I pried it out with my knife. The slug had flattened and was a bit ragged at the edges, but appeared to be the size of a .30 caliber. I slipped it into the coin pocket of my jeans and then waved a fistful of sage over the hip bone and repeated my earlier vow to Ruby that I'd find hers and Jump Diggins' killer.

I walked back to where I'd scrambled down and climbed up the embankment. When I reached the top, I reached for my sidearm.

"Touch it and I'll drop you where you stand," Bull Hammond said over the barrel of a Police Special aimed at my chest.

26

I t wasn't Hammond's gun that made me freeze, it was the snapshot he held up.

"I saw you from the top of the gold mine," he said. "Most men keep a picture of their family in their wallet and the car registration fastened to the visor. What makes you so ass-backwards, like coming here instead of going home?"

"They have nothing to do with this," I said.

"And it'll stay that way if you do what I say. Unbuckle your holster with your left hand and let it drop. Go for your gun and I'll kill you and then drive straight to No Mountain and kill your wife and daughter too. Don't look so surprised. I still got friends in the sheriff's office. They ran your plate. I know where you live."

The Smith and Wesson made a thunk when it hit the ground, not as loud as the one that Wyatt Clark's head made when it struck rock, but the sound portended death just the same.

"Why are you doing this?" I said, keeping my gaze on Hammond, trying to create an opportunity.

"The future. A man gets to my age, it becomes a whole lot

more important. I put in my twenty at the sheriff's and what did it get me? A pension that won't even buy me three squares a day in a nursing home. A man offers me an easy job with a lot more pay and fringe benefits, I'd be a fool not to take it."

"Even if working at the gold mine comes with strings?"

"None that I can't handle."

"Including turning a blind eye to mobsters laundering cash? Killing an old prospector who claimed the mineral rights were his?"

The tip of Hammond's .38 got a little closer as he jabbed it at me. "How do you know all that?"

"A friend of mine prospected with Jump Diggins here twenty-five years ago. His name is Blackpowder Smith. Haven't heard of him? I know you know his closest friend, Harney County Sheriff Pudge Warbler. Pudge said so when I told him about you. He happens to be my father-in-law. Killing me is one thing, but harm his daughter and granddaughter and there's no place on this planet you can hide."

"I should've thrown you in the cyanide pit along with that dead buck," he snarled.

"But now if I disappear, it won't only be Pudge and Blackpowder who know you're responsible. Manning Dobbs will too."

Hammond spit. "Little Manny. I can't believe Jim Coons made him my replacement. He's only one size of long pants away from sitting in his bedroom playing with toy cars while I'm in the next room screwing his mother."

"Why did you kill Diggins? Oro Holdings could've bought him off for peanuts to stay away."

"They tried, but he wouldn't take a dime. He said any gold they pulled out was his. And who says I shot him?"

"If you didn't, then why steal the slugs from the evidence room?"

Surprise showed on Hammond's face. He jabbed the Police

Special again. "You some kind of big city cop got busted down to picking up trash in parks?"

"Why did you take them?"

"Life insurance."

"That's right, Nevada has the death penalty. You can trade the slugs and a confession for a life sentence and the possibility of parole in twenty years."

"I don't need to confess to anything. I never shot anybody in the back in my life."

"Then why do you need insurance?"

"It's an ace up my sleeve if the men I'm holding you for try to double-cross me."

The dots were starting to connect. "And framing Searcher, was that more insurance?"

"A man can't be too careful."

"That policy's void. Dobbs saw the light after I told him about the leather pouch of silver dollars you used to beat Searcher. He let him walk."

Hammond showed surprise again and then sneered. "Next time I'll use this for taming the Indian. Little Manny too." He brandished the gun.

The sun had climbed over Big Mountain and sent waves of heat haze rising from the scrubby desert floor. Despite the glare, I could see more clearly now. "Ray Guzik's boys, Mikey and the rifleman, they killed Diggins. Why?"

"It's the way they do business back home in Chicago. Someone they're trying to work a deal with drags their feet, they leave a body on their doorstep for all to see. Foot draggers tend to come around quick after that. The old prospector happened to be in the wrong place at the wrong time when they needed a calling card."

"But it didn't work for them in Las Vegas," I said. "A man

near a casino. Another by a subdivision. What made them think it'd work up here?"

"Winnemucca's not Las Vegas."

"I guess not. I saw them celebrating with Paul Waiterock last night."

"You've figured out a lot, I'll hand you that."

"I've seen enough to know that Ray will steamroll right over Waiterock despite him handing over a piece of the casino and gold mine. You worked for Waiterock. You don't owe him anything?"

"The only person I owe is me. Why I'm riding off into the sunset of a tropical island."

"Who's behind Oro Holdings, the Outfit?"

Hammond laughed. "See, that's Ray's problem too. He's stuck in the past. Can't see the present. Can't see the future. Think bigger. Much bigger."

"If it's bigger than the Chicago and Las Vegas mobs, then it must be some kind of international gang that needs to launder lots of money. The kind of money that comes from selling drugs and arms."

Before Hammond could put any words together, a dust devil danced above the start of Sagebrush Creek track at Quartz Creek Road. It danced toward us as it followed the spinning wheels of a bronze Mark IV with a white vinyl roof. The suspension on the ground-hugging coupe with the elongated hood was getting a real workout.

"You should've stuck with looking for bighorn sheep," Hammond said.

The car pulled to a stop next to our pickups. Mikey was driving. Heh-heh man was in the passenger seat. Ray wasn't with them.

Mikey got out first. Either he was still wearing the burgundy

suit from last night or he had another exactly like it. His gold
chain gleamed. Heh-heh man was carrying a .30-caliber MI rifle.
His eyes were no less alive than last time, but his pencil moustache twitched when he recognized me.

Mikey hooked a thumb at the car. "What a P O S. The AC
blew. Couldn't keep up with all the dust. And the Landau roof?
Forget about it. Never going to be able to get it cleaned." He eyed
me and then said to Hammond, "This guy, thinks he's a tough
guy, mouthing off to Ray. Ray, he sends his appreciation for
collecting him." He paused. "What's that you're holding?"

"It's a photograph of his wife and kid. I found it in his truck,"
Hammond said.

The twitchy gangster was bobbing up and down, making his
gold chain flounce. He said to me, "Why d'ja leave wifey and
stick your nose where it don't belong?"

"This is my beat," I said.

Mikey made a show of looking around. "What's to police?
There's nothing here but dirt." He laughed out of both sides of
his mouth. "It's Nick, right? Well, Nick. Today's your lucky day.
Hundred percent lucky. Kick that gun belt over to me. Go on and
do it or my associate is going to put a hole through your right
eye. Tappity tap. Right here." He touched his eye lid.

Heh-heh man had the rifle shouldered and aimed at me. I
thought about diving for my pistol, but with the MI and
Hammond's .38 trained on me, I wouldn't even be able to clear it
from the holster.

I raised my eyes to the big sky and said in *Numu*, "Hear me,
my old friend Tuhudda. Hear me, Searcher. Hear me, Forever
Walkers. I need your help."

Mikey scoffed. "What, you Catholic? That Latin? If I was you,
I'd be confessing, not praying."

"It's Paiute," Hammond said.

"What's it mean?"

"How should I know? I don't speak it."

I said the words again.

"Okay already with the blathering," Mikey said. "Kick me that holster or tappity tap."

A calmness settled over me. I committed the three men's faces to memory so that when they cast me into the spirit world, I'd still be able to hunt them down before they reached No Mountain. I kicked the holster.

Mikey picked it up, pulled the gun out, and hefted it. "I don't get a piece like this." He turned toward Hammond, waving my revolver. "It weighs a freakin' ton but only holds six rounds. Here, see for yourself."

Hammond hesitated.

"Go on, I'll hold your piece for you. Nick, he's not going anywhere with the rifle on him. Check this bad boy out. Too heavy for my tastes, but I betcha it packs a wallop."

Hammond took my .357 magnum and handed Mikey his .38. "You're right," he said. "It's too heavy."

"Like I said." And then Mikey pointed the Police Special at him and pulled the trigger three times. Gunpowder banged and the .38 slugs spiraled out of the barrel one after another and smacked into the gold mine security chief's chest and knocked him flat.

"Ray, he sends his regards, Bullwinkle," Mikey said.

Heh-heh man's rifle didn't bobble as he heh-heh-hehed.

Mikey walked over to Hammond and plucked the snapshot of Gemma and Hattie from his dead fingers. "Wifey's pretty cute. Daughter too. Definitely worth paying a little visit." He slid it into the top pocket of his burgundy suit.

Heh-heh man panted another heh-heh-heh.

Mikey turned Hammond's .38 on me. "Here's what we got

here, Nick. We need you to convince a party we're serious about doing business with them. They didn't get the message the first time and so now we gotta send two more messages. You and Bullwinkle." He jerked his chin at Hammond's body. It made his gold chain flounce. He grinned.

Heh-heh man was panting up a storm. I said to him, "That's not Bugsy Siegel's rifle. It's a fake. A Maltese Falcon. How much did you get ripped off for?"

His upside down V pencil moustache flattened. "You're dead already."

"How much?" I said, not taking my eyes off his.

"It's the real thing."

I thought of the gamblers at the Aces Wild, the ones at the craps table putting pay they couldn't afford to lose on the line, the poker players bluffing with two deuces. "I bet you the five thousand bucks you got taken for I'm right. I can prove it."

Mikey looked on with amusement.

Heh-heh man aimed the rifle at my mouth. "I told you it's the rifle that killed Bugsy and a lot of others. It's the one that's going to shut your trap forever."

"I know about M1s. My old man brought his home from France after mowing down Nazis with it," I said, echoing Ron Garzas. "I served in Vietnam. They gave us M1s too until they switched us over to M16s. You're holding a Vietnam-era M1. It was manufactured twenty years after Bugsy Siegel was shot."

"You're lying," he said. But the slightest wobble showed in the barrel tip.

"The ones they gave us in Vietnam all pulled to the right. Same with the one you're holding. Why it took you so many shots to put down the old prospector and his burro."

The M1's barrel wobbled some more.

I pushed the rest of my stack of chips forward, betting I could get him to take his eyes off me, betting I could rush

Mikey before Mikey put more than one round in me, betting I could swing Mikey around and use him as a shield and clamp my hand around his and point Hammond's .38 at heh-heh man and fire when he hesitated to shoot first, not wanting to hit Mikey.

"The serial number will prove it," I said. "If it starts with a six, it's W W two. Anything else, Vietnam. See for yourself."

Heh-heh man raised his cheek from the stock and started to push the rifle away. I got on the balls of my feet.

"Hold it! Stop right there," Mikey shouted. "Nick's BS'ing you. Anybody can see that. Am I right, Nick? Of course I'm right." Heh-heh man tucked the M1 against his cheek again. This time tighter.

"Nick, I gotta say, I respect you for trying," Mikey said. "Hundred percent respect. But you're not only outgunned here, you're outclassed in the BS department. Say goodbye to wifey."

I looked past him. Waves of heat haze were still rising from the hot desert scrub. I was looking for Gemma, looking for Hattie. I wanted their faces locked in my eyes forever. A figure stepped out of the haze.

"Greetings, Searcher," I said.

Mikey snorted. "Lame, man. That's lame. Trying to get me to turn around is so grade school. I don't respect that. Hundred percent don't respect."

"Greetings, Nick Drake," Searcher said.

Mikey's mouth fell open. He whipped around, sending his gold chain swinging. "Getta load of this. Guy's standing there with his schlong hanging out. Okay, we get a freebie. Send a third message. Wait, is that something behind him? More people?"

Heh-heh man swung the M1 toward Searcher and the Forever Walkers. I yanked the Beretta Jetfire out of my front pocket and put two slugs in him before he pulled the trigger.

Mikey wheeled back around and I put two in his heart. The twitchy gangster fell without getting off a shot.

As the light faded from his eyes, I said, "Tappity tap tap." And then I bent down and took the snapshot of Gemma and Hattie from the top pocket of Mikey's burgundy suit and kissed it, relieved that my aim had been true and I hadn't put a hole in the photograph of my wife and little darling.

27

Searcher was expressionless as he looked upon the three dead men. "They now walk alone through darkness. No one will ever sing for them. All they will have forever is their burden of evil that grows heavier with each step they take."

"Thank you for saving my life," I said.

"You saved yourself. You always had *puha* to do so."

"By calling for Tuhudda and you?"

"Believing is *puha*. Asking for help is *puha*."

I stared into the heat haze. The Forever Walkers were murmuring, their footsteps sounding like distant drumbeats as they shuffled in place.

"You knew I'd come back here," I said.

Searcher looked at the gold mine. "Yes, because of the evil hiding behind that. You see through the noise and light. That is your path to walk forever."

"You got here so quickly. How?"

"To walk a path with purpose makes it shorter."

The heat haze was growing thicker around the Forever Walkers. The sound of their feet was barely louder than my breath. I watched, but didn't question what I was seeing.

"Girl Born in Snow told me you are the last of your band. I'm sorry."

"*Mu naa'a* created all *Numu* and so we are all one tribe, one band. It is the same with our brothers and sisters, the *Nuwuddu*. As long as there are *Numu* and *Nuwuddu* in this world, I will not be the last of anything. It will be the same for your tribes, your bands, when you open your eyes to what you share instead of what you take."

A wave of sorrow and acceptance washed over me. "Tuhudda Will died from the fever last night."

"He did," Searcher said.

I gestured at the Forever Walkers. "Is he one of them now?"

"No. Tuhudda walks among the stars and his light shines bright. It guided my way here."

He put his hands on my shoulders. "I must go now. Our paths will cross again because many lie ahead that you and I must walk to bring medicine to heal sickness and medicine to stop evil. Medicine is *puha*."

"Wait, one last thing." I showed him the map Jump Diggins had drawn on his tarp. "Do you know where this is? It's important I find it so the prospector who was murdered here can have peace and shine among the stars. His burro too, a *Nuwuddu*."

He glanced at it and said, "The bighorn sheep will tell you when you take the collar from her neck."

And with that, Searcher turned and followed the Forever Walkers as they disappeared into the heat haze.

Moments later a green-and-white Jimmy sped up the Sagebrush Creek track and skidded to a stop. Manning Dobbs jumped out. He reeled in shock at the sight of the three bodies and me still holding the movie star's gun.

"You're not going to shoot me too, are you?"

"I didn't kill Hammond. Mikey Staz did. He and the hitter with the rifle were going to shoot me next. They're the ones who killed Jump Diggins. They did it under orders from Ray Guzik to scare Paul Waiterock into handing him a piece of the Aces Wild. He also ordered them to kill Hammond and me to scare the owners of the gold mine into giving him a share in it."

I fished the spent .30-caliber slug from my coin pocket. "Hammond admitted he stole the slugs from the evidence room as insurance against Ray. Here, take this. I found it in Ruby's hipbone. It'll match the M1 over there. They're the evidence you need to solve Diggins' murder and the two men who were killed in Las Vegas."

Dobbs couldn't take his eyes off Hammond. I plucked my sidearm from the dead man's grip.

"Bull Hammond can't hurt your mother anymore and he can't hurt you either. You're both free of him. Stu is too."

He was still stunned. I snapped my fingers. "Chief Deputy! We need to roll out."

"But I can't leave his body out here. The others either. It's a crime scene and I need to process it."

"Ray is going to kill Waiterock to get the rest of the Aces Wild. You're a lawman. Your job is to protect the living and arrest the criminals. I'll help you load Mikey and the rifleman into their car and Hammond into his rig. That'll protect them from scavengers until you come back with the coroner. Put their guns in your rig. Secure the evidence."

Dobbs kept staring at Hammond. Finally, he looked up and squared his shoulders. "Okay, let's do it."

After moving the bodies and guns, we jumped in our rigs and tore down the desert roads convoy-style. When we reached blacktop, we hit full speed. My radio thrummed and I picked up the mike.

"I got patched through to the Aces Wild," Dobbs said. "Waiterock isn't there. He's at home."

"Alone?"

"The casino manager didn't know for sure, but did say he's been holding business meetings with out-of-town guests. We'll go straight to his place."

"Waiterock has a pair of armed security guards from the casino. Ray could have other soldiers with him too. It could turn into a shooting war, if it hasn't already."

"That's why I radioed for backup. Three of my deputies will rendezvous with us outside of Waiterock's ranch. I also spoke to Ron and told him what happened and about the Mi. He's faxing over an arrest warrant for Ray Guzik for conspiracy to commit the pair of murders in Las Vegas."

"To go along with the murder of Jump Diggins and Bull Hammond up here," I said. "Did you get a warrant from your Winnemucca judge for those?"

"I don't need one," he said, his voice deepening. "I have a badge."

I nodded at the radio as if he could see me acknowledge his take-charge tone. "Roger that," I said.

Three sheriff's vehicles were idling at the start of a long gravel drive that passed between two stone pillars. The iron gates were already open. Dobbs got out and gave his deputies instructions. One handed him some papers. He walked over to my rig.

"I have the warrant from Las Vegas. My deputies will follow us in. One will remain outside in case anyone tries to flee, the other two will find a back door while you and I go through the front. Do you have a problem with that?"

"Not at all."

"I didn't think you would. Bring your shotgun in case we need to make some noise to get their attention. I'll be arresting Waiterock too. Consorting with a known organized-crime figure is a violation of Nevada state gaming laws."

Dobbs walked back to his Jimmy. His posture was different.

His stride was too. I realized why. He was walking with purpose now.

Waiterock's house was a stone-and-timber mansion that shouted "I'm king of the hill." The circular drive surrounded a fountain with a statue of a horse rearing in the middle. Water spouted from its mouth. The double front door was the size of a cathedral's and unlocked. Our bootheels clacked as we walked across the foyer's marble floor.

Mutt and Jeff scrambled up from two chairs set on either side of a closed door made of oak. By the time Jeff went for the pistol clipped to his belt, Dobbs had already stuck his sidearm in his face.

"Don't," he said.

Mutt started sputtering. I stared him into silence. No doubt my 12-gauge pump helped. We took their guns, shoved the pair into a hall closet, shut the door, and tipped a chair back under the knob to secure it.

Dobbs yanked open the oak door while shouting, "Sheriff's. Nobody move," and stormed in leading with his gun. I was close behind sweeping the room with the shotgun. The two deputies soon joined us. One was the overweight middle-aged deputy who'd escorted the coroner to the gully when we brought up Jump Diggins. Remembering how he'd brownnosed Hammond, I kept an eye on him.

Waiterock and Ray were seated across from each other with a coffee table between them. Both were smoking cigars. Cutglass tumblers were set on cork coasters. Neither appeared to be particularly bothered by our entrance.

"May I help you, Deputy?" Waiterock said.

"That's Chief Deputy and Acting Sheriff Manning Dobbs," the young lawman said. "I have a warrant for Ray Guzik's arrest."

The Chicago mobster's eyes narrowed above his flattened nose. "You don't got squat."

Dobbs held the warrant up. "It's from Las Vegas PD for conspiring to murder two men there. By the time you get to the station, there'll be another warrant from a Humboldt County judge for ordering the murder of Jump Diggins and former Chief Deputy Bull Hammond."

The overweight deputy gasped and rocked back on his heels.

"I never laid a glove on nobody," Ray said. He started to get off the couch.

Dobbs leveled his pistol at him. "Deputy, handcuff this man. Check him for weapons. Read him his rights and get him out of here."

"Yes, sir," the overweight deputy said and moved a lot quicker than he had at the gully.

Ray tried putting on the brakes as he passed me. "You're dead," he growled.

"That's what Mikey and his friend said too. Turned out they were dead wrong. Two hundred percent dead."

Ray's shoulders sagged beneath his vinyl-looking brown blazer and he stopped resisting as he was hustled outside.

Waiterock still didn't show any alarm. He picked up his tumbler and sipped. "Are these theatrics really necessary? I'm confident we can work out this little misunderstanding without my having to call the attorney general."

Dobbs had yet to dip his head or relax his spine. "Paul Waiterock, owner of the Aces Wild Casino, I'm arresting you for violating Nevada gaming regulations by associating with a known organized-crime syndicate and accepting payment for a share in your casino's operations."

The young deputy snatched Waiterock's wrist, causing him to drop the tumbler. He snapped a handcuff right next to the casino owner's fancy wrist watch and yanked him to a standing position, spinning him around and cuffing his other wrist behind him.

"You're entitled to make one phone call after I book you," Dobbs said. "You want to bet your dime the attorney general will take your call from jail after the judge speaks to him first, be my guest."

The chief deputy marched Waiterock out of the mansion. I followed. He put him in the back of his Jimmy and slammed the door. Then he joined me. Water spewing from the rearing horse's mouth kerplunked in the fountain's pool.

"My investigation is going to conclude that Bull Hammond and the two Chicago mobsters killed each other in a shootout," he said. "I want to thank you for all your help, but it's time for you to go back to Harney County."

"Searcher told me asking for help is *puha*. That means power in the Paiute language," I said.

"He did? When?"

"It doesn't matter. What does is you're a good lawman. You're going to need to continue being one because Humboldt County is depending on you. Right now and when Sheriff Coons either retires or dies. Hammond didn't name names, but he made it pretty clear the people behind the gold mine are a lot more powerful than Paul Waiterock, Ray Guzik, and the Chicago Outfit. Since they're operating behind a Panama shell company, my guess is they're South American drug dealers or arms merchants laundering money."

"Then that gives Waiterock and me something to talk about on the drive back to the sheriff's office. My office."

He stuck his hand out and we shook. His grip was firm. "Say hello to Sheriff Warbler for me. Tell him from one lawman to another, I don't hold it against him for shooting my father. He was doing his job."

"I'm sure Pudge will appreciate hearing that," I said.

28

Twice on the drive home I turned off the headlights and steered by the light of the stars, confident that Tuhudda was watching, a knowing smile adding another crevice to his craggy face now residing in my memory forever. No Mountain was buttoned up tight as I passed through, but when I turned off the blacktop to the Warbler ranch, I stopped short of crossing the cattle guard.

I sat in the idling pickup and stared at the hoof-wide gaps between the metal rails. Since leaving Winnemucca, I hadn't dwelled on the two lives I'd taken. Instead, I focused on the lives I'd saved: Gemma's, Hattie's, Searcher's, my own, and who knew how many others Mikey and heh-heh man might've gone on to murder. Still, killing wasn't an easy thing to forget, no matter how justified. Though Searcher had told me the two hitmen were destined to spend eternity wandering through the under-world, I knew the only way to make sure they never reappeared in my life was not to second-guess what I'd done. I replayed what went down for the last time and then clattered across the cattle guard without looking back, confident guilt would never follow.

The floorboards of the front porch didn't creak and the hinges on the door didn't squeak as I let myself in. I went straight to Hattie's room. Starlight poured through the window and illuminated her face. I took in the scene and wrapped myself in the warm embrace of childhood innocence. The stars also illuminated a big ball of fur at her feet. A wet black nose sniffed the air and a tail thumped in recognition of my scent.

"Good boy," I whispered to Jake. I checked his wound and gave him a pat. Then I kissed my little darling on the forehead. "Sweet dreams. We'll go riding in the morning."

Light showed beneath the door to Pudge's home office. The old lawman was stretched out on the couch, a sheaf of papers clasped to his chest. His snores became a snort and his eyes blinked open. "What time is it?"

"Late," I said. "I saw your light was on."

"Paperwork's a stronger nightcap than whisky." He sat up. "Everything in Nevada get straightened out?"

"Manning Dobbs knows who killed Jump Diggins now and two men are sitting in his jail. He sends his regards, not from a son to a man who shot his father, but from one dedicated lawman to another."

"Sounds like he growed up some. And Searcher, you get him sprung?"

"He did that himself. Here, you'd better take this." I handed him Amber's Beretta.

The sheriff sniffed the air like Jake did. He tipped up the gun's barrel and checked the chamber and also the magazine. "I suppose why it's got a smell of fresh gunpowder and four rounds are missing has to do with catching the prospector's killer and the two men in jail."

"The only thing I'll ever say on the matter is, the rounds may be missing, but they didn't miss."

His eyebrows arched. "Okay, son, then the only thing I'll ever say is something the sheriff I served under when I shot Reggie Dobbs told me. Outlaws and lawmen live by the gun and can both die by the gun. The job is making sure it's the outlaw who dies first."

I held his stare and then said, "Are you making any headway with the Wyatt Clark investigation?"

"Butting heads, more than anything. First with Fellows and now the producer. They don't appear particularly upset that a member of their company is dead, not even when I told them he was murdered."

Pudge locked the pocket pistol in his gun cabinet and then sat down in his swivel desk chair. "You know what Wassenberg told me? He said they're going full steam ahead to get the film shot and edited. They want to have it released and showing in a movie house by Christmas. That way it'll qualify for next year's Oscars. Wassenberg says the field's wide open for it to win Best Picture because their only competition is the second *Godfather* movie, and since the first one already won the prize, he's convinced lightning can't strike twice."

I remained standing, glad to be stretching my legs after the drive. "I checked in on Hattie. The dog was asleep on her bed."

"She's taken to him, that's for sure. I'm not looking forward to seeing my granddaughter get her heart broke when the movie folks take him back."

"I was thinking that too, but then I started thinking about something else. The timing of his injury and where he was."

"Early morning in the stable at the Crossed Bars on the same day Clark rode the Pegasus. Yep, I've been thinking the same thing. Why I've been poking around over there. It's where they kept all their tack, his saddle included. I got a hunch Jake got caught crosswise by the person taking a blade to Clark's cinch that morning."

"The blade. There's something about the way Jake was cut

that doesn't set right. If it had been me and I was fending off a big lunging dog, I'd have stabbed him, not slashed at him. Better chance of putting him down before his teeth sunk into my throat."

"Once again we're thinking alike. There is something about the dog's wound. Gemma picked up on it when she was stitching him. She told me later. It's not thick like it'd been done by a knife. Made her think the blade was thin, more along the lines of a scalpel or a straight razor."

"If it wasn't a robber, then it had to have been someone on the film crew. Any suspects?"

"Plenty to choose from. Turns out Clark rubbed a lot of people wrong. The cast, fellow stuntmen, the wardrobe folks, the assistant directors. He was quick with the insult, quick to blame people, and quick to boil over. Orville and me have talked with them all. The only thing we've learned is the actors aren't the only ones who can turn the drama on and off at the push of a button. The whole lot does, right down to the crew preparing the meals and the guys pounding nails on the sets. It's like everyone's auditioning, hoping to get discovered and win a big part."

"Did you question Loq and Dani?"

"Of course. Both came right out and admitted they hated Clark's guts, but they had alibis the morning Jake got cut. They spent the night at the Rocking H with that pinto Loq painted and had breakfast with Blaine and his cowhands first thing in the morning."

"If Loq wanted to kill Wyatt, he wouldn't have launched a sneak attack. It would've been a full-out assault for all to see and he wouldn't have run and hid afterward."

"Loq being a leatherneck like me, I reckon you're right. So, yep, plenty of people didn't like Clark, but whoever killed him had a bigger reason than nursing hurt feelings over something he said or did."

"What makes you say that?"

"Miss Amber."

"I remember her saying Clark's always looked out for her."

"They go back a ways. Worked on a few movies together. Nothing romantic between them, more like a big brother looking after his little sister."

"Did she tell you that?"

"She did."

"Dani told me the two lived in different worlds, that movie stars and stuntmen aren't supposed to mix."

"Maybe so, but Miss Amber was mighty upset when she got the news of his death. I'm the one who broke it to her."

"Not Fellows?"

Pudge's crowfeet hopped. "You could candy that man from head to toe and he'd still be a sour apple. He blows that burning tire of a stogie in my face one more time, I'll sic Smokey the Bear on him."

"How did she take the news?"

"The way you'd expect a person who loses someone who always lent a shoulder for her to cry on. Sure, she's sad and gonna miss him, all right, but she's also scared she doesn't have him to stand between her and the person who's making her life miserable and charging her for the courtesy."

"Does this have to do with what you said about being on the job when you're around her?"

"It does, and although I never like to show my hand while there's still cards in the deck, I could use a fresh pair of eyes. Ears too."

"Asking is *puha*," I muttered.

"What?"

"It's something Searcher said that seems to keep coming around. Okay, deal me in. How can I help?"

"Being able to hear myself talk it through is a start." The

swivel chair creaked when Pudge leaned back. "I got roped into it the very first day I met her."

The old lawman told me how he'd been notified that the movie company had rented the Crossed Bars Ranch and would be filming in Harney County. When the cast and crew arrived, Pudge was invited over to discuss security. Amber Russell sought him out afterward. She started off by telling him he reminded her of a famous actor she once co-starred with, an older gentleman she greatly admired who'd helped her with her career. It was the movie Bobbie Dobbs was watching when I was at her house.

The movie star said she was glad Pudge was going to be around during the shoot and hoped she could rely on him. After that, every time he came to the Crossed Bars or to a location, she sought him out. When he called her Miss Russell, she told him to call her Amber. He settled on Miss Amber. Little by little, she told him how she was the target of a blackmailer who was threatening to expose something she'd done years before unless she paid up.

"What was it?" I said.

"Miss Amber has never come right out and told me exactly what. Embarrassed and ashamed, I expect. She's got her pride. All she says is it's something she did before she was a star and nobody got hurt, but if news of it came out now, fans would turn on her, Hollywood would dump her, and her career would be over."

"Do you believe her?"

"I didn't at first. I thought it was some kind of cat-and-mouse game she was playing at my expense. You know, big city celebrity toys with a small-town lawman to get him to make a fool of himself so when she goes back home she can gets yucks at a cocktail party telling everybody about it. But after a while, my gut started telling me her shame was real.

Especially after she took a shot at Dani. It was more than a cat fight. Dani didn't say anything that deserved getting shot at, it was that Miss Amber was that much on edge." His chair swiveled.

"I told her to have her bank fax me copies of her bank statements, which it did. On the first of every month for the past six months Miss Amber's been going to the bank and withdrawing ten thousand dollars in cash. She told me she mails the money to a post office box in Los Angeles."

"For her to do that, the blackmailer must have shown her some proof of what he's holding over her. Did he telephone her, send her a letter, or show up at her door?"

"It's all been done by letter. Typed. No handwriting. And whatever the proof he showed her was, she won't say. Though I do got my suspicions."

"Like what?"

"Seeing that Miss Amber gets red in the face or all teary eyed every time she mentions it, then it must be something of a personal nature. You know, romantic. Like, a marriage certificate showing she'd been a teenage bride and got a quickie divorce or a birth certificate of a child she had out of wedlock and put up for adoption or photos of her having an affair with a married man. The sort of thing they write about in the gossip magazines they got at the beauty parlor for reading under the hairdryer."

"And Wyatt knew about it?"

"Miss Amber told him at the git go and he even got a bead on who it might be. Before they came to Harney, Clark had been staking out the PO box where she was sending the blackmail money. Like he was some kind of private eye in a movie he was stunt doubling in. He never saw anybody open it the times he was there, but he did talk to the woman who had the box next to it. She was getting her mail one time and he asked her if she'd ever seen her neighbor. Turns out she had and described him.

Right away, Clark knew it had to be somebody in the movie business."

"What made him think that?"

"The woman said the man stuck out because he was wearing makeup and a wig. She could tell because she wore one herself. She's got the cancer and lost her hair from treatments. Clark reminded Miss Amber that everybody working on films has access to wigs, makeup, and costumes and can make themself a disguise."

I glanced around his office. In addition to the desk, couch, and gun cabinet, there were shelves lined with books, a photograph of his late wife, and an oil painting of two faceless cowboys riding in front of Steens Mountain. It was a manly room and the old lawman wore it as easily and comfortably as he did his short-brim Stetson, uniform, and holstered .45.

"That settles it. The blackmailer has to be one of the cast or crew," I said. "Sounds like Wyatt must've zeroed in on the who while they were here and when he got too close . . ." I slashed the air with my hand. "The killer staged it to look like an accident."

"Kind of reads like a movie script, doesn't it?"

"I take it Amber doesn't know who Wyatt suspected."

"He kept her in the dark. Either he was waiting until he got a confession or to protect her in case he was wrong. Problem is, the blackmailer got the jump on Clark before he could tell her." Pudge leaned forward. "I'm not sure hearing myself is helping me come up with a way to solve it. Any ideas?"

"We need to find the blade that was used. If it's something other than a knife, it might be easier to connect to a person. You know, a scalpel to a doctor, a straight razor to a barber. We could also step up the pressure to try and flush the killer."

"As long as it doesn't lead to another killing."

"What about the film they were shooting of Dani and Wyatt

mounting up before the stampede? The killer could've been there to make sure the cut cinch hadn't gotten noticed before Wyatt galloped off. Have you watched it?"

"Not yet. They ran out of chemicals to process it and had to ship in a new batch that got here this afternoon. The film's supposed to be ready for a looksee tomorrow. You want to come along?"

"Sure, right after I take Hattie out riding."

We said goodnight. I walked down the hall and took off my boots before opening the bedroom door so as not to wake Gemma. I should've known she wouldn't be asleep.

"Whatever happened in Winnemucca must've been bad to make you stop and tell Pudge about it before coming to bed," she said.

"He was my second stop. Hattie was the first. Has that dog gotten off her bed since I left?"

"Only to go out and do his business."

"I promised Hattie I'd take her riding in the morning."

"You woke her up?"

I shook my head. "Do you want to go with us?"

Though I hadn't turned on the bedroom light, I could see starlight in Gemma's eyes. "You're working awfully hard not telling me what happened in Nevada," she said.

"I'll tell you what I told your father. Manning Dobbs knows who killed Jump Diggins, has two men in jail, and Searcher walked free. Mostly I figured out casinos, gold mines, and I don't mix. I don't want to live anywhere near them. I like living right here." I finished undressing and climbed into bed.

"How come?"

"Nicer people, fresher air, and prettier scenery." I pulled the blankets up and pulled her close. "And there's you, of course."

"What about me?"

"You're even nicer, smell fresher, and are more beautiful too."

Gemma punched me in the shoulder. "You told that to Pudge?"

"He doesn't smell that fresh."

She laughed.

"We talked about how he's investigating Wyatt's death. We agree that whoever cut the cinch cut Jake. He asked me if I had any ideas."

"Do you?"

"None that he hadn't already thought of. He needs to find the weapon and a witness, and that's going to be hard since the only witness may be a camera that may or may not have filmed the culprit checking on the cut cinch before Wyatt saddled up."

"Better is a live witness who saw the killer cut Jake and the cinch."

"But there isn't one. The dog trainer got there too late and no one else has come forward."

Gemma harumphed. "And you two call yourself lawmen. Aren't you forgetting someone?"

"Who?"

"Jake."

"If only the dog could talk."

"Who says he can't?"

29

Hattie jumped on our bed at dawn. "Wake up, sleepyheads. Time to go riding."

"Too early," I said.

"Is not." She jumped up and down.

"You said you didn't wake her last night," Gemma mumbled, her face half-buried in a pillow.

"I didn't."

"Then how does she know you promised to take her this morning?"

"I dreamt Daddy told me," Hattie said. "*Mu'a* told me to believe my dreams."

"She did, did she?" I said.

"Uh-huh. *Mu'a* said I can see and do things in them too."

"Like what?"

"See Shell Flower and ride her whenever I want." Hattie jumped up and down again. "Come on, let's go."

I traced Gemma's unburied eyebrow with my fingertip. "Our little girl is getting quite the education."

"The same as November gave me when I was about her age."

"Is she still at the Will camp?"

"Yes, but Nagah is bringing her home this morning. He and I have rounds to make."

"Then we'd better get a move on if we're going for that ride."

"Yippee ki-yay," Hattie shouted.

I saddled Wovoka and Sarah while Gemma made a thermos of coffee and put it in a saddlebag along with a tin of biscuits and jar of apple butter that November and Hattie had preserved last fall. The sun was still behind the Stinkingwater Mountains when we set off, but a soft palette of pinks, roses, and yellows was already brushing the sky. Wovoka, sensing he was carrying precious cargo with Hattie sitting in front of me, didn't try to match Sarah's high-spirited pace as he usually did.

We crossed the dirt airstrip and followed the trail to the top of the rise that gave us a view of the ranch, town, and Steens Mountain to the south. It was not dream world and not spirit world, it was our world. Gemma dismounted and spread out a picnic blanket. I got off Wovoka and gave Hattie a flying merry-go-round ride when I lowered her from the horse. After setting her down, she wobbled to the blanket and collapsed.

"I like dizzy," she giggled.

While the pair of cutting horses grazed, we sat on the blanket and ate biscuits slathered in apple butter. I poured coffee into two enamel mugs and handed Gemma hers. When Hattie finished eating, she skipped off to pick stalks of lupine and paintbrush that inked the desert floor in blues and reds.

"We have it all, don't we?" Gemma said as we watched her.

"I'll say."

"And we'll never let anything happen to it, will we?"

"Of course not."

"Especially not to Hattie."

I grew guarded. "What makes you say that?"

Gemma drank some coffee. "You left your clothes on the chair when you came home last night. When I was picking them up this morning, I found the snapshot of Hattie and me in the pocket of your shirt. It has smudges on it. Why did you unclip it from the visor?"

"I wanted to keep it close to me."

"Is that the only reason?"

"It's the only one that counts."

"And whatever happened in Nevada that you won't tell me about, is it going to come back at us?"

"Not a chance."

"What about coming back to haunt you like Vietnam did?"

"It won't."

"Because I could help you deal with flashbacks then, but Hattie wouldn't understand what you were going through if that happened to you now. She's too young."

"You don't have to worry."

"Of course I worry. I worry that you might get in a situation and start thinking too much about what it might mean to Hattie and me, and second-guess yourself and not do what needed doing." Her eyes bore into me. "I know when Pudge went after Reggie Dobbs all those years ago, he had to put my mother and me out of his mind. He's had to do it time and again. It goes with the territory."

I leaned toward her and traced her eyebrow again. "You know what I see? I see you. I see our little girl picking wildflowers. Our ranch down there. Our town over there. All our friends living around here. I see all of that even when I'm not looking at it. I'll never second-guess loving it and I'll never second-guess defending it."

"Good, because I won't let you."

We put our coffee mugs down and kissed. The kiss turned into a long embrace and we fell onto the blanket like a couple of puppy-love-stricken teenagers. Flower petals started to rain on our faces. Hattie was plucking and sprinkling them from a handful of lupine and paintbrush, her smile wider and even more beautiful than the high lonesome that surrounded us.

We packed up and headed back. Hattie held the reins and guided Wovoka for home. Once again, the stallion was acting like he knew how important his littlest rider was. Halfway down the trail, I could see Tuhudda's rusty old sedan with the missing trunk lid parked out front of the house. Nagah had taken over driving his grandfather's junker when Gemma hired him to be her assistant.

"*Mu'a* is home," I said. "Nagah gave her a lift."

"And there's Grandpa," Hattie said. "He runs funny."

One glance at the old lawman fast-stepping toward his pickup with a Winchester in hand told me all I needed to know. I grabbed the reins from Hattie, threw an arm around her, and clicked my cheek. "Go, boy."

Wovoka surged into a gallop with Hattie shrieking, "Faster! Faster!"

We flew down the rest of the trail, across the airstrip, and past the stable and corral. I reined to a stop when we reached Pudge. He had the door open and was putting the lever-action rifle in the gunrack.

"What is it?" I said.

He eyed Hattie before saying, "Another one at the Crossed Bars. I just got the call."

"I'll go with you."

Before I could dismount, Nagah was beside us and reaching up to take Hattie. "Come, little sister. Let's go ask *Mu'a* if she will make us frybread."

Gemma rode up. "What's all the fuss?"

Her father hitched his gun belt. "It's the one who wears all the silk neckerchiefs. Only the one he tied around his neck this morning couldn't stop the blade that was used on Jake and the cinch."

"Tommy Briscoe? Oh no!"

"Orville's going to meet me there."

"I'll take my rig and be right behind you," I said.

Pudge fired his up and aimed for the blacktop.

I looked at Gemma. She touched the corner of her eye. "What we talked about."

I drove so fast over the cattle guard that I didn't feel the bumps or hear the clatter. Pudge was already passing through No Mountain when I caught up to him. He had the lights and sirens on and didn't care if anyone called Bonnie LaRue with a press tip that the sheriff was racing to where all the movie stars were staying.

We zoomed beneath the crossed timbers that marked the entrance to the ranch, our rigs creating double rainbows of dust.

"Orville will be here in a few minutes," Pudge said when we got out in front of the main house.

"The killer could still be here," I said. "How do you want to play it?"

"Let's have a looksee first and then start asking questions. Maybe we can flush him. Keep your eyes open. He might have more than a sharp edge for a weapon. Not all the guns here are props. Miss Amber had a live one and Clark did too."

Tommy was crumpled in the center of the barn's nave. His face was white as a summer cloud and it was hard to tell if his silk scarf was paisley, polka dot, or solid red. The ground on either side of his head was darker and wetter than the rest of the earthen floor. A few people were huddled in groups. I recognized walkie-talkie woman and clipboard man. She was ashen and he looked as green as when he puked after seeing the stuntman fly off his horse. Not John Fellows. His eyes were fixed on his murdered assistant, the anger in them glowing as bright as the tip of his cheroot.

"I sent him to fetch the dailies and this happens." He raised his stubbly chin at us. "He's my first wife's little brother. She badgered me to hire him. I haven't seen her since she moved back to England five years ago and now I got to call and tell her this. What time is it in London, anyway?"

Pudge took his short-brim Stetson off and held it at his side. "Losing folks is hard, especially when they're kin. You have my condolences."

"Whoever did this isn't going to get away with it."

"What time was it when you sent Mr. Briscoe on his errand?"

"Eight a.m. He brought me coffee and today's shooting schedule like he does every morning. I asked him to check on the footage of the stampede you wanted to see. When he didn't come back, I came looking for him."

I glanced at my field watch. Tommy had been alive less than an hour ago.

Pudge asked Fellows if he tried to give him first aid.

"What for? It was clear he was as dead as the heaps of KIA I stormed past at Pork Chop Hill. I went back outside and yelled for help."

"Then what?"

"Lubik was passing by and I told him to call you."

"Lubik being who?'

"My cinematographer."

"He here?"

Fellows backhanded at two men standing together. "Over there."

"The one with the tinted glasses and soul patch," I said.

Pudge glanced over. "I'll talk to him later." Then he asked Fellows what he did after sounding the alarm.

"I came back in here. Even though his sister and I divorced years ago, it didn't feel right leaving him alone."

The sheriff put his Stetson back on. "I'd be obliged if you stayed put while I take a gander at him."

I joined Pudge as he circled the body, studying the ground before stopping at the dead man's feet. He crouched and examined the soles of his shoes. Then he moved forward and looked at each hand. He picked up the right and turned it over to examine the knuckles and fingernails. He did the same to the left.

"Which handed is he?" he called to Fellows.

"Right."

Pudge examined the neck wound next. The cut was straight across, closer to his chin than his clavicle to avoid the scarf. The external jugular veins on both sides were sliced clean through.

Orville Nelson rolled into the barn with a bulky evidence kit balanced on his lap. "Sheriff's Deputy coming through. Move aside."

Pudge brushed his palms off on the side of his pants. "Mr. Briscoe wasn't dragged in here and he wasn't running away when he was killed either. No scuff marks," he said in a low voice. "His attacker took him from behind, cupped his chin, held it up to be out of the way as he pulled a blade straight across his throat. Let him drop right then and there. No skin under his fingernails that says he tried to fight it, no scrapes on his knuckles showing he fought his attacker beforehand. By the time he knew what was happening he was already dead."

"I'll bag his hands anyway," Orville said. "Then I'll search for hair and fibers. The coroner is on his way and will collect the body for a full autopsy. Any idea of why he was killed in here?"

"He must've seen something or the killer thought he did," I said.

"The way his body dropped, he was leaving, not coming," Pudge said. "And being here in the middle of the barn, it wasn't like someone jumped up and surprised him. He must've been talking with the killer and knew him well enough that he wasn't afraid to turn his back on him."

"Does it strike you as curious the killer didn't try to hide the body?" I said.

"It does. Must've been interrupted. Maybe he heard Fellows coming and snuck out the back. Let's go talk to him some more. Keep an eye out for anyone who's trying to get an earful. Might be they're more than curious. Might be they're wondering if they'll hear a reason to make a run for it."

When we reached him, Fellows said, "Who'd want to kill Tommy? He may have been an arrogant little twit, but not enough to drive someone to do this. All he was doing was what I asked him to do."

"You keep all the film you shoot in here?" Pudge said.

"That's right. We use the barn for film storage and processing the raw footage into dailies. It's naturally cool and dark. Plus, there's a storeroom in the corner with running water. I had the set builders convert it into a darkroom for developing the film negatives and printing the positives. It's big enough to handle all the film rolls, chemical tanks, rollers, printer, and drying oven."

"What do you do with the film once it's processed?" Pudge asked.

"In the old days, I'd watch the dailies raw, but on this project I'm using multiple cameras and going through film by the mile and so I make a rough edit first to get rid of junk footage and see what I got. The film is cut and spliced and then synched to sound for viewing. Ask me a couple of years from now and it'll be completely different. Video's going to take over film as soon as they make it good enough. Some say everything will be digital, whatever the hell that means. I don't look forward to that day. I grew up with film. Love the look of it, the sound of it, the feel of it. Hell, I know it better than any of my wives."

"Cut and spliced?" Pudge said. "How's that done?"

"There's a station set up next to the darkroom. It's basically a couple of tables with equipment on them for viewing the processed film. The location film editor cuts the outtakes. Those are underexposed frames or pre-action footage or takes that I had to reshoot. Then he runs it through a film tape splicer. Here on location he uses an old Rivas for the cutting and taping. It's a portable model operated by hand. Everything here is done rough. The real magic takes place in post-production back at the studio where I have the very latest equipment I need for editing, synching sound, and adding special effects along with the titles. That's the easy part. The hard part is getting it past the damn censors at the Motion Picture Association so they don't water it down."

"Let me see if I got this straight. The folks who come in here regular are the ones who develop the film and do the rough edits. How many is that?"

"There's a couple of technicians who develop the film, the editor and his assistant who do the hands-on cutting and splicing. And then there's Lubik and me. We both take a look at the raw, but I'm the final word on what gets cut and what stays. It's my film, my name on the top billing."

"I'm gonna want to talk to all those folks you mentioned."

"Of course. My assistant will get you a list—" Fellows stopped himself and then glanced at Tommy's body. "I don't know what I'm going to do without him. Poor kid."

"What about the cast?" Pudge said. "The actors and actresses ever come in here to see what you shot? Stuntmen, doubles?"

"Some do, some don't. Some like to watch the dailies of the scenes they were in for helping stay in character for the next day's shoot or they're plain in love with seeing themselves. Others could care less. I know an actor who never watches the feature films he stars in, much less views the dailies. Once he's in character, he doesn't want to get out of it, and seeing a daily would do that. He goes so far as to never get out of costume either and makes everyone on set call him by his character's name. Once the movie's completed, he doesn't watch it because he never wants to see that character again. He buries him so he won't show up in his next role. It must work for him because he's won Best Actor twice."

"Garth Scott, Amber Russell, and Dani Reyna, they all look at their dailies?"

"They do."

"What about Wyatt Clark?"

The cheroot bobbed up and down. "Wyatt was always searching for a way to make a stunt look even better."

"I'm also gonna need a list of where everyone was this morning. Say, from seven a.m. to right now. No one touches anything in the barn either until I say so. And my previous order of no one leaving Harney County sticks."

Fellows flicked an ash from his cheroot. "What about Tommy?"

"Coroner's on his way. Now, before I begin talking with folks, I need to view the film you sent Mr. Briscoe to fetch."

"When?"

"Right now."

30

J ohn Fellows scratched his stubble and then barked orders. He told walkie-talkie woman to make a list with everybody's name on it and where they were that morning.

"If they were at breakfast, I want to know what they ate," he growled. "If they were still in bed, I want to know who with." He pointed to Lubik and the other man. "You two stay. Everybody else, vamoose."

Orville continued with his evidence collection. His camera's flash bloomed like white carnations inside the gloomy barn. Pudge and I followed Fellows and the others to the editing station. The man with Lubik was introduced as the location film editor.

"Run the footage the techs processed last night," Fellows said.

The editor threaded a reel into a machine and the tiny monitor it was connected to flickered to life with a long shot of Dani galloping. The contrast of her dressed all in black atop a white mare set against the stark backdrop of the high lonesome was stunning and I felt myself tense at how fast she was riding even though I knew she wasn't going to get hurt. The mare's tail streamed straight out and her hooves flew over the ground.

The tension built when Wyatt galloped into the frame astride a black stallion. He was riding full tilt too, thundering across the rough terrain, the gap between him and Dani narrowing with each piston-like pounding of his horse's powerful legs. Wyatt rode leaning forward, the reins in one hand, his six-shooter in the other. The camera captured the velocity of his ride by showing the front brim of his cowboy hat pushed up against the crown.

I braced myself when the stuntman rode right in front of the camera and abruptly went airborne. His boots left the stirrups and his hands clawed the air trying to grab hold of something that wasn't there. When he hit the ground and his head smacked against the rock, Lubik exhaled loudly. "Real American tragedy."

The camera kept rolling as I rode into view and clipboard man and walkie-talkie woman yelled at me to get out of the scene and I yelled back that Wyatt was dead and they ran over and she signaled to kill the camera.

"Helluva thing to see and one helluva action scene," Fellows said as the little screen faded to black. "I'm definitely going to use it to honor Wyatt. I'll do whatever it takes to get it past those lily-livered MPA censors."

Pudge said, "That there, what we watched, has it been cut and spliced?"

The film editor answered no. "It's raw footage from start to finish. I didn't touch it because it's very dramatic. I've worked with John on his last three films. I knew he'd want to use it."

"Let's see the bit before that, any film that shows the two riders before and after they mount up."

"It was shot by another camera. I'll need to change reels."

The monitor came to life again. The first frames were of the ground. Then the camera was raised and focused. No sound played. Several people milled in and out of frame. The camera paused on a woman touching up Dani's makeup and the focus was sharpened. Dani stuck out her tongue at the camera. Next, a man and Lubik came into view. They were pointing at the horizon. I recognized it as the direction where the two riders would intercept the stampede.

"That's my second-unit director," Fellows said. "Westerns are in his blood. He interned on *Little Big Man* and Robert Altman hired him for *McCabe and Mrs. Miller*. He's written a screenplay about an aging gunfighter. John Wayne would be perfect for the part if he can be talked into playing something other than a white hat."

"I've always liked the Duke," Pudge said. "Especially the movies where he's courting and sparking with Maureen O'Hara. She has that red hair and the temperament to match." He turned to Lubik. "What were you two talking about?"

The cinematographer ran his finger over his soul patch. "I tell him where other camera. How make light stay same. One sequence, two location of sun, two camera. Difficult."

The footage became herky-jerky as the camera was repositioned again. It caught the white mare and black stallion being led out of a trailer for a second or two. While the shot was cock-eyed, I could see both were unsaddled. Black screen flashed and then the camera zeroed in on the second-unit director giving instructions to Dani and Wyatt. He was using his hands to mime horses galloping and the gap between them narrowing. Wyatt wore a bored expression. Dani was breathing in and out as if doing a transcendental meditation exercise.

"He's giving them final direction," Fellows said. "He uses my technique. Tell them to visualize the action beforehand so it unfolds like the way they saw it, to dig deep into their souls and relive a time when they were fearful and hateful. Do that, it'll come out on screen."

Black flashed again and then sound came on as a young woman holding a clapperboard stepped in front of the camera and read aloud the scene and take. A voice off-camera said, "Ready and action."

The monitor filled with Dani's face. She was frightened and furious and then looked over her shoulder. The camera pulled back to reveal she was already in the saddle. "Bastard!" she cried and her arm came down and she whipped the white mare's haunch with the leather quirt. The horse shot directly at the camera and then passed it by. The camera swiveled and tracked horse and rider as they galloped away. Dani looked back over her shoulder again. The screen filled with her face. Her teeth flashed as she cried, "I'll kill you!" and whipped the horse again.

The camera swung back and zeroed in on Wyatt. He had one boot in the stirrup and was making a show of getting on the skittish black stallion. The horse took off with Clark swinging aboard and the camera tracked them as they galloped after Dani. The stuntman never looked back. The two riders grew smaller and smaller and then the monitor faded to black.

"That it?" Pudge said.

"It's actually quite a lot," Fellows said. "By the time it gets edited, run time will be ten seconds, twenty tops. The money shots are Dani's face, her yelling at the rancher who tried to rape her, and her whip coming down. Every man in the audience will feel its sting on his backside."

The old lawman sucked a tooth before saying, "And those black spots, what caused them?"

"They're cuts and splices," Fellows said. He motioned to the film editor. "You cleaned up the raw on this one."

"I had to. There was a ton of garbage. The cameraman pulled the trigger too early and didn't turn it off even when he was repositioning. So much for a twenty-to-one ratio. He blew through a lot of film."

"What's that mean, the ratio?" Pudge said.

"Minutes of film shot to minutes on screen," Fellows said. "The average filmmaker uses one minute for every twenty minutes he shoots. That's why their films are *average*. I shoot as much as it takes and damn the bean counters. They won't complain when a naked gold man is perched on Morty Wassenberg's desk."

I asked him what they did with the film they cut.

"We keep it. I've found diamonds in the rough before."

"Where?"

"It gets rolled back onto reels, labeled, and sent back to the studio with the good stuff. All except for little scraps. They go in the dustbin."

I flashed on the three dumpsters back in Winnemucca and wondered if I'd find a map to the killer when I combed through the barn's trashcan.

"I didn't see you in any of that footage," Pudge said to Fellows. "Weren't you there?"

The director reached under his poncho, pulled out a fresh cheroot, but didn't light it. "I was, but early on and only long enough to confer with my assistant director. I had to get over to Bone Ravine with the first unit where the real money shots were going to be had."

"But you were there," Pudge said, chinning at Lubik. "You're on film."

"Yes."

"Did you check on all the camera locations or only that one?"

"All. My job."

"How do you get from location to location?"

"Real American Jeep. Same as Fellows. Only faster." His soul patch spread as he grinned.

"You direct the cameras, does that mean you cut and splice what they shoot?"

"No. I pick best shot. He do rest." Lubik pointed at the film editor.

Pudge asked him if he was at the location too. The editor shook his head. "Why not?"

"Too many cooks in the kitchen as it is," he said without looking at Fellows and Lubik.

Pudge turned to the director. "How many folks do you reckon were up there total?"

"At the second-unit location? I'd say a dozen. In addition to the unit director and actors, there are grips, lighting, sound, makeup, props, and the wrangler who hauled up the horse trailer. The production manager will have a complete list of names. Got to keep track of everyone's hours. Guild rules."

"Okay, I need to talk to each one to find out if anyone saw what I'm looking for."

"What's that?"

"Evidence." Pudge counted on his fingers. "Let's see, that list will include the second-unit director who loves Westerns, Miss Reyna, Clark, only I can't talk to him, can I? The folks working behind the scenes. Am I missing anyone?"

Fellows said, "Garth and Amber. They drove over while I was there."

"What for? They weren't in the scene, were they?"

"No, but Amber is married to the rancher who tried to rape Dani and she's in love with Garth. She winds up killing her husband. Amber wanted to use what he does to Dani as motivation for hating him even more."

"Are you talking about Miss Amber the real person or her character? And is it Miss Reyna or her character? Same with Clark. Was it him the stuntman or the bad guy husband he was doubling for? I forget the name of the actor who plays him. All I know he's a ringer when it comes to playing horseshoes."

Fellows chomped his unlit cheroot in annoyance. "Their characters, obviously."

"The reason I ask is, you said you get actors to forget they're actors and become their characters and use something from their past to work up fear and hate. Maybe when they're doing all that, they mistake the person they're pretending to want to kill for who they really hate." The wily old lawman let it sit.

Fellows didn't answer. Lubik chortled.

Pudge turned his gaze on the cinematographer. "What about you? Did you see Miss Amber and Mr. Scott there?"

"Yes."

"Did they leave before or after you?"

"Don't know. Only think next shot."

"And this morning, Fellows said you were walking by the barn when he called for help and you went and called my office. Where were you coming from and where were you going?"

"My room to breakfast. You want know what I ate?"

"I reckon you didn't eat anything. You made the call and then came back to the barn to see what was up, right?"

"You smart sheriff. Real smart."

"When was the last time you were in the barn here? You know, to look at the film that was shot?"

"Last night. You got question. I answer. Simple "

"As Simon," Pudge said. "I got a lot more, but we'll talk later. Right now I gotta talk to a man about a horse."

31

The old lawman strode out of the barn. He paused briefly as he passed a sheet-draped body on a gurney being loaded into the back of a paneled van.

"Got everything you need?" Pudge said to the rumpled county coroner.

"I came for a corpse and wind up getting handed a couple of pieces of evidence from Orville along with his new-fangled notions of what they mean." He held up two plastic baggies. "Your deputy's going to do me out of a job before I have a chance to retire."

"If he doesn't do me first," Pudge said.

A Ford half-ton with a US Fish and Wildlife decal on the door was parked across the drive. Loq was leaning against a horse trailer hitched to it. As we walked toward him, Pudge said, "I radioed your partner on the way here. Asked him to bring Clark's horse from the Rocking H where he's been stabled since the stampede."

"I remember Loq and Dani leading him back," I said.

"Loq saw him chasing after Miss Reyna's mare. With no rider aboard, he knew something was wrong and rode that pinto he'd painted straight into the stampede. Grabbed the stallion's reins before the panicky beeves shoved him into Bone Ravine."

When we reached him, Loq said, "Did you find the bighorn?"

"Not yet, but I know where she's at," I said.

"But you found who killed the prospector and his *limi'lam t'shíshap.*"

"Who told you that?"

"You wouldn't be here if you hadn't. I knew you'd catch the killer. It's why I didn't go to Nevada. You already had all the help you needed."

"From Deputy Dobbs and Searcher," I said.

Loq looked down his high cheekbones. "Among others." I knew he meant the Forever Walkers.

Pudge said, "If you two could stop jawing for a second and start helping me get the horse out of the trailer, I can take a gander at his belly without getting stomped, kicked, or bitten."

Loq asked him why he wanted to do that.

"Because my gut woke me up early this morning like someone had tightened a cinch around it. Told me the one on Clark's saddle didn't get cut the same time Jake did."

Loq opened the doors to the trailer. The black stallion and pinto were inside.

"Why did you bring the pinto?" Pudge said.

"The pony is teaching the stallion not to forget he's a four-legged."

He waded between the two and rubbed the pinto's muzzle and said something in *Maklak*. The pinto backed out of the trailer. Loq did the same to the black stallion. The big horse balked. Loq repeated the words. This time, the stallion obliged and backed out.

We watched as Loq stroked the stallion's muzzle again and spoke more words in *Maklak*. Then he leaned against the horse's left shoulder and ran his hand down the front leg and clicked his cheek. The horse lifted his hoof. Loq grabbed hold above the pastern until the horse's knee was fully bent. Then he clicked his cheek and the horse took a three-legged step backward. Loq let go of the leg. When the horse had all four hooves back on the ground, Loq clicked his cheek again. The horse lowered his head, buckled his knees, and knelt. Then he rolled onto his side.

"Looks like the pinto isn't the only one teaching him," Pudge said. He stepped slowly toward the stallion with his palms out. "Atta boy. Let's have a gander."

He examined the horse's belly and traced a line with his finger. "Right here. He's got a scratch like he jumped over a dead cottonwood and the tip of a branch raked him. Only this particular branch made a cut as straight and sharp as a razor."

"That proves the cinch got sabotaged after he was unloaded and saddled at the second-unit location," I said.

"Looks like it, and whoever did it knew how to keep the blade from slicing even deeper into horseflesh. Somebody with a lot of experience using it." Pudge stood. "Too bad we don't have film that shows 'em in the act. All I got now is a list of who was there. Seeing that each and every one of 'em fancies themselves as an actor no matter what their job is, could be a might tricky picking out which one's pretending when they say they're not the killer."

Loq clicked his cheek again and the stallion rolled onto his back and rubbed in the dirt like a dog and then rolled back and got to his feet and shook the dust off. He let out a contented whinny.

"I got half a mind to join you," Pudge said. "I got an itch to put somebody in jail before they kill again that needs scratching."

A woman's wail rented the air. Amber ran across the yard, her untied ivory silk bathrobe billowing like a sail. She reached the van and pounded the side with the heels of her hands. "No, no, not Tommy! Please tell me it's not him."

"Oh Lord. Exactly what I don't need right now," Pudge muttered.

He went over and she buried her face in his burly chest. "It's all my fault. All of it."

Pudge patted her back. "There, there, Miss Amber. Don't you worry. I'll catch who did this."

The actress gulped for air. "You will?"

"Sure as Sunday." Pudge gently untangled himself.

Loq said to me, "Nightgown and slippers, she's only now getting out of bed?"

"Gemma told me it's in her contract. No rehearsals or close-ups in the morning. That and bottles of French sparkling water and fresh cucumbers delivered to her room that she slices and puts on her eyes to prevent wrinkles."

"I like wrinkles on a woman's face. Means she's seen a lot, knows a lot. There's a story in each one, a story that will hold you a lot longer than her arms and legs will."

"I can't argue with you there."

"If Amber's trying to hide wrinkles, maybe she's trying to hide something else."

"Maybe so. She doesn't get up early as a rule, yet she was up early enough to be at the Rocking H for the stampede shoot."

We watched as Pudge went over to Orville, said something to him, and then returned to the actress and guided her toward the wing of the ranch where the stars had rooms. Orville wheeled over to Loq and me. The pinto and black stallion eyed his chair, but didn't spook.

"What did Pudge tell you?" I said.

"That Fellows is getting a list of everyone who was with the second unit and they're all going to assemble for questioning. In the meantime, we are to return to the barn and search for evidence."

I asked what else Pudge was going to do.

"After he takes Miss Russell back to her room and gets her settled down, he is going to make some phone calls. To whom and about what, he did not tell me. He said he will meet up with us before conducting the questioning."

Loq tied the two horses to a hitching rail and we went inside the barn. No one was there. We stopped in the nave where Tommy had died. Loq crouched next to the spot, his eyes searching the ground. I asked Orville about the evidence he gave to the coroner.

His boyish face lit up. "Two things, actually. The first was stuck to the sole of the victim's shoe."

"Pudge didn't spot it? I saw him look at Tommy's feet."

"It is easily missed because it is transparent. I found it using a magnifying glass from the evidence kit."

"What is it?"

"A small piece of cellophane tape."

"Scotch tape, you mean."

"This is no ordinary kind of tape. It has perforated holes on the top and bottom."

"Like film does?"

"Precisely. I believe it is the kind used for taping two ends of film that are being spliced together. The holes in the tape are matched to those in the film and allow the spliced section to run through a projector unimpeded."

"Tommy must've gone to the editing station, saw something he wasn't supposed to see, and when he was leaving, whoever was back there, killed him to keep him from talking."

"What wasn't he supposed to see?" Loq said.

"My guess is something on the reel of film that was shot where Dani and Wyatt began their chase. Maybe it shows the person doctoring the cinch. Whatever it was, it got cut from the reel Pudge and I watched."

Loq stood. "This is a killing ground, but there's no sign of struggle. Why didn't Tommy fight back?"

"Some people go their entire lives without realizing there's always a danger of losing it."

"Then it's better he never went to Vietnam because he wouldn't have lasted a day."

I blinked away the image of Private Danbaby's face as he lay dying and asked Orville what else he found on the body.

"There were no nicotine stains on his fingers or teeth."

"Tommy wasn't a smoker, so what?"

"The back of his head smelled like tobacco smoke. I took some samples of his hair for the coroner to test."

"I'd be surprised if Tommy didn't reek of it. His boss was always chain-smoking those cheroots around him."

"There was more than the smell of smoke in his hair. I found flecks of tobacco. They could have ended up there if someone who smokes cigars or unfiltered cigarettes was standing close behind him and spit or coughed or was breathing heavily. Any of those actions would have discharged tobacco residue left on their lips or tip of their tongue."

"Let's go take a look at the darkroom and editing station. Maybe we'll get lucky and find the outtake showing the killer cutting the cinch."

32

The door to the darkroom was barely wide enough for Orville's wheelchair to pass through, but he managed without scraping his knuckles. I followed him while Loq prowled the barn. The deputy flicked a switch that bathed the room in red light. He ignored the cartons of chemicals stacked against the wall and a series of tanks filled with different solutions, and went straight to a clothesline strung across the room. Two strips of film dangled from it like a pair of black socks. He pulled one down and held it up.

I asked him what was on it. Orville pulled the second down and examined it before answering.

"The first strip is frames of a clapperboard with the movie's title *High Lonesome Showdown* on it. I believe it is a master negative they print duplicates from and splice to the beginning of each reel for identification and copyright purposes. The second is a panoramic shot of the Crossed Bars. It could be a souvenir someone is saving. Instead of postcards of places tourists have visited, locations where movie people have worked."

He reclipped the filmstrips to the clothesline and poked

around the printer and rifled through a cabinet. I searched the counters and floor.

"Cleaner than November's kitchen," I said.

"Dust is a darkroom's enemy, second only to unwanted light. There is nothing incriminating in here." Orville closed the door to the cabinet.

We exited and went to the editing station. I found a cardboard box being used as a trash can beneath one of the tables. As I emptied its contents, Orville pushed aside the chair in front of the editing equipment and scooted forward. It was a far cry from his electronics-ladened U-shaped desk back at the sheriff's office that he'd dubbed "The Bridge" in honor of the Starship *Enterprise*. It took him less than a minute before he was replaying the reel of footage shot by the second unit.

I picked through the pile of crushed soda cans and crumpled cigarette packs. The discarded film cuttings were no longer than five or six frames as measured by the four perforations on each side of a frame. All were overexposed.

Orville stopped the film reel on the scene of the white mare and black stallion being led out of the horse trailer.

"See, they haven't been saddled yet," I said.

"I was hoping we could identify who was leading them out, but all this shows are their halter ropes extending past the edge of the frame."

"It had to have been the wrangler who drove the horse trailer. He probably saddled them too."

The deputy advanced the reel frame by frame and froze it again when the monitor filled with black. He reversed and forwarded it a couple of times. "The black frame is not the end of the footage of the horses leaving the trailer but the front butt of the section that has been spliced to it. Look, when I freeze it, you can see the tape. We need to ask the editor what followed the horse trailer scene and why he decided to cut it."

"If he's the one who did."

Orville studied the projector and monitor apparatus more closely. "This is only for playing and viewing. There must be something else for doing the cutting and splicing."

"Fellows said he uses hand-operated equipment when he's on location because they're only making rough cuts for dailies. All the sophisticated equipment is in a studio back in LA."

Orville searched the table and then looked behind the monitor. He slid out a black metal object the size of the rotary-dial telephone in the old lineman's shack. "It says Rivas on it. That must be the name of the manufacturer." It had a moveable bar. The deputy raised it and pushed it back down. "This is definitely used for cutting film."

I handed him the longest scrap from the trash pile. "Give it a try."

Orville raised the bar, placed the film down on a fixed metal platform etched with guides, and then pressed the handle down. The film was sliced in two.

"Chop," I said. "Like a guillotine."

Orville studied the cutter. "The blade is removable either for sharpening or replacement purposes." He fiddled with it and then held up a two-inch-long silver blade. Light caught the razor-like edge and made it shimmer.

Loq joined us. "Attach that to a toothbrush and you have a shiv like cons use in prison." He shrugged. "I saw it in a movie."

"And I saw Jake, the cinch, and Tommy's throat. That blade's sharp enough to slice all three."

"Not this one," Orville said. "At least not the latest victim. The killer would not have had time to remove it, slit his throat, and put it back. There must be a box of replacement blades."

It didn't take long to find a carton containing new rolls of splicing tape and bottles of glue. Beneath them was a partially filled box of brand-new film-cutting blades, their sharp edges wrapped in protective sleeves.

"Maybe the film editor is the murderer," Orville said.

"It has to be someone else," I said. "He wasn't at the second-unit location when the cinch was cut that sent Wyatt flying."

"Someone who went out the back door after killing Tommy because Fellows was coming through the front," Loq said.

He gestured at the wooden slider that hung from an iron rail behind us. It screeched when I slid it open. I walked clockwise around the outside of the barn, paused at the double doors in the front, and then continued back to the open slider.

Orville asked me what I found.

"The back door doesn't line up with the front because we're in the corner here. If you're using this to reach the ranch's main building and bunkhouse, then it's shorter to walk counter-clockwise."

"What does that prove?"

"Only that if you walk the long way around like I did, no one can see you until you get to the front. And when you're there, you're walking toward the bunkhouse, not away from it."

"What exactly is your point?"

I was about to explain when Pudge hailed from across the barn. "Anybody home?"

"Back here," I said.

Orville greeted him by holding up a plastic evidence bag where he'd put the film-cutting blades. "I believe we found what the murder weapon is."

Pudge took a look. "Could be, but finding those in here doesn't mean our killer is one of the folks who works in here. Barns are never locked. Anybody could've helped themselves to one or brought a blade from home. Until we get a confession, we can't rule out another kind of weapon either."

Orville was too good of a lawman to argue or voice disappointment. "I also found tobacco residue on the back of the victim's head. It is plausible that it came from the killer as he clenched him from behind."

"Good work, but I'm afraid that doesn't narrow down the field all that much. These movie folks are walking smudge pots. It must do with them being high strung. That and all the hurry up and wait that goes along with movie making. It was one of the reasons why so many of us leathernecks took up coffin nails during the war. 'Course it didn't hurt they put a four-pack of smokes gratis of the tobacco companies in every C ration. Shipped us out as soldiers and came back as customers."

"Tommy was the exception," Orville said. "He did not smoke. I checked his fingers and teeth."

"He was particular about his appearance, I'll grant you that. What else did you boys find?"

I told him about my walk around the barn and what Lubik had said about passing by out front when Fellows discovered the body.

"Might mean something, might mean nothing," he said. "What does mean something is Fellows has rounded everyone up from the second unit and they're on their way here. I'd usually question them one at a time, but considering these folks create make-believe for a living, I figured I'd do them all at once. See what kind of performances they give and what kind of reaction they get from their coworkers who'll be their audience along with us. You three keep a lookout in case one starts acting squirrely for real."

Fellows entered the barn followed by Amber Russell, Lubik, Dani Reyna, Garth Scott, the second-unit director, and a half dozen crewmembers. They lined up in that order, careful not to step on the spot where Tommy died.

Fellows made introductions. I recognized a couple of faces

from the reel of dailies we'd been watching. Then he turned it over to Pudge.

The old lawman walked up and down the line the same way a drill instructor did inspecting a crop of new recruits. A couple people met his gaze. A couple looked away. The others remained stone-faced. Pudge took three steps back.

"I appreciate you coming in to help sort out poor Tommy Briscoe's death. I also want to offer my condolences for the loss of your friend and colleague." He waited while a few choked back tears. "I meant to everybody here but the one who put your pal Tommy in a headlock, drew a blade across his neck, and severed his jugulars. Yep, everybody's got two sets. You get 'em both slit, you bleed out twice as fast."

Some people in line gasped. A couple wobbled.

"But Tommy wasn't our killer's first victim," he continued. "No sir. Wyatt Clark was. Now, I know the story's been it was an accident, but that was spun to keep the press from nosing around. Word gets out there's been two deaths? They'll be nosing around plenty. Why we're gonna solve this right now."

The lawman sucked a tooth. "And when I say we, I don't mean my deputy and the two rangers standing here. I mean all of you. The way we're gonna do this is, I'm gonna start asking questions to each of you. Since you all work together and know each other, I figure you'll be able to tell if the person answering is lying. The rules are simple. You hear a lie, butt right in and tell me."

Lubik drew a finger down his soul patch. "I butt in. Is okay?"

"You got something to say, spill it."

"You not tell something."

"What do you mean?"

"Why someone kill Wyatt and Tommy. Who next? Me? Dani? Amber?"

"That's why we're here, so there won't be a next one. And the why those men were killed is because someone here is black-mailing someone else. When Clark and Tommy got a little too close for comfort, the blackmailer killed 'em to shut 'em up."

"Who is blackmailed? Why for?"

"That doesn't matter. The only thing that does is identifying and stopping the killer."

Lubik's shoulders shrugged beneath his black leather jacket. "Okay. We stop killer."

Pudge said, "Now, you've all heard about President Nixon and his secretary Rose Mary Woods and how eighteen minutes of what must be a pretty darn incriminating recording tape got erased. Well, we got our own Watergate right here." He hooked a thumb toward the editing station.

"During the filming by the second unit, the camera was left turned on. I believe it filmed the killer cutting the cinch on Wyatt Clark's saddle that caused him to get throwed. The film editor told me when he watched the entire reel before starting to cut and splice it, there was no scene of the horses being saddled or anyone monkeying with the cinches. But when he was editing it into a daily, the film came apart in his viewing machine right after the shot of the horses being unloaded from the trailer.

He eyed the lineup. "Turns out there was a tear in the film. The editor didn't think much about it and went ahead and spliced it back together. I guess rips happen. But after talking to me, he now believes someone cut it before he saw it, took out a part, and spliced it back together. Only they were a little too hasty pushing down the tape. My guess is the killer had intended to get rid of the whole scene of the horses coming out of the trailer and getting saddled and the cinch getting cut, but later, after viewing what they cut and took, realized they'd left a few frames and came back to cut them out too. That's when Tommy came in and saw what was going on and, well, we all know what happened. What I need to know is, if anyone saw someone doing something to that black stallion's saddle before Clark rode off."

Without taking a breath, the sheriff jabbed his finger at the wrangler. "Did you haul the horses up there?"

The wrangler was gangly and wore a plaid shirt with pearl snaps, "Yes, sir. It's what I get paid to do."

"And did you saddle them?"

"Yes, sir."

"When?"

"Right after I unloaded them and their tack."

"Where?"

"We'd scouted the location the day before and put in a hitching post. It wasn't that far from where I backed up the trailer."

"What did you do after you saddled them?"

"I went and had a smoke and a cup of java at the canteen they set up there."

"Did you see anybody with the horses after you saddled them?"

"Nope."

"Did you have eyes on them the whole time they were hitched?"

The wrangler hesitated. "Nope."

"Why not?"

He worked his jaw and studied his boots and then looked up. "Well, Sheriff, I'm around horses all day every day, but I'm single and Dani Reyna is the purtiest woman I've ever laid eyes on. I watched her get her makeup put on. I never seen nothing like that before. It's a sight that's gonna stick with me a lot longer than any old horse. If that's a crime, then lock me up 'cause I'm guilty, but I ain't repentant."

A couple of people snickered. Dani blew him a kiss. Amber pouted.

Pudge moved to the cameraman who had surfer-blond hair tied in a ponytail and wore an aloha shirt. "You turned the camera on and forgot to turn it off while you were moving it around. There's some footage of the horses coming out of the trailer. Did you see that?"

The surfer cameraman flinched. "Hey, man, a lot was going on and I was busy setting up. I didn't see anything."

"But the camera did."

"If you say so. I turned in the reel, but I don't know what's on it."

"You don't look through the Brownie when you're snapping a picture? How do you know you're taking what you want to take and not your thumb?"

"Are you jiving me, man? I don't use a Brownie. I use a Panavision. And FYI, it's not like I got my eye glued to the lens the whole time I'm shooting. Dude, the camera's like an extension of me. Like my head or my arm. My soul. It's the same with my board when I'm surfing. It's, like, Zen."

"Answer the dang question. Did you see the horses getting saddled, either through the camera lens or through your soul?"

"No, man. I didn't see it. If it's on film, then only the camera knows."

Pudge continued going up and down the line asking if anyone had seen anyone around the horses. Garth and Amber said they never noticed them. They were only focused on watching Dani and Wyatt get into character and listening to the second-unit director coaching them. Dani said she only remembered the wrangler bringing her the white mare and holding its bridle while she mounted up. Fellows said he'd left before they were saddled. The rest of the crew members said they hadn't seen a thing. No one challenged anyone.

The sheriff turned, nodded at Orville, and then looked back at the lineup. "Raise your hand if you smoke." Everyone did except for Dani and Amber. Pudge said, "Are you sure about that, Miss Amber? I seem to recall seeing an ashtray on the table in your room right next to that cute little knife you use to slice unpickled pickles."

The movie star's chin quivered. "It's a secret. My fans can't know I smoke. It's part of my contract."

"Which brand?"

"Virginia Slims, but only a couple a day. I'm trying to quit. Honest." She fluttered her eyelashes.

"We'll see about that. How 'bout you, Miss Reyna, you don't smoke?"

"My father smoked four packs a day and died of lung cancer. As he took his last breath, he made me promise never to smoke. I honor him still."

"The rest of you, hold out your smokes so I can see 'em."

Fellows pulled a cheroot from beneath his poncho and clenched it between his teeth without lighting it. The second-unit director held out a cheroot exactly like it. The rest showed cigarette packs. Pudge inspected them. He stopped in front of Lubik.

"Camel man, huh?"

"Real American cigarette."

Pudge returned to Dani. "You said when Clark was chasing you, you knew he was firing live ammo. Why do you think he did that?"

The actress shrugged. "Maybe he wanted to kill me."

"That makes me wonder if you're the blackmailer and he knew it."

"But I'm not." She tilted her chin at him. "Maybe Wyatt was the blackmailer. Maybe the blackmailer put live rounds in Wyatt's gun when he cut the cinch to throw suspicion on him. So many maybes. So few answers."

The sheriff blew out air.

Fellows said, "What do you think, Sheriff? Is any of this helping or is it a waste of time? The reason I ask is, I called Morty Wassenberg to tell him about Tommy. He said with one phone call to the White House, he can have a plane full of FBI agents here within an hour. The sooner this is solved, the sooner we can get back to work and make our end-of-the-year release deadline."

"Tell Mr. Wassenberg, thanks but no thanks, Nixon or no Nixon. Federal agents have no jurisdiction with these murders. They were committed in my county." He patted his badge. "I already said what the motive and opportunities are. I've also identified the means. What's it called again, Deputy Nelson?"

"A film-cutting blade from a Rivas." Orville held one up for all to see.

That caused some gasps among the cast and crew. Both Loq and I studied faces, but no one averted their eyes or bolted for the door.

"All that's left is to identify the culprit and I got a special agent of my own that's gonna do that. In fact, coming in right now."

Everyone looked at the open barn door except for Pudge. His eyes remained fixed on the lineup. Gemma stood in the wide doorway. Silhouetted against daylight, it appeared she was holding a large duffle bag. It was only when she stepped inside that I could see the handle was attached to a makeshift sling that went under Jake's belly and allowed her to help the big dog walk on three legs while keeping his bandaged one off the ground.

Pudge said, "You all remember Jake. Being in the movie business, I'm guessing you also know who Rin Tin Tin is. Starred in plenty of Westerns. And how 'bout Bullet? Helped Roy Rogers catch loads of bad guys. Both had that police dog sixth sense about them."

The lawman pushed his short-brimmed Stetson up. "Well,

Jake's got it too. I know because he's been living at my ranch ever since my daughter here patched him up after he got sliced by the . . . what's it called again, Orville?"

"A Rivas film-cutting blade."

"Right. Jake got hurt when he surprised someone 'bout to cut the cinch on Clark's saddle in the stable next door. It's why the killer had to risk finishing the job on the set and then came back here to cut out the footage that showed him doing it. While Jake was hurt bad, he hasn't forgotten who did it to him. He's gonna come over here and give everyone a looksee and a sniff. When he recognizes who cut him, I'll try my best to hold him back before he puts the bite on, but no guarantees he won't sink some teeth."

Gemma scratched Jake between his ears and started to bring him to her father, but halted when Amber screamed. Lubik had grabbed her and shoved her in front of him. He pressed a stubby revolver against the side of her head.

"Stay back! Everybody stay back," he shouted, his Hungarian accent suddenly gone. "I'm walking out of here. Anybody tries to stop me, I shoot her. Don't go for your gun, Sheriff. Tell your men to stand down."

The cinematographer pointed the gun at Pudge and then Orville and then Loq and me as he shuffled toward the barn door while using Amber as a shield.

"You? You're the one blackmailing me?" Amber gasped.

"Consider it payment for making you look pretty in every shot," Lubik said.

"Reminds me of a scene from *Dodge City Drifter*," Fellows drawled around the unlit cheroot clenched between his teeth. He reached under his poncho for a match.

Amber moaned and then swooned. Her dead weight caused Lubik to stumble. A gun banged and the cinematographer grunted and staggered backward. He dropped his revolver as he sat down hard, clutching his side. Pudge rushed forward and stepped on the fallen gun as Orville, Loq, and I drew our weapons. I smelled singed wool and looked around. A bullet-sized black hole was smoking in the front of Fellows' poncho. He swept it aside to reveal an Army Colt in his hand that he'd pulled from a cross draw holster. Amber, who'd slumped to the ground, quickly jumped to her feet.

Fellows holstered the Colt, struck a match with his thumbnail, and lit his cheroot. He blew a smoke ring at Amber. "I was hoping you'd remember that scene. It was one of your finest performances. This was even more convincing."

"And *Dodge City Drifter* was one of the best pictures you've ever directed," she cooed. "I'll never forget you showing Clint that move with the poncho."

"I need a doctor," Lubik groaned.

"And you'll get one," Pudge said. "A real American jailhouse doctor." As he pulled the killer upright and slapped the cuffs on him, he said to Fellows, "You always strap while on the job?"

The award-winning director blew another smoke ring. "I make Westerns, Sheriff. You never know if one of the snakes on location is going to have two legs."

33

The black phone in the old lineman's shack rang the next morning.

"Ranger Drake, I am afraid I have devastating news," F.D. Powers said. "President Nixon will not, I repeat, not be coming to Harney County."

"I can't say I'm surprised, sir. Two murders is hardly the kind of press he needs right now."

"They were the proverbial icing on the cake. In doing routine background checks, the Secret Service had already discovered unsavory information about some of the people associated with the film."

"Such as?"

Powers hesitated. "I suppose helping solve the murders earns you a right to know. John Fellows was called to testify in front of the House Un-American Activities Committee twenty-some years ago. He avoided it by enlisting in the Army and, ironically, served with distinction against the Red hordes in Korea. Garth Scott is a homosexual. Amber Russell appeared in a pornographic film prior to changing her name and becoming a star. The cinematographer is not a Hungarian national. He is from New Jersey and has a lengthy criminal record. The list goes on, but what do you expect in that business."

"Will the president be going elsewhere?"

"Yes, to the Middle East on a peace mission along with a little saber-rattling in hopes it will change the mood in Washington. General Haig believes the public will rally around a leader when national security is at stake, but I fear it will not work this time. I spoke with the president last night. His state of mind is, well, naturally he is saddened. He told me confidentially that he will resign rather than be impeached."

He sighed. "It is over. His presidency. The era. Everything. Mark my words, Saigon will fall within a year. Nothing goes on forever."

I pictured a line of Paiutes walking a trail with no end to escape sickness and disease, but opted not to contradict him. "And you, sir, what will you do?"

A ballpoint pen clicked a couple of times. "Another reason for my call, Ranger Drake. I am also resigning."

"Isn't that a bit rash?"

"Quite the opposite. It is an act of loyalty to President Nixon. Rest assured, I will continue to serve this great nation. As a matter of fact, I am moving to California at Mr. Wassenberg's urging. Governor Reagan is an old friend from his acting days. His last term is drawing to an end and Morty and others have convinced the governor he would make a great president. I am signing on as his chief campaign advisor. If I help secure a Ronald Reagan victory, I may get that cabinet secretary job after all."

We wished each other farewell and good luck. I was still staring at the phone wondering what impact his departure would have on me when Loq arrived.

"Powers is resigning," I said.

The Klamath looked down his high cheekbones. "Why?"

"He's going to try to get the governor of California elected as president."

"I hope Reagan treats Indians a lot better from the White House than he did in his Westerns."

"How are things at the Crossed Bars?"

"Everyone's packing up."

"I thought they had more scenes to shoot."

"They do, but Fellows said it'll be faster on a set built in LA. They can also film on a nearby ranch that's been used for Westerns before."

"The Spahn Ranch?"

"I'm not sure of its name. Why, is there something special about that one?"

"Long story. What are you going to do?"

"Fellows says he needs me for a couple of more scenes. I said I'd do it in exchange for the pinto."

"Will he agree?"

"He already has."

"What about Dani?"

"We're driving down together."

"So, you're going Hollywood after all."

"No, I'm getting a free pony."

"Are you taking him with you?"

"It's too gray for him down there. I'll leave him with you until I get back. Your corral's got plenty of room and Hattie can ride him for me while I'm gone."

"How long will that be?"

"As long as it takes."

"If we get a new boss before you return, I'll cover for you until the fall migration. If you're not back by then, I'll put in a requisition for a new partner. It's a busy time of year around here."

"The pony's in a trailer out front. I already hitched it to your rig."

"Thanks."

"Don't mention it." A grin creased Loq's usually stoic face. "See you around, brother."

"I'll look for you on the red carpet."

I finished up some paperwork and then headed for home, making a stop at Blackpowder's on the way. The movie crew hadn't removed the hanging oil lamps, roulette table, or other props. The proprietor was sitting on a barstool, a glass of amber liquid in his grasp.

"I heard the movie people are pulling up stakes," I said.

"That they are. Why I'm sitting here having a farewell drink to them all by my lonesome."

"Looks like they were good for their word and left you the movie trappings. At least you'll have those to remember them by."

"I got more than that, young fella. I got a personal invitation to opening night. *High Lonesome Showdown* with yours truly starring in it is goin' play at that Chinese theater. I'm finally goin' get to see all those handprints my fellow stars put in cement."

"I have something I'd like you to take a look at." I placed it on the bar.

Blackpowder put on his half-frame reading glasses and studied it. "It's some kind of map. Where'd you git it?"

"From the canvas tarp that covered Jump Diggins' pack-saddle on Ruby."

"Well, I'll be. Seeing it makes me feel like I'm seeing those two again after all these years. What's it to?"

"I thought you might know."

Blackpowder took a sip of whisky and examined the map more closely. "Can't say I rightly do, but that R is definitely his way of marking the spot, so buried treasure is a safe bet. That

Paiute directional he drew there, you think he copied an actual one carved in a rock?"

"Probably, but there are thousands throughout the Great Basin. It could be anywhere."

"You goin' back to the Sheldon anytime soon?"

"Tomorrow. There's a bighorn population study I need to complete. It's long overdue."

"Well, ol' Jump spent most of life right around there. My advice is, put yourself in his boots and walk where he would've walked from Quartz Creek toting a heavy sack of gold nuggets. Stands to reason he wouldn't have gone very far to bury it. Who knows? You might get lucky."

"If I do, whatever's in it is rightly yours."

Blackpowder's billy-goat beard shook back and forth. "Jump and me already divvied up our take long ago. I got all the riches I need right here. You keep it and put it to good use."

I got back in my pickup and drove home. The pinto didn't whinny when the horse trailer bounced over the cattle guard, but Wovoka and Sarah made noises as soon as I got him out and led him to the corral. The buckskin stallion laid back his ears, snorted, and pawed the ground while the sorrel mare nickered and put her nose over the top rail to sniff him.

"That's right. He's got Loq's scent on him. That means he's a friend. He's going to be staying with us for a while. Treat him like family."

As the pair of cutting horses calmed down, Hattie came running out of the house at full gallop. "You got me a pony!"

I told her he was Loq's but we could ride him together while he was staying with us.

"And Jake can go with us," she said.

I crouched to be at her level to deliver another disappointment. "No, like the pinto, Jake's not ours. He belongs to the movie company and they're leaving today. That means we need to say goodbye to Jake because the trainer is going to take him with her."

"Is not."

"He has to go back with the other two dogs that are in the movie."

"Uh-uh." Her pigtails whipped. "She said we can keep him because he can't be a movie star no more."

I tried to figure out what to say next when Gemma walked up. "Hattie won't listen to me. You tell her."

"You're the one who's not listening. Hattie's right. The trainer already came and went. Because Jake got hurt performing what he'd been trained to do, she can't trust he won't have a flashback and attack an actor for real next time."

"Dogs have flashbacks?"

"Like even the best soldiers. Maybe you can help Jake get over them." Her eyes sparkled. "That's right, hotshot. We got ourselves a dog."

I opened the gate to the corral and shooed the painted pony inside as Hattie climbed up on a rail to pet him. "Guess our little family is growing."

"We're only getting started. Sarah is with foal. If it's a filly, Hattie's dream of Shell Flower will come true before the year's out."

"I never would've guessed she's pregnant after watching her during the stampede. She ran faster than ever."

"Sarah's a strong horse. With Wovoka as a father, the foal will be doubly so."

We watched the horses for a bit and then I told her I planned to return to the Sheldon. "There's the bighorn study that needs completing. Searcher told me the radio-collared ewe is on Blowout Mountain."

"When are you leaving?"

"In the morning."

"Why not right now? The sooner you go, the sooner you get back."

"What's the rush? Do you have a ranch full of sick cows you need to get to?"

"I always have patients that need doctoring, but this appointment is different. You need to be there too."

"How come?"

"The adoption agency called. They want to meet us."

"You contacted them already? I thought that was something we were only talking about. Do they have a kid lined up? Is it a boy or a girl? Do I need to build another bedroom? What about a name? Does it come with one or do we get to pick it?"

"Whoa! This is only a get-to-know-you appointment. We'll take it one step at a time. Don't sweat it."

"Who says I'm sweating?"

"Your brow." She put her arm through mine. "Come on, I'll help you pack. You have three days to find your bighorn. Make them count."

34

I left the horse trailer hitched and loaded Wovoka. With food and gear stowed and a new snapshot of my little darling clipped to the visor, I kissed Gemma and Hattie goodbye and pulled away from the ranch house. November was standing in front of the cattle guard. The old healer was holding a bundle.

"Is that more medicine for the elders? Hop in. I'll take you."

"It is for you," she said.

The bundle was comprised of four layers of cotton fabric, each a different color: yellow, red, black, and white. Wrapped inside was a pinch of tobacco, packet of sugar, and small bag of coffee grounds.

"Thanks, but you didn't need to go to the trouble. I won't be gone that long and packed plenty."

"These are for when you are on top of what white men call Blowout Mountain. The cloths are prayer ties. Our Lakota and Cheyenne brothers and sisters are not the only people who use them. They have much *puha*. Put the tobacco in one, coffee in another, sugar in another, and fresh sage you pick in the fourth.

Tie them to the tallest bushes to mark the four winds and sit in the center."

"Then what?"

"Open your mind and free your spirit. Tuhudda will join you. He is your guide now and forever more."

"I don't understand. I'm not *Numu*. I thought . . . "

"That *Numu* can only be spirit guides for other *Numu*?" November's tsk was gentle. "What kind of people would we be if we did not share our knowledge with others? Do we not have wisdom from walking this land for tens of thousands of years and living with *Nuwuddu* close to earth and sky?"

"You're right. As usual."

"Tuhudda chose you because of what you did many years ago for his son Louder Than Wolf, Nagah's father. Your gift set Tuhudda and Nagah free that day from a life of shame, and you and Gemma are helping Nagah as he continues his path to manhood. Tuhudda now gives you a gift. You must honor him by accepting it. Listen to his songs. They will help you understand the many journeys you must take. Some will be easy, others hard. Some will bring joy, others deep sorrow. You must face both for that is your path."

The old woman returned to the house. Her words mingled with those of Searcher's, but I had a long drive ahead to ponder them, and so I put boot sole to pedal and sped south. This time I didn't take the two-lane down to the border at Denio, but turned off in Catlow Valley and followed a series of rough dirt tracks to the tiny panhandle of the Sheldon refuge that was in Oregon.

I slipped across the Nevada border and proceeded to a perennial spring in a clearing that was as high as a vehicle could drive up Blowout Mountain. Wovoka seemed relieved to be free from his jarring ride in the trailer when I stopped. He shook the kinks out of his muscles from all the bracing he'd had to do by trotting circles around my rig.

While he helped himself to free graze, I packed the saddle-bags with the VHF receiver and headphones along with food and water. I double-checked that November's prayer tie bundle was safely secured. Then I whistled the buckskin over, saddled him, tied a bedroll behind the cantle, and slid the Winchester into the scabbard.

"Come on, boy," I said. "Let's find that bighorn and maybe even a treasure box full of gold."

We spooked a herd of mule deer as we made our way up the mountainside. I thought of the buck poisoned by the gold mine and the series of deaths in Nevada that followed. The only ones I mourned were Jump Diggins' and Ruby's. The way steepened the higher we climbed and before long I had to dismount and lead Wovoka.

It was an hour shy of sunset when I pitched camp, gathered wood, and made a small fire ring. Then I knotted the tobacco, sugar, coffee, and a handful of fresh sage in the prayer ties and fastened them around the camp in the direction of the four winds: yellow was east, south red, west black, and north white. With Wovoka picketed close to my bedroll in case cougars prowled, I turned on the receiver, clamped on the earmuff-like headphones, and listened for a signal. Holding the directional antenna like a Lady Liberty torch, I walked toward the highest point on the mountaintop, since bighorns tended to bed down in groups on the steepest slopes. A hum filled my ears as I hiked.

As darkness gathered, a faint pulse broke through the hum. I paused, turned full circle in place, and then heard the pulse again. It was coming from the silhouette of an escarpment etched against the skyglow. I walked toward it. The radio collar's pulsing signal grew louder. I took off the headphones and heard grunting. The smell of sheep urine wafted through the air. The ewe was close by, but it was too dark to see her or the rest of the band. I'd have to wait until first light.

Wovoka welcomed me back with a whinny. I touched flame to wood and put a pot of water on to boil. My stores were in better shape than the last time I spent the night in the Sheldon when all I had to eat was a stale piece of bread slathered with peanut butter. This time I'd brought fried chicken and a container of cooked wild rice that only needed reheating.

After supper, I threw a handful of coffee grounds in the pot of boiling water, let them steep, then took the pot off, added a cup of cold water to sink the grounds, and filled two mugs. I added two heaping spoonfuls of sugar to one and placed it on the other side of the fire. I sat down on my bedroll inside the circle of prayer ties, closed my eyes, and remembered all the times I'd been with Tuhudda. After a while, I don't know how long, a familiar voice joined the crackle of burning wood.

"Nick Drake. I knew you were coming before you left."

I looked through the flames and the tongue of woodsmoke curling toward the sparkling heavens. "Hello, my old friend. I'm honored you found me here."

"Where else would you be but where you are needed. That is your way."

"Searcher said a hawk told him where I could find the bighorn."

"Searcher has powerful medicine and Hawk is a powerful spirit bird."

"November said you would teach me about such things."

"Girl Born in Snow has powerful medicine also."

"Then I am ready to learn."

"You have already begun. This is so."

The Dusty Trail, as Tuhudda called the Milky Way, shined brighter than I'd ever seen it, and the campfire burned late into the night as I listened to his songs about many things, including the Forever Walkers and Searcher. "With time, you will see more, understand more," he said.

When the campfire started to die, he invited me to add the prayer ties to the flames as gifts to the Great Spirit. I watched them burn and breathed in the smoke of sage, tobacco, coffee, and sugar until the embers turned to ash. As dawn crept over the eastern horizon, Tuhudda and I said our goodbyes until next time. I felt refreshed, renewed, and full of purpose.

With first light, I rose and quietly retraced my footsteps to the escarpment where I'd detected the bighorn sheep. Several ewes and lambs were still bedded down on patches of bare ground between boulders, but the matriarch was already up and climbing onto the rim of a sheer rock wall that soared above tree line. As she took up her sentinel position, she turned and looked at me. I held her gaze and walked toward her.

"It's okay, sister. I'm here to remove that collar and hear from you whatever you wish me to know."

She allowed me to unfasten it, shook her head when it was off, but did not run away. From her perch, I could see every member of the band of ewes and lambs. I committed their number to memory. I also counted the young males in a nearby bachelor herd along with a mighty ram with curling horns that stood alone on the highest ground of all, ready to take on all challengers.

"Your family has grown," I said.

The ewe was staring across the great expanse of peaks, tablelands, and lonesome desert. I looked east too and picked out Big Mountain, Sagebrush Creek, and Virgin Valley. From my vantage point, the valley formed an almost straight line with a half circle at the top and a diagonal slash to the right where the half circle rejoined the straight line. Terms from a grade school penmanship workbook came to me. Stem, arm, lobe, tail. They were the parts of a letter, and suddenly I could see it plain as day. Virgin Valley was a capital R.

I thanked the bighorn and fast-stepped back to camp,

saddled Wovoka, and rode quickly back to my pickup. The knobby tires kicked up plenty of dust as I sped across the refuge. Despite searching high and low until dark, I didn't find Jump's treasure that day. I made camp next to the hot spring where I'd seen Searcher emerge and soaked in its soothing waters to ease my muscles that night. As dawn broke, I went back to work.

The key was finding the ancient directional carved in a boulder that protruded in a desert meadow halfway between the old opal diggings at Rainbow Ridge and Royal Peacock. I got off Wovoka, placed Jump's canvas map against the petroglyph and lined up the directions. The X was ahead of me and the R behind. I turned around. A steep cliff of pink sandstone rose from the valley floor. Water spilling from the top had left a streak the shape of an arrow pointing toward the ground. I remounted and rode toward its tip, keeping the ancient directional lined up to my back and careful not to veer off course.

When I reached the cliff wall, I searched its base. A slab of pink sandstone the size of a grand piano had broken away and slid straight down. Carved on the top edge was a tiny R. Smaller rocks at the base had collected in the gap between the slab and cliff. I pulled one loose and then another and another until I was able to reach behind. Something hard, something rectangular met my fingertips. I grabbed an edge and slid it toward me.

The strongbox was made of metal and stained with rust. It bore no lock. A leather strap that looked like it had once been part of a packsaddle's rigging tied it shut. I undid the knot and lifted the lid. Inside was a packet wrapped in oilskin that contained a clothbound ledger. An envelope was stuck between the cover and first page. I opened it.

Two faded black and white photographs stared back. One was a wedding portrait of a handsome groom and beautiful bride, the other showed the same couple several years older posed with three children in front of a two-story white clapboard house. The parents were beaming with pride. The kids were grinning.

A yellowed newspaper clipping was also folded inside the envelope. It was from the *Carson City Daily Appeal* datelined December 26, 1939. The article was brief. Elias Waterton, a local businessman, was driving home from a Christmas dinner celebration when the family sedan veered into oncoming traffic and was struck by a big rig. Waterton was thrown clear of the wreckage. The automobile burst into flames. His wife Marcia and their three young children, Elias Jr. and twins Ricky and Janey, were trapped and perished. Waterton was arrested for drunk driving. Funeral services were pending.

I slipped the photographs back into the envelope along with the clipping and then thumbed through the rest of the ledger. Pressed between each page was a dried wildflower and the date and year inked above it. I counted thirty-three flowers, thirty-three Christmases. No gold nuggets and no mining claims to Quartz Creek or anywhere else were inside the strongbox. There was only the record of the real treasure Jump had lost and been unable to reclaim.

I folded the map he'd drawn on the canvas tarp that covered Ruby's packsaddle, placed it in the ledger, rewrapped it in oilskin, and laid it in the strongbox. After shoving it behind the pink slab of sandstone and sealing the gaps with stones, I stared across the desert meadow at the directional carved thousands of years ago by wise people to help others find their way. Then I looked up at the big blue sky that went on forever and prayed Jump Diggins had finally found what he'd spent his life running from and running to.

The buckskin sidestepped when I swung back into the saddle and pointed him toward the pickup and horse trailer parked beside the hot spring.

"Let's go, boy. We got family waiting for us."

Wovoka stretched out his neck and I clamped down my hat and we raced to meet whatever came next. No matter if good or evil, lost or found, sorrow or joy, I vowed to face it head-on or die trying.

AFTERWORD

Infectious diseases have been a trail of tears with no end for indigenous peoples. Coronavirus disease 2019 has been the latest in a long history of pandemics that have impacted them disproportionately and laid bare historic discriminatory government policies and continuing health care disparities.

The mortality rate among Native Americans and Alaska Natives from COVID-19 has been two and a half times higher than that of Whites and Asians. With tribal elders more likely to die, it has also taken a heavy toll on indigenous cultures by severing the human connection of language, history, and tradition passed on from the old to the young. In the Navajo Nation, for example, coronavirus ravaged the ranks of *hataalii*, the elderly singers who serve as traditional medicine people.

The history of infectious disease in the Americas dates to the arrival of European explorers, traders, and colonists who brought with them Old World viruses such as smallpox, measles, and influenza. Indigenous peoples had never experienced those pathogens and, consequently, had no immunity to them. The resulting epidemics are estimated to have killed seventy percent or more of the native population.

Smallpox was extremely deadly. Colonists landing in Plymouth, Massachusetts, in 1633 infected local communities. The disease spread quickly, reaching the Mohawk people in New York the next year. By 1690, the Iroquois living in Quebec had suffered twenty-four epidemics. Eight years later smallpox had crossed the Mississippi and nearly annihilated the Quapaw in Arkansas. By the mid-nineteenth century, the disease was rampant among the peoples of the Plains. The Lakota called smallpox the "rotting face sickness." An epidemic in the Pacific Northwest resulted in a death rate of more than fifty percent among coastal native peoples from Puget Sound to Southeast Alaska.

Lack of immunity was only partially to blame for such devastation. Colonialism and intolerant government policies conspired to create social conditions that left indigenous communities additionally vulnerable to disease. The Indian Removal Act of 1830 was particularly barbarous. The Cherokee, for instance, were stripped of their homeland and forced to march twelve hundred miles from Georgia to the Indian Territory in Oklahoma. Denied adequate shelter, food, clean water, and hygiene along the way, four thousand men, women, and children (out of sixteen thousand) died from whooping cough, dysentery, and measles. The death rate was even higher for the Sauk and Meskwaki. By the time they reached Oklahoma from Illinois, their population had been reduced by eighty-five percent.

The impacts from prejudicial government policies and the resulting disproportionate poverty and discrimination in the delivery of health services continue as of this writing. American Indians and Alaska Natives born today have a life expectancy that is five and a half years less than the US population as a whole. They die at higher rates than other Americans in many categories, including heart disease, chronic liver disease, cancer, diabetes, and suicide.

The COVID-19 pandemic, with its associated higher-than-average death and hospitalization rates among native peoples, amplified the health inequities because of chronically under-funded and under-resourced health care systems, limited access to services, and poor infrastructure. For indigenous peoples, fighting the virus has been a continuation of their battle against a centuries-old legacy of discrimination and dispossession.

A NOTE FROM THE AUTHOR

Thank you so much for reading *The Forever Feet*. I'd truly appreciate it if you would please leave a review on Amazon and Goodreads. Your feedback not only helps me become a better storyteller, but you help other readers by blazing a trail and leaving markers for them to follow as they search for new stories.

To leave a review, go to *The Forever Feet* product page on Amazon, click "customer reviews" next to the stars below the title, click the "Write a customer review" button, and share your thoughts with other readers.

To quote John Cheever, "I can't write without a reader. It's precisely like a kiss—you can't do it alone."

GET A FREE BOOK

Dwight Holing's genre-spanning work includes novels, short fiction, and nonfiction. His mystery and suspense thriller series include The Nick Drake Novels and The Jack McCoul Capers. The stories in his collections of literary short fiction have won awards, including the Arts & Letters Prize for Fiction. He has written and edited numerous nonfiction books on nature travel and conservation. He is married to a kick-ass environmental advocate; they have a daughter and son, and two dogs who'd rather swim than walk.

Sign up for his newsletter to get a free book and be the first to learn about the next Nick Drake Novel as well as receive news about crime fiction and special deals.

Visit dwightholing.com/free-book. You can unsubscribe at any time.

ACKNOWLEDGMENTS

I'm indebted to many people who helped in the creation of *The Forever Feet*. As always, my family provided support and much patience throughout the writing process.

Thank you Karl Yambert for proofreading and copyediting. Kudos to designer-extraordinaire Rob Williams for creating the stunning cover.

Additional thanks go to the Harney County Library's Claire McGill Luce Western History Room and Archivist Karen Nitz.

I humbly offer my respect to the Burns Paiute Tribe of the Burns Paiute Indian Colony of Oregon for your inspiration and to the Klamath Tribes, whose mission is to protect, preserve and enhance the spiritual, cultural and physical values and resources of the Klamath, Modoc and Yahooskin Peoples by maintaining the customs and heritage of their ancestors.

Any errors, regrettably, are my own.

ALSO BY DWIGHT HOLING

The Nick Drake Novels

The Sorrow Hand (Book 1)

The Pity Heart (Book 2)

The Shaming Eyes (Book 3)

The Whisper Soul (Book 4)

The Nowhere Bones (Book 5)

The Forever Feet (Book 6)

The Jack McCoul Capers

A Boatload (Book 1)

Bad Karma (Book 2)

Baby Blue (Book 3)

Shake City (Book 4)

Short Story Collections

California Works

Over Our Heads Under Our Feet

Made in the USA
Las Vegas, NV
02 March 2022

44851808R00187